**FUJINO
OMORI**

ILLUSTRATION BY
**SUZUHITO
YASUDA**

VOLUME 4

FUJINO OMORI

ILLUSTRATION BY SUZUHITO YASUDA

YEN
ON

NEW YORK

IS IT WRONG TO TRY TO PICK UP GIRLS
IN A DUNGEON?, Volume 4
FUJINO OMORI

Translation by Andrew Gaippe

DUNGEON NI DEAI WO MOTOMERU
NO WA MACHIGATTEIRUDAROUKA vol. 4
Copyright © 2013 Fujino Omori
Illustrations copyright © 2013 Suzuhito Yasuda
All rights reserved.
Original Japanese edition published in 2013
by SB Creative Corp.
This English edition is published by arrangement
with SB Creative Corp., Tokyo, in care of
Tuttle-Mori Agency, Inc., Tokyo.

English translation © 2015 Hachette Book
Group, Inc.

Yen On
Hachette Book Group
1290 Avenue of the Americas
New York, NY 10104
www.hachettebookgroup.com
www.yenpress.com

Yen On is an imprint of Hachette Book Group, Inc.
The Yen On name and logo are trademarks of
Hachette Book Group, Inc.

First Yen On edition: December 2015

ISBN: 978-0-316-34016-8

10 9 8 7 6 5 4 3 2 1

RRD-C

Printed in the United States of America

VOLUME 4

FUJINO OMORI
ILLUSTRATION BY **SUZUHITO YASUDA**

PROLOGUE FASTEST BOY IN THE ALLENS

The Guild Headquarters was filled with the chattering of a lively crowd this morning.

The traffic of adventurers coming and going through the headquarters' wide lobby was always at its peak between sunrise and noon. Of course some were visiting their adviser before heading into the Dungeon, but most of them spent their time reading notices that had been posted on the Guild's announcement bulletin board overnight or talking with fellow adventurers.

Most of the notices contained information about new items on sale from the mercantile *Familias* or requests for specific drop items from the Dungeon. However, announcements about the strength of each *Familia* as well as sightings of rare monsters in the Dungeon were posted as well. The Guild posted all of this to assist adventurers in their travels.

What the adventurers learned today from this notice board could determine their luck tomorrow, not to mention their pay. Obviously, they couldn't afford to ignore it.

Bathed in the strong sunlight coming in through the high windows of the Guild lobby, many races of human and demi-human swiftly went about their business.

"Whew…So many adventurers showing up today."

"We're working now. No time for small talk."

Eina Tulle gave her coworker Misha Frot a light warning without getting up from her chair at the counter window.

Just as Misha said, more adventurers than usual were visiting the Guild on this particular morning. Eina and her coworkers knew that this was no accident; something had spurred the adventurers into action. She herself had been busy since early that morning and was just now able to catch her breath.

Usually around this time, adventurer traffic would be slowing down to the point that some of them would try hitting on the cute receptionists at the Guild. Most days the girls would just roll their eyes, but today the would-be suitors were mercilessly shot down and shown the door so that those needing advice could come to the front.

"Denatus is coming up, so it looks like adventurers who leveled up are waiting around…But it has to be the news about you-know-what—that Minotaur that showed up on the ninth level."

"…Yes, it certainly looks that way."

Three days ago, there was an announcement that had made Level 1 adventurers' eyes lose color.

It read: MINOTAUR SIGHTED IN UPPER LEVELS.

The notice, issued by *Loki Familia,* sent waves of fear through more than half of the adventurers in Orario. Demands for more detailed information had been coming in nonstop ever since.

Monsters appearing on floors where they weren't normally seen was nothing new. In most cases, the monsters were encountered two floors above or below their recorded origin point. But this Minotaur was spotted on the ninth level, meaning that it had somehow journeyed up from the Middle Fortress. The earliest floor where Minotaurs were usually encountered was the fifteenth, six floors below.

The fact that this was not the first time a Minotaur had been seen in the upper levels was what really made the adventurers' blood run cold.

It had been about one month ago—the day that Bell met Aiz—that the beasts had been spotted much higher than normal.

That particular incident had been caused by an accident during *Loki Familia*'s return from an expedition. Guild employees had explained this many times, but adventurers were not that easily convinced. Some adventurers claimed there had been a change in the Dungeon's design that allowed Minotaurs to be born in the upper levels.

Eina and her coworkers were unable to dismiss it as an exaggeration.

For Level 1 adventurers, this was a matter of life and death. If monsters from the Middle Fortress were roaming the upper levels, they couldn't work. Understanding their fears all too well, the Guild accepted the fact that many would panic and did their best to quell the adventurers' fears.

…Haven't heard from him since that day, either. Is he all right?

Eina hadn't seen Bell during the rush of adventurers, and it made her extremely nervous.

It had been less than a week since his last visit to the Guild, so she knew it was too early to be anxious…But Bell had nearly been killed by a Minotaur recently. Just hearing the monster's name might make him take more precautions than necessary, though she couldn't blame him.

Thoughts of Bell running through her head made Eina feel restless, an uneasy pulse throbbing in her chest.

"Ah, Eina's favorite adventurer spotted, twelve o'clock."

"!"

Her friend's needlessly long-winded voice caught Eina's attention, and she looked up.

Sure enough, the boy's signature white hair stood out from the crowd as he weaved his way toward the reception counter. Once he noticed Eina's gaze, Bell blushed a little as he flashed a toothy grin.

"What's this—doesn't he look like he's in a bit better mood than usual?"

"…"

This time Misha's words rolled in her left ear and out the right. The warmth of relief ballooned within Eina, her pinkish lips curling into a smile before she took a deep breath and pulled herself together.

Watching Bell maneuver through the crowd like a rabbit through a meadow, she was a bit irritated that the boy had made her worry. However, relief won out.

"Good morning to you, Miss Eina!"

"Morning, Bell. It's been a while. I probably don't have to ask but…Working hard in the Dungeon?"

"Yep! Giving it my all! Although it's been a few days!"

"Heh-heh, breaks are important, too. The body needs to rest, so a few days sounds about right."

An even bigger smile bloomed on Eina's face as she talked with Bell.

Sitting next to her coworker, Bell's infectious good mood made Misha grin as well. She left her chair at the counter to give Eina some space. Sitting down at her desk, she set to work sorting the documents on it.

Eina's eyes softened as she asked another question.

"So, did something good happen?"

"H-how did you know?"

"One look at you and anyone could tell."

Eina giggled for a moment as Bell put a hand to his reddish cheeks.

She knew from the look on his face that Bell couldn't wait to talk about whatever it was that had happened. Eina blinked her emerald eyes slowly and nodded her head, as if to say, "Go ahead." The boy nodded back brightly. He hadn't looked this happy since the day that he'd officially become an adventurer. Just behind Eina, Misha fought back a smile by biting her lip. The human girl backed away from the mountains of paperwork on her desk and slowly stood up, inching ever closer to the conversation.

He really can't tell a lie, thought Eina as she waited for Bell's next words. A calm, warm feeling swelled within her; it was as if she were looking at her own younger brother.

"W-well, you see…"

"Yes?"

Then Bell flashed his teeth again in another happy smile and a twinkle in his eye before saying, "I'm Level Two now!"

Misha's paperwork fell to the floor with a great *swish* sound.

The human girl froze like a statue, her back toward Eina and Bell.

Misha had seen Bell's paperwork on Eina's desk before, so she knew that Bell hadn't been an adventurer for even two months yet.

Eina smiled.

It was a beautiful smile.

A moment later, shock took over her face as she, too, froze.

To be more precise, time had stopped.

It was as if the two ladies were in a bubble; the usual noise of the lobby couldn't reach them.

"...huh?"

Did I hear that right? That was the only thing she could think of to explain what she just heard. A dumbfounded smile still stuck on her lips, her head tilted to the side as her mind raced to find answers.

A corner of her mouth started twitching.

"Like I said, I'm Level Two! Me! Since three days ago!"

In too good a mood to notice Eina's state of shock, Bell happily repeated himself, loud enough to be heard over the din.

The tension in her body that had built up passed her breaking point, causing her to shudder in her chair at the counter.

"Level Two?"

"Yes!"

"Three days ago?"

"Yes!"

"And that's the truth?"

"Yes!"

"Bell, when did you become an adventurer?"

"A month and a half ago!"

Bell's words hung in the air.

The human and half-elf shared a smile, the conversation fresh in their minds.

Another wave of adventurers had arrived and stood in line behind Bell, looking agitated and impatient as they waited.

Since Misha hadn't budged an inch, the reception counter had become gridlocked.

Squeak! Eina shot up from her chair—and exploded.

"LEVEL TWO IN SIX WEEKS?!"

Her shrill scream cut through the commotion of the lobby.

Every Guild employee sitting in the office behind the reception counter suddenly jumped to their feet as Eina's voice thundered through.

Taking the brunt of the blast, Bell broke out in a cold sweat as he leaned away from her.

CHAPTER 1

D
E
N
A
T
U
S

© Suzuhito Yasuda

"I'm so sorry!"

Eina clapped her hands together with a loud *smack* and bowed her head.

They had moved from the Guild Headquarters reception counter to a small conference room just off the Guild lobby. This modestly decorated room was normally used for one-on-one conversations because it was soundproof.

Bell and Eina sat across from each other on either side of the desk as she apologized over and over.

"To scream like that when there were so many members of other *Familias* there…I'm very, very sorry!"

Just minutes earlier, Eina had yelled personal information at the top of her lungs. All who were within earshot now knew that Bell had leveled up.

No matter how surprised she had been by the news, just thinking about the looks she had received after her outburst was enough to make her face burn bright red.

She had failed to protect an adventurer's personal information. Eina was so ashamed by her actions that even her ears seemed to blush.

"I-it's not a problem, Miss Eina. Adventurers' levels always get announced, anyway…So a few people found out a little early. That's not a big deal, is it?"

The half-elf hadn't even tried to raise her head, and it was starting to make Bell feel uneasy. His voice shook as he searched for the right words.

A worried look appeared on his face as she finally made eye contact with this boy who couldn't grasp the real problem.

That's true…But the issue here isn't the fact you leveled up; it's the speed at which you did it…

Reaching Level 2 in just over a month was by far and away the fastest level-up on record. Even putting it into words was absolutely ludicrous.

Leveling up required a grand act—such as slaying an enemy stronger than yourself, and overloading the container that is your soul, with excelia. Eina was one of the few people who knew how fast Bell has been growing, but for even his Level to go up this quickly…It was as if he had shattered the most common of common sense.

Even though this information would have been announced eventually, Eina would've liked to have kept it a secret for as long as possible.

It was an unlikely story to begin with, and many would not believe it…The gods and goddesses, however, loved this sort of "never been done before" story.

Images of the deities of Orario staring at Bell and drooling with excitement popped up in Eina's head. She started feeling a bit queasy.

"Um, Miss Eina…?"

"…It's nothing. Sorry, I spaced out for a moment there."

Trying to shake off the visions of gods and goddesses chasing Bell around the city, Eina straightened up and forced an awkward smile. Letting out a quick sigh, she returned her attention to the matter at hand.

"Bell, I must apologize again, but I have a request. I know you came all the way here to talk to me…but I have some work to do."

"Y-yes, sure. What can I help with?"

"I want you to tell me everything you've done as an adventurer up to this point."

"Huh…?"

"Even a rough outline is okay. The kind of monsters you fought, the quests you completed, things like that."

Eina pulled a pen and notepad out of the desk as she spoke.

The Guild collected and announced data on how adventurers leveled up, so long as it didn't cross the lines set by each *Familia* pertaining to the personal information of their members. This was all to help increase the collection rate of magic stones from the Dungeon.

Since Bell had just achieved the fastest level-up on record, Eina wanted to focus on the way he gathered excelia. His name would most likely be well known soon, and a record of his exploits would be something no one would overlook.

In short: "This is how Bell did it. Follow his example and get stronger."

Eina wanted to get this information because casualties would decrease if other adventurers knew how to grow as fast as Bell. Careful not to break any more rules, she listened carefully to everything he had to say.

Bell finally reached the events of three days ago.

For the second time that day, Eina's head started to spin.

"A M-Minotaur..."

Thump. Eina's head tilted limply over before she brought her right hand up to support it.

—Three days ago, ninth level, encountered a Minotaur, slew it.

Every word out of Bell's mouth made Eina more and more light-headed. Everything he said matched *Loki Familia*'s report perfectly.

When she'd asked the messenger to tell her who had taken care of the monster, he'd sounded a bit ambiguous. Eina could remember his muddled words as she stood behind the counter at the Guild. Naturally it would have been hard for anyone to believe that a Level 1-ish adventurer could slay a Minotaur.

Eina closed her eyes for a moment to shake off the dizziness before opening them in a blaze of anger.

She glared accusingly at the boy as if to say, *After all those times I told you not to go on adventures!* Bell broke out in a cold sweat, his body shrinking in the chair.

Just what kind of magic did he use...?!

She spent almost an hour trying to get a clear answer of exactly how a Level 1 adventurer managed to take down a Level 2 monster like a Minotaur.

"...Whew. I've got a pretty good idea now. A pretty good idea of just how little you actually listen to what I say."

"Huh?! No, that's—...I'm sorry."

Anger still radiating off of Eina, she closed her eyes as Bell tried to explain himself. However, his voice trailed off halfway through and he ended up apologizing and hanging his head.

Opening one eye to see a very depressed Bell sinking in his chair, Eina couldn't help but feel a little put off by his childish way of regretting his actions.

On the other hand, she was glad to know that Bell fully realized what he had done.

If he had been off by so much as one second at any point during that battle, he wouldn't be here to reflect upon it now.

"...Bell. I wasn't there, so there is a chance I could be wrong. Perhaps your decision not to escape was the right one after all."

"Miss Eina..."

"I might not have the right to scold you...but still—please don't ever forget this one thing: Everything is meaningless once you're dead."

I'm begging you, she said to the boy with her gaze.

She couldn't hide her own conviction that coming back home alive was the most important thing of all.

Bell hadn't moved in the slightest from his position on the chair, but he slowly raised his eyes to meet hers and nodded.

Their eyes locked for a long moment before Eina lightly cleared her throat. In an attempt to clear the slightly gloomy atmosphere that filled the room, she leaned over the table and extended her finger all the way up to Bell's eyes.

"In any case—just don't be reckless, understand?"

"Y-yes!"

Eina bopped her finger on the tip of Bell's nose before smiling and returning to her seat.

That's enough reprimanding for today, she thought to herself.

Her brown hair swishing just above her shoulders, she looked at Bell with a warm smile.

"...Bell, congratulations on your advancement to Level Two. You've been working very hard."

His nose still slightly indented from Eina's finger, Bell's face lit up as he smiled from ear to ear.

He wasn't a particularly conceited person, but those were the words that Bell really wanted to hear just then.

"Thank you very much," he said with red cheeks. His adviser Eina, who had watched him grow since his very first day as an adventurer, couldn't help but feel proud.

"Should we leave it at just the level-up announcement for today? Is there anything else you wanted to ask me?"

"Ah, that's right...Actually, there is something I wanted to ask you about, Miss Eina."

Now that Eina had calmed down considerably, Bell remembered the main reason why he'd come to the Guild today.

"It's about Advanced Abilities..."

"Oh, I see. So you're not officially Level Two yet, are you, Bell?"

Advanced Abilities worked together with Basic Abilities to increase an adventurer's overall strength and power.

However, these abilities could only be acquired when a person with a Blessing from a god or goddess leveled up. They were different from Basic Abilities in that they were specialized to the profession of the user.

"In that case, it sounds like you have a few options to choose from."

"Yes. I've already talked with my goddess, but I thought it would be a good idea to get your opinion as well, Miss Eina..."

Eina gave an affirmative nod of understanding.

The Advanced Abilities that a person could learn were based on the type of excelia they had collected up to that point. In a way, they had control over what kind of abilities appeared because of their Falna, their deity's blessing.

Certain Advanced Abilities wouldn't be available if the right type of excelia wasn't present when an adventurer leveled up. At the same time, the blessed person would have a choice of abilities as long as they had the excelia for them. Only one Advanced Ability could be learned with each level-up, so these decisions opened some doors and closed others.

Such abilities appeared above an adventurer's status when they leveled up, so Bell had yet to reach Level 2.

Bell's leveling up had been postponed to allow some time for him to consider his options. He had fulfilled the requirements; all that was left to do was for Hestia to complete his new Status. Bell was in a kind of limbo.

"What abilities are there to choose from?" Eina asked.

"There are three of them. But there's one that I don't really understand..."

Eina nodded again a few times as she prepared to jot down Bell's options on her notepad.

The first one was a very basic Advanced Ability that prevented the effects of monster poison and other ailments—an ability known as Immunity. It wasn't the flashiest of abilities, but in a place as dangerous as the Dungeon, many adventurers considered it extremely valuable. Due to the large number of purple moths in the upper levels, many adventurers had inhaled their poison spores. So Immunity was a relatively easy Advanced Ability to acquire.

Next, there was the anti-monster ability called Hunter. Basic Abilities temporarily increased when fighting a type of monster with which that adventurer had experience. Since Hunter could only be learned at Level 2 and required an absurd amount of excelia from the same monsters, it was one of the more difficult ones to learn. Of course, it was a popular choice among adventurers but was also highly valued by the gods because of its rarity.

And then the third one...

"...Luck?"

"Yes..."

Eina's pen stopped mid-writing, and she blinked.

Despite all of her experience and expertise in advising adventurers, she had never heard of this one.

The question was, exactly how would good luck take effect?

"Well, what did Goddess Hestia have to say about it?"

"She didn't know much, either..."

Well, that makes sense, Eina said to herself.

Everything that was known about statuses had been discovered long ago, when the gods first came down to the lower world and verified it many times over.

Even the gods who granted a blessing had no way to know what abilities a particular child would learn. Except for in the very beginning, a Status was completely dependent on excelia. It showed the possibilities of the people of Earth. The gods became like parents, watching their children grow and change right before their eyes. This was why it was said that even the gods didn't know what would happen in this world.

All the more reason for the gods and goddesses to be interested in a rare skill. The unknown made living in this realm interesting, and they couldn't get enough of it.

So much for keeping a low profile, Eina thought somberly to herself.

An ability that had never been recorded in the Guild's records— nor had she ever heard of it with her own ears.

In other words, it was an honest-to-goodness rare ability.

More than likely, Bell was the first adventurer in history to discover this Advanced Ability.

If his options had been just "Immunity" and "Hunter," then she could have offered some advice. However, she could only guess at the meaning of something she'd never heard of before.

"Ah, but…" Bell suddenly remembered something and raised his voice as he wandered the forest of his own thoughts. "My goddess did say that she thought it would be something like…'protection.'"

No matter who she was, a goddess's insight was not to be ignored. If that's what Hestia thought after seeing Bell's new ability, then she was probably on the right track.

Protection…A force that moved to defend someone without their knowledge. It could be like a divine shield that looked after the user.

While that was just speculation, if any of it was true then it was more than enough reason to acquire this new ability.

"Hmm," said Eina quietly as she gathered her thoughts. She decided that for the time being she wouldn't file this information with the Guild. There was enough attention on Bell already.

"Well—that's one possibility. But there are other areas where Luck would be useful for adventurers...like more drop items, maybe?"

"Ah, yes, that's true."

"But that sounds a little bit too money-related. I'm sorry, but I don't think I'll be of much assistance."

"B-but—!"

Bell waved his hands in front of his chest, shaking his head no.

Feeling very apologetic that she couldn't do more, Eina decided to ask about *Hestia Familia*'s opinion.

"What would you and Goddess Hestia like to do, Bell?"

"My goddess wanted me to learn Luck. She made a fist, kind of like this, and shouted, 'You need this ability!'"

Sounds a bit risky, thought Eina as she raised an eyebrow at the young boy.

It was a bit late to be asking now, but she was getting very curious as to what exactly Bell had done to learn this new ability.

Meanwhile, Bell couldn't understand why he was feeling over-whelmed by the look in Eina's eyes.

"...What about you, Bell?"

"Hunter is cooler...I mean, no, but, it's just, I can't ignore it, and yeah..."

"Heh-heh. I understand what you're getting at. And then?"

"Um, then again, just as my goddess said, I can't just ignore Luck, either......"

Despite his indecisiveness, she had a pretty good idea of what Bell was thinking.

Hunter was indeed a very strong ability. Adventurers who faced the dangers of the Dungeon firsthand day in and day out would all most likely jump at the opportunity to acquire it.

The other option was Luck—a never-before-seen ability with unknown effects. But it was in human nature to react quickly to the words "rare ability," especially if you were the only one who had it.

Considering that Immunity could be acquired the next time he leveled up, most likely Bell was leaning toward choosing Hunter.

Truth be told, he probably wanted both.

She could relate to Bell's situation, his having to make a hard decision. Eina couldn't help but grimace.

"I've often said this, but the one who has to make the final decision is you, Bell. So I don't want to say anything that would make you lean one way or the other. Therefore, I'll give you something else to think about beyond the choice itself."

"S-sure."

Eina waited for Bell to fix his posture before she continued.

"The simplest way is to think about what the differences between your goals might be."

"My goals?"

"Yes. If you would like to powerfully and thoroughly work your way through the Dungeon, then Hunter will serve you very well, Bell. If you want to crawl the Dungeon with great efficiency, then I highly recommend it."

Eina paused for a moment before looking directly into Bell's ruby red eyes.

"But if your goal is something loftier—to get somewhere that is currently beyond your grasp...That path has nothing to do with mere ability. I believe that Luck might be a better ally when the time comes."

"..."

"In which case, I think that you might indeed need Luck."

The room was silent for a moment.

Bell took a deep breath before looking down at the palms of his hands.

As the boy flexed his fingers into a fist, Eina felt that he had reached a decision by the look in his eyes.

"There is no wrong decision here. So it needs to come from you, Bell. Whichever one you choose, it will come through for you when you need it."

"...Yes. Thank you."

Bell held his chin high, a look of determination on his face as he nodded to her one last time.

He might have reached Level 2, but he still had burning questions on his mind.

Eina looked at the boy who had just made his decision and decided it might be a good idea to look after him a while longer. A gentle smile rose to her lips.

"Goddess, I'm home—!"

I push open the door to my home, a hidden room under an old church.

The goddess lifts her face out of a book that she's been reading on the sofa the moment I say hello, and smiles.

Tap tap tap—her feet smack the floor as she gets up and walks over to greet me.

"Welcome home, Bell. Well then, have you decided? What ability will it be?"

"Yes. I would like to learn Luck."

Eina's advice helped me make up my mind.

It's not about now. I'll take the future.

I don't know for sure whether or not I'll need this Luck ability, but Eina's words really hit home. I believe them.

The goddess happily grins at me and lightly whispers, "All right.

"So, shall we? You're still not leveled up."

She walked all the way up to me just to say that? I'm pretty nervous but I nod in agreement.

The two of us go over to her bed and start preparing for my last Status update as a Level 1 adventurer.

"At long last you're Level Two, Bell…is what I'd normally be saying, but in your case, it was so fast I didn't have time to feel nostalgic."

"R-really?"

"Yep. I remember it like it was yesterday—that time that you slew a goblin right after joining my *Familia* and came back all smiles. Kind of a strange feeling, actually."

The goddess keeps on talking, going on and on the way she does. I can't get a word in edgewise, except for the occasional "wow" and "yes."

I'm becoming Level 2.

For some reason every little movement I make on the sheets is really noisy. It's very comfortable, though. The thought of leveling up is making me a bit full of myself. I know many have done this before me, but still.

Other than that, nothing's really going on in my head, and my body feels normal, too. Well, actually, everything from the neck down feels pretty warm, now that I think about it.

I'm not nervous or anxious; I'm just quietly waiting and listening to my heartbeat...Then suddenly the moment comes.

The goddess's fingers stop moving.

"!"

"...It's done."

I sit up as soon as I feel her get off my lower back.

Sitting on my heels in the middle of the bed, I take a look at my hands.

I can feel the goddess's eyes on me from my side, watching as I open and close my fists.

"...I don't feel all that different."

"What were you expecting? The sudden urge to yell, 'The power flows within me...!' up at the sky?" The goddess acts out the scene in front of me, skillfully pretending to shake with newfound energy before giggling.

It might be a little rude of me to say my true feelings, so I just nod.

I leveled up, but I'm still the same.

I thought my body would be lighter. I thought I'd feel like the world was different. Or something like that. But there is nothing. I feel no different than I did the moment I got home a few minutes ago. Where's the feeling of accomplishment that comes with leveling up to Level 2?

This is really disappointing...Like all the wind in my sails just disappeared.

"It's not like the structure of your body changes, you know?

Sorry if I made you think you'd have some kind of dramatic transformation."

"Ah, no, it's not that…"

"Ha-ha, but your Status improvement is the real deal, you know. The 'container,' your spirit, has gotten much bigger. It's very obvious to me and any other gods. You might not realize it now, but the next time you're in battle, it'll feel like you flipped a switch. You'll pull off attacks that you never knew you could."

The goddess laughs to herself again as she starts writing my new Status in Koine, the common language of humans and demi-humans.

I know that when an adventurer levels up, all of their Basic Abilities return to zero. I've heard that those points don't just disappear, but instead are hidden in the new Status as "extra points." What was it the goddess had called it—a "hidden parameter"?

Since I know that it will be all zeros on my new Status, there isn't really any point in looking at the sheets the goddess is holding right now…But what's the harm in checking?

I tilt my head to the side a little as I get up from the bed. My usual undershirt was torn to shreds in the battle against the Minotaur, so I grab a spare and put my arms through the sleeves.

My eyes meet the goddess's gaze the moment my head pops out of the collar of the shirt, and she hands me the paper.

"It was going to be a surprise, but I think I should tell you first."

"?"

The goddess beams with happiness as I take it from her.

I don't even have a chance to glance at it before she says, "Good news, Bell." I'm about to ask her what it is, but she's faster. "A Skill."

"Huh?"

"It's your sec— No!…I mean, um, you know. It's what you've always wanted: your own Skill!"

Several moments pass in silence.

Her words sit in my mind for a few seconds before everything suddenly clicks and my eyes race to the paper clutched in my hand.

I can feel the pupils of my bloodshot eyes pounding as I will them to focus on her handwriting.

Then,

Bell Cranell

Level 2

Strength: I O   Defense: I O   Utility: I O   Agility: I O   Magic: I O

Luck: I

Magic:

"Firebolt"

- **Swift-Strike Magic**

Skill:

"Heroic Desire, Argonaut"

- **Executes automatically with an active action**

My eyes have never been this wide.

There's something in my Skill slot.

My head snaps up. The tiny goddess, much older than I am, is looking up at me with a gaze of approval. She silently mouths, "That's right."

My cheeks pull back into a smile all on their own. Happiness floods through me. This is definitely the highlight of my day!

The muscles in my face are refusing to relax. Even I can tell my eyes are shining as I take another look at the paper in my hands. That's when I notice something.

…"Heroic Desire"?

All of the joy in my body suddenly evaporates, my eyes stuck to that one spot of my Status.

That seems rather exaggerated for a description…Every corner of my brain has cooled off and is now sending up red flags.

…*Wait a second.*

My lips go numb. My smile disappears.

I've heard that the Skills and Magic in an adventurer's Status are not only affected by excelia but by the blessed person's personality and aspirations as well.

Even the name of the Skill…So an adventurer's Status is like a reflection of their soul?

And now the phrase "Heroic Desire" is literally carved into my back…That means the cat's out of the bag that, even at my age, I want to be a hero…

Creeeeeaaaak. My head rises from the sheet of paper with about the same efficiency as a rusty door, my ears burning red.

And standing directly in front of me, the goddess with her warm gaze and perky smile—

"—Guh, DAAAAHHHHHHHHHHHHHHHHHHHH?!"

I scream at the top of my lungs as the goddess looks at me like she could burst out laughing at any moment.

Throwing the piece of paper into the air, I spin around and collapse into the fetal position on the floor, hands covering my ears.

No, no no no—!

She knows! The goddess knows that even now I want to become a hero like the ones in the picture books! She knows!!!

This is pure agony. I feel just as ashamed and embarrassed as all the times I messed up in front of Aiz. I'm sure my face is just as red. My soul is on fire, cooking me from the inside out.

I'm dying! Something please put me out of my misery!

"Bell."

Zing! Her voice shoots through me like a firecracker, my body shaking.

But her voice is gentle. I can feel her soft fingers on my shoulder.

She's right behind me; I should at least look up at her. Trying to blink the tears out of my eyes, I turn to face her, fearing the worst.

She's wearing a very bright and loving smile.

"—That's so cute!"

"Uwaaaaaaaaaahhhhh!!"

Why, Goddess, why—?!

"Uoohhh…"

"Hey, how long do you plan on sitting there?"

I'm still in the corner of the room, hugging my knees to my chest.

Falling from heaven all the way into hell leaves a pretty deep wound. The scar'll probably stay on my heart forever.

© Suzuhito
Yasuda

I hear the goddess's voice behind me as hot tears roll down my cheeks.

"Oh, get up, already. What's the problem with you idolizing heroes anyway? Do you know how many children can stay that pure in this day and age?"

"I can see you biting your lip, trying not to laugh, Goddess!!"

The way she said "children" as well—so patronizing!

The echoes of my half scream bounce around the room. I'm really upset here.

The goddess grins and leans down over me, smiling, and says, "I apologize if you're hurt." I'm being comforted by a goddess who looks like a child. Good thing no one else is here because this would be the most pathetic sight ever. Just imagining it makes me feel even worse.

"Feeling any better?"

"I'll get there..."

I force my knees to straighten and stand up. I'm *not* feeling any better, but she'll never understand, so what's the point?

Flexing the muscles in my neck to keep my head up, I lean down to pick up the sheet with my Status off the floor and have another look.

Argonaut...That's its name, but I don't know anything else about this Skill...There's nothing written here to go on. There's barely any information at all.

It was the same with Firebolt, too. Why is it that whenever I learn something new, there's never enough explanation on how to use it? I don't have a clue what this thing does...

"Goddess, do you know what this Skill's effect is?"

"Hmm, it's a bit hard to explain. It's not one that's constantly turned on...instead, it's an Active Action, so basically when you choose to make a move, it will have some kind of effect."

"Choose to make a move...?"

"You know, like attacking or defending yourself." She adds, "But in that case, I don't think it will do anything for counterattacks."

Huh? I kind of get it, but I kind of don't...

It's no use. I'm not smart enough to work this out on my own.

"So, in the end you'll just have to try and figure it out in battle. That's a little bit of a vague way to put it, though."

"Don't worry about it. It's my Skill, anyway..."

After all that, it looks like I'll just have to wait and see.

Feeling a little bit put out, I take another look at the paper.

I don't know very much about the Skill itself, but the name Argonaut...I know a lot about that. Well, maybe I should say that I *remember* a lot about it.

"Argonaut."

It's a story about a hapless young man who ventures out to rescue a beautiful queen from a ferocious bull monster.

The main character gets fooled by many people, and he doesn't have a clue. He just ventures forward like an idiot and by some miracle manages to arrive at the feet of the monster he's seeking. If I remember right, the queen he's trying to rescue saves *him* from the monster in the end.

Out of all the heroes and the stories I've read, he stands out as the least heroic.

It was probably based off a play, but I distinctly remember reading the picture book and raising an eyebrow. He wasn't cool at all... Could there be a hero who dreams about being a hero?

But Gramps, he loved the story. He'd say things like, "This guy's best days are ahead of 'im," and stuff like that. All I can remember thinking was the story's over.

To think I'd run into something as random as that from my childhood at a time like this...It's all so confusing.

"Sorry, Bell. It's time for me to leave now."

"Eh? You're working today, Goddess?"

The goddess's voice brought me out of my memory pool in time to let me know she was leaving the room.

I was sure she had today off, so I ask her about it.

"Well, you see, today is a Denatus—a meeting of the gods that happens once every three months."

"Denatus...Isn't that...?"

"Yep, that's right. It's a get-together for the gods with nothing to do…We choose titles for adventurers who level up."

Titles. The word makes my shoulders tense up.

It's just like Aiz's second name, "Kenki." It was chosen for her by the gods.

Which means there had to have been some kind of discussion when her nickname was decided. That had to be the Denatus.

If the goddess is going to some kind of gathering like that…

"Since you leveled up to Level Two, Bell, I'm allowed to attend. More than likely we'll decide your second name."

I knew it!

That's just what I was hoping she'd say. I don't know how many times I've been excited today, but this takes the cake!

"W-w-well, well then, me, too? I'm going to receive a name like Aiz?!"

"…Enthusiastic, aren't you?"

"Of course I am!"

A title is like an adventurer's banner!

Only adventurers who level up get one; it's proof that the gods have recognized your abilities! There's no doubt in my mind it's a great honor!

And then there's…!

"All of the titles that the gods and goddesses come up with are so cool and refined! Nicknames like 'Fallen Seraph of Black Flame, Dark Angel' are so awesome that they even *sound* strong!"

"…Oh, that's what you mean."

Despite my passionate ramblings, the look in the goddess's eyes becomes distant, a weak smile on her lips.

To put it simply, it's a very sad smile. She looks far away.

Wh-what?

What happened to that warm gaze she had just a moment ago…?

"That's right. It's still too early for the children here…"

"Um…wh-what do you mean by that…?"

"No, it's nothing. I'm sure the day will come when you'll all understand, Bell."

The meaningful words hang in the air as the goddess falls silent and makes her way toward the door.

So many questions spring into my mind that my face starts contorting into different questioning looks.

Is the Denatus...something completely different from what I thought it was?

I've heard that it's a meeting where divine wills clash in a solomn atmosphere, but...?

"Well, I'll be back later."

"O-okay."

The goddess is standing in front of the door, waving.

She looks like a soldier preparing for death, and I can't help but stutter.

She looks at me again as the muscles in her face suddenly tense. She opens her mouth to speak.

"I don't care what I have to do; I swear I will win an acceptable title for you, Bell...!"

For you...! Her words ring in my ears.

Creak—She closes the door behind her.

I couldn't tell if she was motivated or desperate, but that wasn't the goddess I know. My body breaks out in a cold sweat as her footsteps disappear up the stairwell.

The Denatus was originally a meeting of retired gods and goddesses that was held because they had too much free time.

Their *Familias* had built up a certain level of power and influence, and these deities wanted to forget the stresses of work and enjoy full-time relaxation. Since they had nothing to do, they decided it would be fun to gather others like themselves and talk about trivial matters to kill time.

While it was nothing but a small party, the important thing was that all of these extravagant gods and goddesses needed a place to meet. And one was soon established.

As years passed and the number of participants grew, the purpose of these meetings started to change. The pointless conversation became a way to share the latest news. It didn't just stop with
exchanging information among *Familias,* and once the Guild
became involved, the Denatus became a meeting that had far-
reaching effects all over Orario.

While the meeting was known by name only, the gods and goddesses who participated in a Denatus became more powerful, their
voices directly affecting adventurers.

The naming process was one such influence and had become a
customary event.

"Looks like many children leveled up this time."

"Yeah, I've heard it was a great harvest. This is gonna be fun."

The meeting place for Denatus was on the thirtieth floor of the
skyscraper in the middle of the city—Babel Tower.

The entire space had been completely remodeled, with only the pillars supporting the high ceiling remaining from its original design.
A large, round table sat in the middle of the room surrounded by a
ring of chairs. The rest of the floor was completely empty. The outer
walls had been replaced with glass, encasing their meeting within
the clouds above the city.

Due to the extremely high ceiling, it looked almost as if the gods
met in a temple floating in the sky.

"More of us here than usual this time."

"Heh-heh, quite a few have stopped showing up as well."

As the last of the deities made their way toward the table, it didn't
take them long to realize that more than thirty gods and goddesses
were in attendance. Each one of them had at least one advanced
adventurer—Level 2 or above—in their *Familia,* meaning there
were just as many influential *Familias* inside Orario.

There were many faces around the table. One god wore a blank
expression, unable to hide his nervousness. Another mysterious one
wore a large elephant mask. A blond goddess laughed with those
around her, her eyes closed with glee.

Completely different from a Celebration, there was no dress code.

Hestia made her way through the colorful ensemble to the seat that had been prepared for her.

"You seem rather calm."

"I've got nothing to be nervous about, do I?" Hestia quickly answered the question as the crimson-haired, crimson-eyed goddess Hephaistos gazed at her.

The refined goddess wore a thin black blouse, her sparkling crimson hair flowing down her back. With her clothes that would be more fitting for a man, male and female deities alike were drawn in by her charm.

She looked over at Hestia, a patch covering her right eye, and slowly shrugged her shoulders. "I thought you'd be a little more anxious. You know, scrunching up your face like you always do."

"...If something's going to change I'll make plenty of noise. But all that does is just provide entertainment for everyone else, right?"

"You're not wrong..."

Hephaistos could feel Hestia grimacing as deity after deity came up to her to squeeze and pinch her puffy cheeks. Hers was a new face, and many of the gods and goddesses around her were drawn to her side like moths to a flame. They didn't bother to hide their intentions.

They would do the same even if it weren't Hestia. Their way of thinking was obvious.

They were congratulating her, in their own way. It was almost a miracle that her extremely small *Familia*'s status had gone up.

"I'm going to say this now: Don't expect any help from me. With this many of us here, my voice is but one among many."

"Yes, I know." Hestia fidgeted a little bit in her chair after Hephaistos's warning.

"Let's get the ball rollin'!" came a voice from across the table.

All conversations came to a sudden halt. The owner of the voice got up, her vermilion-colored hair swishing as she stood.

"'Bout time we started up the one thousandth Denatus. Today's hostess is none other than yours truly, Loki! Nice ta see ya!"

A chorus of whistles and thunderous applause erupted throughout the room.

Loki, her light red hair tied into a short ponytail, smiled with narrowed eyes as she waved her hands to settle everyone down.

Meanwhile, Hestia looked at her from her seat on the opposite side of the table and muttered with the utmost dissatisfaction, "Why does Loki get to run the show?"

"She wanted to. Most of her *Familia* is out on an expedition and her home is almost empty. Basically, she was bored."

"Ohhhh, she has time to be *bored...*"

Hestia was not particularly fond of Loki, and her disdain came out in her voice.

Whether she heard Hestia's angry mumbling or not, Loki cast her squinty gaze over in Hestia's direction but decided to ignore the young goddess and continue with her duties.

Hestia was surprised by this turn of events. Normally, Loki would've charged headlong straight for her.

"Alrighty, let's get to it. First off, any news that needs hearin'? You got something interestin' ta say, speak up!"

"Oh, me, me! Poor little Soma got a warning from the Guild. He had to give up his one and only hobby!"

"Whad'ya say—?!"

"Eh, what was Soma's hobby anyway?"

"Not a clue."

"Ah—probably the work of little Miss Eina..."

"To think we'd be talking about that loner Soma!"

"What happened next? Tell me, tell me!!"

"Apparently he won't come out of his room. He's just sitting in a corner, rocking back and forth."

"I wanna seeeeeeeeeee!!"

"I'm going to go cheer him up!"

"Hey!"

"You're just going to rub salt on his wounds, aren't you?"

"My apologies. Sorry to change the topic so suddenly, but there is an urgent matter we need to discuss. There is information that the Kingdom of Rakia is preparing to invade Orario."

"Very sudden, indeed."

"Don't tell me it's that Ares guy again."

"Isn't it about time we do something about that idiot? He's getting to be a real pain in the ass, seriously."

"Why is Ares worshipped so much in that country, anyway?"

"Maybe it's because he's got a personality that's hard to hate? The children love that kind of thing."

"It has to be his amazing good looks. His visage is almost on par with the goddess of beauty. I'm in the Freya camp, though."

"Got muscles for brains, too."

The table erupted with conversation ranging from pointless joking to absolute seriousness, and back again two or three times.

Each of the gods continued to say their own opinions, the atmosphere relaxed and unhurried.

While she had an idea this was what went on, actually seeing this chaos with her own eyes was frustrating for Hestia.

It looked nearly impossible to regain any kind of control, but—"Y'all pipe down, now!" Loki's voice suddenly rose above the din. With a reaction speed that Hestia could barely comprehend, all the deities went silent.

"All right, then. Here's what we got. Need ta keep our eyes on Rakia, inform the Guild. Then again, knowin' old man Uranus, he'll figure it out himself. For everybody else, give yer *Familias* a heads-up. That clear ta y'all?"

"Understood."

Loki sorted through all of the information and summarized the important points. Since the gods and goddesses from all of the most influential *Familias* in Orario were in attendance, making sure that all of them heard the most important information was part of her job.

Loki then went around the table, asking for any other news that needed to be shared. As soon as her questions fell on deaf ears...she clapped once, her face scrunched into a catlike grin.

"Time ta proceed ta the Namin' Ceremony."

The room was suddenly tense.

The moment that Loki uttered those words, many of the gods who had up until that point been very vocal in the discussion froze, their faces one shade paler. Hestia was among their ranks.

As for the others, they drooled in anticipation.

They were used to how these Denatus meetings were run, and their favorite part was coming up. Several of their faces looked broken as ugly smiles burst forth from their lips.

Their party, and the others' tragedy, was about to begin.

"Everybody's got the handouts, yeah? Then let's raise the curtain! Today's top batter is…Seto's boy, an adventurer named Ceti!"

"P-please, please go easy on him…?!"

""""""""""DENIED""""""""""""""""

"Noooooooooooooooo!"

The sensibility of the gods, as with the people below, had changed to match the culture on Earth. Both were very similar up to a point. Being from Deusdia, it was common knowledge to Hestia that the gods and goddesses possessed senses that transcended human comprehension. However, that was not necessarily so, and there were many similarities between the ways gods and the people of Earth thought.

However.

The deities had a completely different sense of what made a good name when it came to bestowing titles.

Were the gods strange, or were the children foolish?

Were the gods too radical or were the children too old-fashioned in their respective ways of thinking?

While the truth had yet to be determined, the fact was that many names that made the children's eyes light up with pride made their gods' heads droop in shame.

"—That's final. The adventurer Ceti Selty shall be known as a dragon knight of the dawn: 'Burning Fighting Fighter'!"

"Whhhyyyyyyyy?!"

Another "regrettable name" had just been created.

The deities with less-than-generous personalities loved to watch others squirm as their favorite children were, one by one, given these regrettable names. The children who received them, however, would be in awe of the images that these nicknames produced.

The deities would first enjoy watching other gods and goddesses go mad with embarrassment, with their second course being watching the children's reactions to their uncouth nicknames. Today was a great day because they would spend most of it rolling on the floor with laughter. The best part was many of these names would live on in the children's legends.

"This is too cruel…"

"I understand all too well…"

Hestia's scared voice squeaked out of her throat. "I was the same at first," said Hephaistos with a slow nod. Her crimson left eye was looking off into the distance.

Deities attending Denatus for the first time, especially the Naming Ceremony, were treated with the utmost cruelty.

Sharing useful information might have been the main purpose of the day's meeting, but the hazing of newcomers had now begun. Hestia's face turned sour as she watched some gods scream out in despair while others laughed, clutching their ribs. The disparity between the two groups was sickening.

"Okay, next up. Takemikazuchi's…ohh, quite the cutie, this gal. Hmm, she's from one of those Far East places, so her name's backward…Little Miss Yamato Mikoto!"

Loki took another look at the Guild's paperwork in her hands, scanning it with her eyes.

It included the profiles of every adventurer to be named, as well as a sketch of that person's face drawn at the time they registered with the Guild. The sound of paper suddenly fluttered around the table before a chorus of "Ohh?" rose from their collective mouths.

"Look at this one…Pretty damn good."

"Black hair is so nice—"

"Hmmm, and she's just a little kid, we can't really…"

"Oh yeah, just thinking about doing something to a girl of this tender age…makes me really excited! Just kidding, it'd weigh on my conscience."

"A-are you serious?!"

There were two ways for a god at Denatus to avoid the drama of the second name.

The first way involved paying off some of the more influential gods and goddesses before the meeting even started. However, this was nearly impossible for most of the lower *Familias*.

Therefore, in these cases the influential gods and goddesses would look at the person in question and find a characteristic that they liked, as was taking place right now. Girls tended to get better names with this method than boys.

Like a sunbeam piercing through storm clouds, the male gods in the room quickly focused on the girl's hair color. Takemikazuchi couldn't sit still, and he jumped to his feet.

"Takemikazuchi, you're hopeless, you bastard!"

"Natural-born gigolo, that's what you are…"

"A goddess, a child, doesn't matter to you, does it? You pull them into your scheme just the same…"

"You got a Lolita complex or something?!"

"Wh-what the hell are you talking about?!"

"Poor Mikoto—her, too…"

"If the thoughts don't get through, then how about something a little more physical…Ha-hee-hee."

"Damn you all…!"

There was nothing more whimsical and unpredictable than a god.

Takemikazuchi gritted his teeth. His frustration with the other deities had gotten to him.

"I shall be the one to deliver a requiem for Miss Mikoto! Future of the Milky Way—'Fortune Galaxy'!"

"Dear Mikoto, you were such a good girl, but your god is just hopeless. You're a fallen saint—'Last Heroine.'"

"Enough! Stop this at once! I've done my absolute best to raise up and guide my little angel!"

"'Little Angel,' then!"

""""""That's it!""""""

"Please...have mercy..."

This was what the gods came to Denatus to see.

Hestia and Hephaistos also tried to give a few suggestions, but they were completely ignored.

"This gal Mikoto's nickname is... 'Eternal † Shadow.' That sittin' well with everybody?"

"No objections."

"Uwahhh, gggaaahhhhhhhhhhhhhhhhhhhhhh!!!!"

Hestia felt sorry for her friend as he threw his head back, hands over his ears, and wailed at the top of his lungs in humiliation. She swore to herself that she would take him out for a stiff drink that night.

Even after Takemikazuchi, a god of military arts, stopped crying tears of blood, the victims of the Naming Ceremony kept piling up.

The pandemonium continued until all of the adventurers from lower and middle class *Familias* had been given a title. Now it was time for the cream of the crop.

Adventurers from *Hephaistos Familia*, *Ganesha Familia*, and *Ishtar Familia* were on the list to be named.

"...*Freya!* Not a single one from your house has leveled up. So you came here for leisure only? Why is it that the Almighty Freya would even bother showing her face in a place like this?"

"Why, yes. Even in Tenkai, retirement is the poison that will kill us all. I was just out for a little stroll, Ishtar."

Any deity who received an invitation to Denatus had the right to participate in any meeting from then on.

If no one in their *Familia* had leveled up, then there was almost no point in their attendance other than for the entertainment. A good example would be the many gods and goddesses who took the lead in suggesting second names during the ceremony.

Despite Ishtar's poorly disguised mockery, Freya brushed off her fellow goddess of beauty's words with a cold smile.

"Oh, is that right? And speaking of time to burn, one of your house seems to have that as well. Just roaming around the middle levels, dueling Minotaur after Minotaur for fun, yes? The apple never falls far from the tree, now does it?"

"Hee-hee, you may be right."

"Ah, yes. While we're on the subject, I heard about a Minotaur that came into the upper levels...Could this have something to do with your house, Freya? If by chance it does, what will the Guild have to say about it?"

"Why don't you ask, Ishtar? I've heard that while my child was playing with those Minotaurs, he was attacked by a group of Amazons wearing masks...Don't you find that a little rude? I'd like to have a word with their mother..."

"...!"

Ishtar's face contorted, the brown skin under her very revealing outfit tensing up all over her body. On the other hand, Freya laughed quietly to herself and closed her eyes to signal the end of their conversation.

The truth behind the Minotaur incident that was making waves in the adventure community was still shrouded in mystery. All of the gods in this room were aware of that.

The other gods at the table watched the two goddesses of beauty trade verbal jabs while giggling to themselves.

"Amazons. Does that mean Ishtar is trying to butt into Freya's affairs?"

"Well, could be. It's not like this is the first time. Ishtar has always considered Freya to be her rival."

"Even so, Freya is just toying with her...Seems like arguing which one of the two is the most beautiful would be a very fruitless discussion."

"Don't say that to Ishtar's face."

Hestia and Hephaistos whispered quietly to each other, but the young goddess's eyes were locked firmly on Freya.

Since Bell had become directly involved in the Minotaur incident, this wasn't just someone else's problem...However, while she couldn't just take Freya's and Ishtar's words at face value, she wasn't in a position to press them for answers, either. She didn't want to make any false accusations.

Despite her mind firing on all cylinders, Hestia decided to stop trying to figure out the meaning of Freya's words. She did not, however, take her eyes off the silver-haired goddess for a moment.

"Alrighty, then, enough chitchat. Time to pick back up again. Next on the list is…nu-hee-hee, the hometown hero, my Aiz!"

"The Kenki's back again!!"

"The princess is just as beautiful as ever."

"You mean she's Level Six now…?"

The Naming Ceremony had been in danger of breaking down, but a big name like Aiz Wallenstein's was just what they needed to get back on track.

Each of the deities flipped through their paperwork to find an extremely detailed picture of a young girl staring back up at them with eyes like a doll.

Every time someone leveled up, they received a chance to correct their second name. Even if their first title was rather strange, as long as they leveled up again it could be fixed at the next Denatus Naming Ceremony.

"Don't you think that Aiz's name is good enough as it is?"

"Agreed."

"It could be changed to something like *holy sword*—'Kensei'?"

"Hunh?"

"Aiz's image is completely different, don'cha think?"

"Well, the be-all and end-all would be *Daughter of the Gods*—'Our Lady.'"

""""""Agreed!""""""""

"I'll end y'all."

"""""""Our apologies!!""""""""

Another way to avoid an embarrassing second name was for the god or goddess to bring up how powerful their *Familia* was within Orario.

In short, they had to make the others think that picking a fight would be a very bad idea.

None of the gods were foolish enough to get carried away when they knew the wrath of Loki was waiting for them.

Every single one of the deities who had gotten caught up in the moment slammed their heads to the table in a deep bow in Loki's direction, in order to escape her glare of death.

"Seriously, ya gotta know who yer dealin' with. Anyhoo, next... Hmm, last one, yeah?"

Hestia suddenly went tense, gulping down her last breath.

There was only one last page left in the prepared handouts. The level-up had occurred just before Denatus was scheduled to take place, so only the most basic of basic information had been prepared in time.

It was for an adventurer who belonged to *Hestia Familia*, who had been completely unknown until recently.

Bell.

"So that child really did become Level Two..."

Hephaistos whispered quietly to herself as she looked at the Guild's seal of approval on the paperwork clutched in her hands.

Her friend's words barely making it into her ears, Hestia looked around the table.

There were many smiles. However, they were the dirty, drooling smiles of people who had just eaten a full-course meal and were about to get their dessert.

Her moment of truth had arrived.

She had said all those things to Bell before leaving but had failed to prepare a strategy, thinking that everything would work out by believing in the power of their love and courage...!

—Right after that.

Loki quietly got to her feet.

"...Loki?"

"Before we get to namin', there's somethin' I'd like ta know, Shorty."

No one objected, as the normally squinting Loki opened her eyes wide enough to let everyone know she had a bone to pick.

"He did that much with our blessin' in a month an' a half—you expectin' me ta believe that?"

WHAM!

Loki slammed the palm of her hand onto her own paperwork on top of Bell's face, glaring daggers in Hestia's direction.

"It took my Aiz a year to level-up fer the first time—a whole *year*! And this boy does it in a month an' a half?! What're ya tryin' to pull?"

It was eight years ago.

A relatively clueless eight-year-old had become the fastest adventurer on record to reach Level 2. Not only that, she was human—a race that was physically and mentally weaker than many of its counterparts.

News that such a person had set a record like that had spread throughout Orario and the world like wildfire.

"It's not like a blessin' is anythin' special. A child that levels up that fast ain't natural. There ain't no shortcut, all of them bust their tails workin' hard ta level up."

Loki went on to say that Falna, the power of a blessing, was not instant.

A Status only gave the children a chance. Falna manifested itself differently in each person, based completely on their own experiences and desires.

Abilities, Skills, Magic. All of them developed based on Characteristics lurking within an individual. Even those characteristics were built up from a personal history—and the excelia gained from those experiences warped the power of a blessing, or degenerated it, into its new shape. It was similar to how the size and shape of a flower growing out of the ground can differ depending on its environment during development.

Therefore, it was a stimulant.

Falna was completely unaffected by outside forces. To be completely blunt, it was the ultimate key to unlocking inner potential.

"So, spill it, Shorty."

"..."

Hestia could have sworn Loki was breathing fire; the black-haired goddess was drenched in sweat.

This is bad, very, very bad.

The moment that the other gods and goddesses learned of Bell's Skill, "Realis Phrase," this place would become an absolute zoo. She hadn't told Bell about his own Skill for this very reason; she knew exactly how the others would react—. Add to it the fact that he just set a new record for the fastest level-up, and every god in this room would swarm him.

She had to fulfill her duty to protect the boy. However, in order to do that she would have to imply that Bell was special without outright saying it. Her best option was to give Loki a believable explanation, but there was no way she could come up with something good enough to satisfy her on the spot.

She was stuck between a rock and a hard place. Swinging her arms as if she were trying to swim through the air, Hestia's mind raced to come up with anything believable.

"So ya can't say? Ya wouldn't happen ta be usin' yer divine power, now would ya?"

"O-of course I'm not!"

"Okay then, out with it. If yer conscience is clean, this should be easy as pie."

"Ah..."

Loki had accused Hestia of using Arcanum, divine power, to accelerate Bell's growth. A near-panicked Hestia couldn't string enough words together to defend herself.

Hephaistos sat next to her friend with a very troubled look on her face. Her mouth was open, as if she were about to speak but couldn't figure out what to say.

Every set of eyes around the table was now trained on Hestia. Extremely interested in what was going on, all of the gods and goddesses leaned in to catch every single word. Hestia felt as though the room were closing in on her. She had never sweated this much in her life.

I'm finished, said a little voice in her head as she gave up hope. Just then.

"My my, what's the big deal?"

A beautiful soprano voice echoed throughout the room.

"…Huh?"

"Whassat?"

All eyes left Hestia in an instant and instead went to the owner of the voice.

Freya was leaning back in her chair, an aloof expression on her face.

"As long as Hestia hasn't violated our laws, then there's no need for her to explain herself, yes? It is, after all, taboo to reveal the inner workings of any *Familia*. That includes the Statuses and Abilities of any members."

Looking at a lock of her hair, she pulled it back behind her ear. Freya appeared disinterested, as if she were only talking common sense. But it stopped Loki in her tracks.

"…But one month? Can't ya wrap yer mind around that, ya air-headed vixen?"

"Hee-hee, why does this bother you so much, Loki? Your attitude seems rather strange to me…Is this jealousy, perhaps? Is it because Hestia's boy broke your favorite little girl's record?"

"Like I care," Loki retorted with a sneer.

"I wonder," Freya responded with her ever-present smile.

Loki's pretty face contorted in rage as she opened her mouth to speak, but nothing came out. Just as Loki had done to Hestia moments ago, Freya had twisted Loki's words into a corner from which she couldn't escape. The look on Loki's face made it all worth it for Freya as she smiled smugly in her chair.

Tsk! Loki clucked her tongue in Freya's direction, looking at her with the utmost fury.

"Of course it's difficult to believe my ears when I hear those numbers…But this boy, by some miracle, managed to defeat a Minotaur despite his low level."

"…"

"If I had to wager a guess, then I would say this Minotaur is the reason. If, perhaps, defeating a Minotaur meant something special to him, then the excelia he gained could also have had more influence than usual…That's what I think."

Every one of Freya's words sent ripples through the meeting room.

Each deity looked down at the paperwork in front of them and under the "personal history" column, only to find that this was, in fact, the second time the adventurer Bell Cranell had encountered a Minotaur. But he had defeated only one of them. One by one, the gods and goddesses around the table started murmuring in agreement with Freya's opinion. Even Loki couldn't deny that it made sense, but she wasn't too happy about it.

It had been nearly a thousand years since the deities had come down from the heavens and begun bestowing blessings on the children.

None of them could hope to predict what possibilities were hidden within each of the people of the world below. Even strange occurrences like this happened every now and again—all Freya did was point it out.

She let a moment of silence fill the room.

Then she went on to say that while she was extremely interested, there was no reason to force an answer for Bell Cranell's unusual development speed. Soon other gods around the table were saying that it would be against the rules to do so.

Freya quietly smiled again and gracefully looked over at Hestia.

It took her a moment to notice Freya's silver gaze. All Hestia could do, however, was blink, her body still in a state of shock.

An instant later, Freya stood up from her chair.

"Oh, are ya leavin', Freya?"

"Yes. I have something urgent to attend to, so I shall excuse myself now."

"Since you're here, why don't ya leave after we've given Loli Big Boobs's child a name? It's the last one, anyway."

"Hee-hee, I apologize, but I can't. Still…" Freya reached down to the table and picked up her copy of the paperwork. She took a look at Bell's face and said, "Just be sure to name him something cute."

""""""""""OKAY!!""""""""""

All of the gods around the table suddenly looked refreshed as Freya flashed her biggest smile of the day at each of them in turn. The goddesses, however, glared at their male counterparts, as if they were looking at rotten garbage.

Freya turned her back to the table and started to walk toward the door, sending one last grin over her shoulder.

"Well, shall we get down to business and choose a title for this boy?"

"Sounds good."

"But this human…I haven't heard anything about him."

"It's the ones you overlook who surprise you."

"There are no rumors about him at all."

The suddenly serious gods began discussing the boy immediately.

Hestia had finally recovered from the abrupt changes of mood during the Denatus and looked up at Hephaistos sitting next to her. Her eyes asked exactly what she wanted to know: "What happened?"

The crimson-haired goddess shrugged her shoulders, a look of frustration on her face as she responded. "I don't have a clue."

"There's not enough information here. Nothing to go on. The Guild was really lazy with this one."

"He leveled up just two days before the Denatus, so they had to squeeze him in. Can't be helped."

"Let's see…White hair with red eyes…A rabbit…How about 'The Good Rabbit, Pyonkichi'?"

"No, that name is already used. A smith named Wel-something used it for a piece of armor already."

"Thought of it before us…!!"

"Wel-something…Just what is he?"

"Hmmm, Ganesha, do you have any thoughts?"

"……I am Ganesha!"

"Yes, yes, Ganesha, Ganesha."

"As we try to find a more suitable name, nothing really jumps out at me!"

The discussion continued with the male gods taking center stage in a somewhat unproductive conversation.

Hestia tilted her head in relief that the greatest danger seemed to be behind her.

A heartbeat later, a shadow fell over her body.

"...Loki?"

"..."

Loki was standing beside her. She had left her seat on the other side of the table and was now staring directly down at Hestia.

There was no doubt she was in a bad mood, but she forced her mouth open and said:

"...Watch yer back, Shorty."

"Huh?"

"Keep yer eyes open, is what I'm sayin'. As much as it pains me ta warn ya like this...I can't stand watchin' that idiot do as she pleases. Gotta stop it now.

"She's underestimatin' me," said Loki with an annoyed sneer.

Loki jerked her head toward the door to grab Hestia's attention. Looking in that direction, she saw the last of Freya's silver hair flow out of sight.

"W-wait a second, here! What do you mean by 'warn me'?"

Unable to understand Loki's words, Hestia asked for clarification. Loki's eyebrows twitched in frustration before she took another step toward the young goddess.

"Are ya that thick?" asked Loki as she leaned down to Hestia's eye level, their noses almost close enough to touch.

"Idiot! Wake up, willya? She just covered fer yer boy."

"...?"

Still unable to connect the dots, Hestia could only look back at Loki with dumbfounded eyes.

Loki stood back up, sighing through her nose. She'd had enough.

"Woah, y'really don't know. Ah well, not my problem anyway. Such an idiot," Loki said under her breath on her way back to her seat.

Under Hephaistos's watchful gaze, Hestia's eyes followed Loki as she went around the table. Then she looked over toward the door that Freya had just exited.

She mulled over Loki's words.

And then she remembered the look that the goddess of beauty had sent right at her.

…Freya…protected him?

The moment she realized the possibility of a certain scenario, the table of gods and goddesses around her erupted as one.

""""""""""""""""""IT'S DECIDED!!"""""""""""""""""

🔥

The atmosphere wasn't exactly bizarre, but it definitely wasn't normal.

An air of tension had descended upon one of the largest rooms in the Guild Headquarters.

"Why does everyone look like they're going to kill something?"

"I don't think that's what's going on…"

Misha whispered into a pointed ear. Eina responded quietly under her breath.

The two of them had left their usual workplace in the lobby and gone upstairs to the second-floor office room.

An intense stillness had taken over a space that was normally in constant motion.

"Tulle, are you listening?"

"Ah…m-my apologies, sir."

A voice from directly in front of her yanked Eina out of her thoughts. Misha snapped to attention beside her.

There was a male animal person sitting in a chair in front of the two girls, holding in his right hand a document that Eina had recently prepared. His eyes fell from his subordinates back down to the paperwork and narrowed with discontent.

"At the risk of repeating myself, publishing this would be the same as telling all Level One adventurers to die."

"Umm…"

"I realize you put forth much effort to collect this information, but the Guild cannot under any circumstances allow it to become public. I'm shelving the plan to use Bell Cranell as a model for adventure development."

I was afraid of that, thought Eina as she pulled her shoulders just a little farther back.

—While working solo, slay a large amount of killer ants before taking down a Minotaur in one-on-one combat.

That was a very brief summary of how Bell reached Level 2.

Should this strategy be made public and used by many low-level adventurers as a method to level up quickly, then there was no doubt the number of casualties would be off the charts.

Low-level adventurers would think the Guild was making a joke at their expense.

"…We'll need to sweep this under the rug. I'll take care of the higher-ups myself."

"I'm very sorry, sir…"

Eina's boss, a gentleman with thin features, took one last look at the document before shutting it deep in the bowels of his desk. Most likely, no one would ever see it again.

Lightly scratching the long ears on top of his head, the man turned away from his desk and back toward the girls with a very disgruntled look on his face.

"Tulle, one more thing. "

"What is it, sir?"

"Please try to keep your emotions in check from now on."

"…Yes, sir. I will be more careful."

After being scolded for that last incident of the morning—when she had shouted Bell's personal information in the crowded lobby—Eina deeply lowered her head in apology.

Grateful to her superior for overlooking the incident, she sighed quietly to herself.

The man took a moment to clear his throat and said, "Next, Frot," looking toward the human girl.

"Y-yes?"

"…The quality of paperwork submitted to the Denatus was extremely poor. Especially the last one, for adventurer Bell Cranell."

"B-but, sir—. He leveled up so soon before the meeting that I had no time—! I did the best I could with my back against the wall, so please don't question the effort that I put into making it!"

"I understand what you're saying…but I'm talking about the whole project. Should we receive any complaints from the gods, it will be your job to talk to them alone, Frot. I can't help you if it comes to that."

"Waaaah—Eina—," sobbed Misha as she wrapped her arms around her friend's shoulders. Eina sighed for the second time in as many minutes. Their supervisor turned to face his desk with a very curt "You may leave." The two of them backed away from him and started walking toward the exit.

But rather than returning straight to the lobby, they decided to stop at the break room in the corner of the office.

Using a magic-stone machine they had operated many times before, both of them had a cup of hot tea in their hands in no time at all.

"Ugh…Tell your little brother I said 'thanks a lot'…"

"Little brother…? He's not the only reason for what happened today, Misha."

"Not listening! Can't hear a word you're saying!"

Swish. Eina could only look on in astonishment as her human friend's shoulders slumped, turning away.

Misha's pink hair swung lightly around her chin as she sipped tea and tried to make herself as small as possible.

She hasn't changed at all since our school days, thought Eina with a grimace on her face.

"Not to change the subject, but what was with all of them? Everyone seemed really uptight."

"Hmm, well, they aren't usually like this…"

They couldn't find a single relaxed face among the Guild employees from their vantage point at the corner of the office.

Many of them were up, pacing back and forth in front of their desks. Those who were sitting in their chairs kept looking at the clock as if it were about to explode. The office was normally filled with pens racing across parchment, but that sound was nowhere to be heard.

Actually, the two girls had a pretty good idea of what was causing the heavy mood.

"It's just past three in the afternoon...It's over, right—the Denatus?"

"Most likely. The results should have been delivered by now..."

This was the usual scene on the second floor of the Guild after a Denatus meeting.

The Guild employees were very interested to know the titles assigned to adventurers. The people of Gekai had to take their hats off to each of the names given, and nobody could wait to see what the gods and goddesses would think of next.

Seeing their superiors like this was nothing special to Eina and Misha, they had seen adventurers do exactly the same thing in the lobby many times.

"Are you excited, too, Eina? I wonder what names came up this time."

"I...Hmm, yes. I'm a little interested this time."

"So it's true? Actually, one of my adventurers leveled up, too, so I can't wait to see!"

Their conversation was interrupted without warning by a *BANG!*

An office door had been flung open, slamming into the wall behind it. All eyes in the room turned to face the doorway.

A man stood in the frame, trying to catch his breath and carrying a bundle of paperwork.

"It's here—the Denatus results are here!"

"Finally!"

"Hey, open it up, already!"

All the employees dropped everything and rushed toward the door. The mob encircled the man as he passed out sheet after sheet of documents containing the second names of adventurers.

Voices of praise and amazement started ringing out almost immediately.

"Take a look at this one, this nickname."

"Woah! Awesome…"

"They never disappoint."

"Ahh, we'll never measure up."

"The gods really are different from us. The Hand of Strength and Grace, 'Biolante'…Gives me goose bumps just reading it!"

"This is so exhilarating!"

"The gods just come up with this stuff off the top of their heads. They really are worth looking up to."

The Guild office was suddenly alive with excitement, especially the male employees.

Eina and Misha's supervisors seemed to be all in agreement, standing in a circle and talking as though they were of one mind. A group of women from another department arrived on the scene, their higher-pitched voices joining in the mix of enthusiastic chatter.

Misha stood just outside the break room, separate from all of the energy across the room. A sudden shiver ran down her spine, twitching her shoulders.

"T-they're starting without us…! Let's go, Eina!"

"Ah, sure."

Eina followed her into the fray. Making sure not to lose sight of Misha's pink hair as the human girl fought her way to get a copy of the name list, Bell's face suddenly popped up in Eina's mind.

Ohhh, a softer name would be better for him…

What if they named him something like "The Crimson Adventurer, Bloody Guy"? Suddenly she could see herself telling him—with Bell puffing out his chest with pride and her sweating—as she chose her words very carefully.

While not necessarily feeling that such a gallant name would be completely unsuitable for Bell, somehow it didn't fit his image. Biting her lip, she did her best to calm down and prayed that she wouldn't have to face that situation.

"Eina, I got it! Quick, have a look!"

Misha waved her over, a big smile on her face and the list in her hand.

There were several documents containing the titles selected for the adventurers. The two of them started at the top sheet, their eyes working down the list through the second and third sheets.

Eina finally found what she was looking for at the very bottom of the final paper.

"—Ah-ha-ha-ha."

"Oh? Bell's name?"

Eina couldn't control the laughter pouring out of her.

Her pinkish cheeks tightened, her lips quivering into his soft smile.

Misha leaned over the list, trying to find his name. Eina read it to her out loud.

"It's 'Little Rookie.'"

CHAPTER 2

NEW RELATIONSHIPS CHANGING ENVIRONMENT,

"…"

I'm lying here, looking up at the white ceiling.

I'm the only one in the room under the church, and I'm sprawled out on the sofa.

There's really nothing for me to do besides zoning out and letting the day go by. *Ticktock ticktock.* I can hear the gears inside the clock on the wall as it marks the steady march of time.

It's been three days since the fight with the Minotaur.

This is becoming a habit. I'm getting used to daydreaming for long periods of time, motionless.

I slept for two days at the hospital inside Babel Tower after that fight.

It took a heavy toll on me…Neither my body nor my mind held out at the very end, and I just shut down. Apparently I slept like the dead, nothing but a bump under the sheets. However, I was awake enough at one point to see a look of relief on the goddess's face, and Lilly's, too. That's the only thing I can remember after the battle.

After that the goddess and Lilly half carried me back here. I spent the rest of that day on the sofa—exactly like I am now.

"Level…Two…"

I'm a Level 2 adventurer.

Hearing that I leveled up brought a smile to my face. The proof that I'm closing the gap between me and *her* is now etched into my back.

…But I just can't get over the fact that I won, I beat that Minotaur.

It's like a never-ending transparent reverberation, unrelated to the heat of victory. But it's not a langorous sensation—more a feeling like water rising up out of a flowing spring.

Saying it feels like accomplishment would be an overstatement, but it doesn't feel like I've been released from a burden, either.

Loss…Yes, I feel like I've lost something.

I can't put it into words very well, but something about that Minotaur meant a lot to me.

Of course, leveling up is important, but the fact that I slew a Minotaur feels heavier somehow.

"..."

I reach down beside my hip, grab what I'm looking for, and raise it up to the light.

A sharp point, its charred surface having a few cracks. It's a horn that looks a little bit like a long dagger.

The drop item "Minotaur Horn."

Lilly told me that when the Minotaur turned to ash, only the magic stone and this horn remained. She'd already exchanged the magic stone for money, but she held on to the horn for me.

Holding it under the magic-stone lamp, I scrape off some of the burned surface.

I watch as the grayish dust falls off the surface, exposing a reddish layer underneath. I wonder if that's how it originally was or if my magic had something to do with it.

It's a very robust horn.

To think the Minotaur was thrusting it at me right at the very end.

Somehow, the fearsome roar that has been in the back of my mind since that day a month ago seems distant now.

All that's left is the silent horn in my hand, like some sort of parting gift.

"...Okay."

I get off the sofa. My body is surprisingly light.

I've got to pull myself together. Clenching my jaw, I put the horn down out of sight. Enough of this brooding.

I need to move around. First thing I do is check the clock.

Actually, I'm going to a party today. It's at my usual bar and café, The Benevolent Mistress.

Truthfully, the party is to celebrate my leveling up...

I told Syr that I'd leveled up this morning, when I went to return a lunch basket, and next thing I knew I was going to a party at The Benevolent Mistress.

I think she wants to get me to spend money. It does sound like one of her plans, and I don't really need to hold back…but it just feels strange.

Would have been nice if the goddess could have come…

I don't think she has time. She said that she and some other gods are going to go out for a drinking party of their own. I'm not sure if it's a Celebration or if they're trying to cheer somebody up, I just know she's busy.

When she came by after the meeting, she told me my title was "Little Rookie."

Little Rookie…Hmm. Well, the goddess seemed happy about it. She threw her arms around me and yelled, "This is great, Bell! You got a good one!" So I'm not…disappointed.

I've been alone with my thoughts since then. But now it's six o'clock in the evening. Time to get a move on.

I leave the hidden room under the church and make my way outside onto the street.

The western sky is already turning red. It's almost night.

I make my way through the side streets and out onto the busy Main Street.

"—Thereeeee heeeee iiiiiiis!!!!"

"Eh?"

It happens just as I'm about to join the crowd.

A sudden loud voice fills my ears.

Wh-what? I don't even have time to look around before a wave of people surrounds me.

They're—gods…?!

"Couldn't find the Loli Lady's home anywhere, and we've been lookin' real hard, too…"

"But it was worth staking out this area…"

"Lying in wait is the key to hunting, you know."

"So you finally came out of your hole, Li'l Bunny."

—I'm scared.

They're getting closer, surrounding me. I don't know why, but alarm bells are going off in my head. Especially that last one. My blood ran cold when he winked at me.

What the hell is going on?

What are they doing here, what are they talking about? I'm so confused.

"First come, first serve! Bell, want to join my *Familia*? If you come with me right now, everyone will greet you with open arms!"

"Hey, idiot! You sound way too desperate! Wait your turn, why don't you? That's why your *Familia* is still so tiny…!"

"Blabbermouths, out of my way. Bell, come to me! For it is you who has stolen my heart, you naughty bunny!"

"What do you have in mind for this child?!"

They're arguing with one another and coming closer, step by step. I have to say something, so I clear my throat. "Ahem."

…A *Familia* welcoming me with open arms? Why now?

Every single one I went to when I first came to Orario showed me the door without a second look…

"I, um, already have a goddess…I'm a member of *Hestia Familia*…?!"

"All previous relationships are meaningless in the eyes of love. Don't you think so?"

"You're too good for the Loli Lady!"

T-they aren't listening…!

"But a serious question: What's the secret to your fast growth? Raw talent? A Skill? Or perhaps foul play?"

"A rare skill, a rare skill? Is it true, is it true? It has to be a rare skill!"

"I really wanna know what's written on this boy's back."

"If it's okay with you, would you take those clothes off? Just the top is okay! I'll even pay you?…Hee-hee."

"We could always force him out of them…"

"—Fu-heh-heh-heh."

—I run away with all speed.

"He's here, meow!"

"Ah-ha-ha! Fashionably late, aren't you, Mr. Adventure."

The sky is completely dark and the moon shines brightly over my head by the time I reach The Benevolent Mistress.

I reach out to support myself against one of the pillars by the front door, hunching over to try to catch my breath. *Huff...huff...huff...* I'm going to need a moment.

I flew through the back streets, doubling back many times to try and shake my divine pursuers. I only lost them just a few minutes ago.

I should be in much better shape than them...So what was that? They almost had me a few times; it felt like I was running for my life. I've never thought of gods and goddesses as scary before.

Why all of a sudden...?

"Syr 'n' everyone's been waitin' for you, meow! The kitchen's really busy, too, we're bending over backward to accommodate you, meow! So get in here, meow."

"S-sorry..."

"They couldn't start without the guest of honor. Go over there, quickly."

Two waitresses—Ahnya, a cat person, and a human—come out to meet me and usher me inside. If I remember right the human girl's name is...Runoa. She's laughing, too.

I wipe the sweat from my face and stand up straight before setting foot in the bar.

"Mr. Bell! We're over here—!"

I swear there's a customer in every single seat in here! But just over the lively mass of humanity, I see Lilly standing on a chair and waving with a big smile on her face.

I invited Lilly to come tonight. It's not every day that I get to do something like this, and she responded with a resounding "Yes!" so I asked Syr to prepare a seat for her.

...It would have been nice for Aiz to be here as well—wouldn't that be something? But she's somewhere in the lower levels of the Dungeon right now on an expedition, so inviting her wasn't an option. Trying to get the what-ifs out of my head, I give a quick nod and wave back at Lilly.

The table they reserved for us is close to my usual counter seat. Syr and Lyu are sitting beside Lilly, dressed in their nice-looking waitress uniforms.

Syr's eyes meet mine as I work my way through the crowd. I bow my head, mouthing, "Sorry I'm late!" over and over.

"Bell...?"

"*Hestia Familia*?"

Just as I'm making progress toward the girls waiting for me, I suddenly feel all the eyes in the bar lock onto me.

The topics of the conversations around me change without warning, like a spark igniting an inferno.

I don't stop moving as I look around in every direction.

"A white-headed human...That's him, all right. What did they call him...? 'Little Rookie'?"

"That punk-ass kid?"

"You heard? He's the record holder now."

"Who said he's gonna keep it? The gods're just awestruck, nothin' more. One month is nothin'!"

"Ya got tha' right!"

"But I've heard that he really did slay that Minotaur. You know the one, the lower ninth."

"So he took out one Minotaur, big frickin' deal!"

"Could you kill a Mino at Level One? On your own, I might add."

"Who in their right mind would try something that stupid?"

Eyes glinting at me from every direction, I weave my way through the maze of tables as quickly as possible. The air around me is swirling with hushed whispers.

Being the center of attention like this is overwhelming! I must look like a criminal or something. A man stops talking on the spot when my eyes happen to meet his.

With ice flowing in my veins, I duck down as low as possible and quickly escape to my destination.

"You've become the talk of the town, Mr. Bell."

"R-really? I can't relax anymore...Even on my way here, I was chased around the city by a group of gods..."

"That is the fate of all adventurers who become known. You are not being singled out, Bell. Please put up with it for the time being."

I can feel all the muscles in my face droop. I must look pretty funny because Lilly's trying hard not to laugh at me.

I scratch the back of my neck with my left hand out of habit, making small bows to everyone in turn.

"Well, now that Bell is here, let's get this thing started, shall we?"

"Um, Syr and Lyu, are you sure it's okay for you guys to be here with the bar like this...?"

" 'I'll lend 'im the two of ya. Make sure he's well fed' was Mama Mia's instruction. That and 'spend yer cash.' "

Hearing Lyu imitate the owner's—Mia's—accent in her calm voice makes me chuckle to myself.

As for Mia, I look over my shoulder to see her standing behind the bar, waving her hand and giving me a hearty smile. Must be her way of telling me to live it up tonight.

It's not long before we say "Cheers!" and clink our glasses together.

Mia suggests that I try ale for the first time, being a special occasion and all. For now, I've got a small jug of the stuff in front of me.

Syr's holding a citrusy cocktail, Lilly's gotten sick of ale so she's drinking fruit juice, and Lyu refuses to drink anything except for water. Wait a second...Syr and I are the only ones drinking alcohol?

As soon as food starts arriving at our table, all the eyes around the bar finally turn away. Such a relief! Ahnya and Chloe drop by our table a few times for some friendly banter and we start to have a genuinely good time.

I know that Lilly and Lyu have a little bit of bad blood from an incident when Lilly was still a thief, but it's never come up, and Lilly is laughing and looks like she's having a great time. Syr is smiling ear to ear, while Lyu is responding to their questions as seriously as ever.

I wonder if something happened before I got here. I keep catching Lilly looking at me out of the corner of her eye.

"Now, Bell, drink lots and lots. You're the star of the show tonight. Or maybe, would you like something to eat?"

"T-thank you..."

Suddenly Syr is at my side, waiting on me hand and foot.

Getting me more ale, loading up my plate with food, filling my jug, she's zipping around all over the place. And for some reason, Lilly's usual smile is scary.

Even though I'm feeling kind of awkward, Syr looks like she's enjoying herself.

"I could be wrong...but you seem to be in a very good mood, Syr."

"Do you really think so?"

I think she blushed a little bit just now. I can't tell anymore because she's hiding her cheek with her hand and giggling behind her shoulder like someone's tickling her.

"It might be a bit bold of me to say this but...I feel like I helped you when I gave you that book. And thinking about that makes me, I don't know, happy."

She must be talking about the grimoire. She won't take her warm gaze off of me.

Our eyes meet and she smiles even wider. It's almost intimidating.

The muscles in my face are locked in place. What does it look like right now?

"If I may say, Mr. Cranell, congratulations to you. To think that you would be able to level up on your own...I seem to have underestimated you."

"I-it's nothing..."

At the same time, I get a compliment from the other side of the table.

Lyu's expression hasn't changed at all, but I'm still embarrassed.

"M-many people helped me out; it's all thanks to them. Even you, Lyu..."

"There is no need for modesty. Of all the level-two categorized monsters, defeating a Minotaur is worthy of praise. Mr. Cranell, you are allowed to be proud of your accomplishment."

Lyu said everything in a very deliberate, serious voice. She looks at me with a refined gaze from across the table.

I just noticed something about myself: I'm not good at taking compliments.

© Suzuhito Yasuda

My face is turning red and my throat is so tight that getting the word "thanks" out of my mouth takes everything I have.

To top it all off, Syr is giggling at me…

"Lilly was worried sick about you. Her heart was breaking over and over…"

"I-I'm sorry, Lilly…"

"…But you looked really cool, Mr. Bell."

I can't take much more of this…

Lilly leaning up to my shoulder with her big smile is the finishing blow.

Her cheeks are rosy pink, and those large, chestnut-colored eyes of hers are so close I can see myself in them.

It could be the alcohol, but my entire body feels hot.

"Mr. Cranell, what is your plan going forward?"

"?"

"I am curious about what the two of you are planning."

After talking with Lilly, I hear Lyu's voice again as I'm trying my best to fight off the effects of the ale. Without really taking time to think about her question, I start talking about my plan for tomorrow.

"Well, tomorrow Lilly and I are going to go buy some new equipment. My old armor was completely destroyed."

"…About that, Mr. Bell."

"What is it, Lilly?"

"There are many things at the shop where Lilly is staying that need to be done…It doesn't look like she will be able to join you tomorrow."

"What, really?"

I can see Lilly shrinking in her chair, looking very apologetic. But considering all the shop has done for her after everything that's happened, it can't be helped…so I tell her not to worry about it and start thinking about what I should do.

I want to start going into the Dungeon again soon, and I need new armor in order to do that.

I should be able to find new equipment on my own, right? I could go by myself tomorrow.

Sure, I'm not as good at judging quality…but this will be a good learning experience.

"In that case, are you going to go shopping alone tomorrow, Bell?"

"It looks that way."

"Then, would it be all right if I came with you?"

"Huh?!" Syr's suggestion catches me off guard; I can only choke up a surprised response.

Lilly jumps, too, but soon crosses her arms and lowers one shoulder at Syr. She looks like a boxer before a fight…

"Wh-why do you ask?"

"I need to buy some things pretty soon anyway…I might get in the way, but if it's okay with you, Bell, I want to go shopping with you."

"No, Mr. Bell! Miss Syr only wants you there to carry her bags! That's right, Lilly can see your hidden agenda! Mr. Bell, she's planning to make you carry so much that your bones will crack! Turn her down!"

"I-I'm not going to buy that much…"

A bead of sweat rolls down my face after Lilly's outburst. She's standing right next to me, so I look up in Syr's direction.

But she seems unfazed and smirks at Lilly. "Why would I do something like that?" says Syr, with her light gray eyes gazing warmly down at me.

Wh-what do I do…?

I don't mind going shopping with her, and I'd feel bad to refuse her invitation…Ah—then again, things tend to happen when I go along with her suggestions. There was the night when I came here for the first time…And just a few days ago I ended up washing dishes to help her out.

I'm trapped between Lilly's objections and Syr's warm smile. Just as I'm about to crumble under the pressure— the wooden floor creaks.

A large shadow falls over Syr from behind.

"Don't push yer luck!"

"Ugahh!!"

Wham! A tray appears out of nowhere, slicing through the air at an angle, and slams into the back of Syr's head.

It's Mia. She's standing and glaring menacingly down at Syr. She must've hit her pretty hard; Syr is holding her head, with tears bubbling up in the corners of her eyes.

"Don' be thinkin' you can take time off that easily, ya little brat. Gettin' full o' yourself, eh? What's the big idea, playin' hooky whenever ya feel like it," Mia growls under her breath.

Supporting her shaking body by putting her elbows on the table, Syr looks back, only to see Mia's burning death-stare.

She twists her body to face Mia directly. I can't see her face, just her light gray hair tied into its usual bun with a ponytail coming out the middle. But based on her aura, I'd say she's glaring right back at Mia.

"Those eyes'll get'cha nowhere. Here, I'm the law, got that? Lyu, keep an eye on 'er tomorrow."

Mia's nostrils flare in anger as she turns on her heel before Lyu can answer, going back behind the bar counter.

Our table becomes a silent island in the middle of the sea of happy voices.

The tension continues for a few moments before Syr turns to face me.

"Bell, I've become damaged goods. Would you please pat my head and cheer me up?"

"So, Mr. Bell! Enjoy your shopping trip tomorrow and find some good stuff *alone*. Lilly can't wait to see what you buy!"

I'm worried that these two will never be able to sit at the same table again.

"Mr. Cranell, what about after that?"

"Eh?"

"My question is, what are you planning to do after you have found suitable equipment?"

"What do you mean...by that?"

"I'll take a more direct approach. Mr. Cranell, Miss Erde, do you intend to go to the middle levels as soon as you return to the Dungeon?"

So that's what she's been asking all this time.

Lilly and I look at each other for a moment—we are in the same party, after all—before looking back at Lyu.

"For starters, I'd like to test out my new strength on the eleventh level. If everything goes well, I'd like to go to the twelfth."

"Yes, that is very wise."

I go on to tell her that I want to test my leveled-up abilities in the upper levels, and the best place to do that is on the twelfth level. Lilly and I had agreed that after warming up on that level, so long as everything looks good, we'd go to the middle levels together.

Lyu might be worried about us, I think.

"It may not be my place to say this…but I believe that you should not proceed to the middle levels at this time."

"In other words, Miss Lyu, you believe that Mr. Bell and Lilly aren't good enough to make it in the middle levels?"

"It was not my intention to insinuate that you are weak. That being said, the upper levels and the middle levels are *very different.*"

Of course Lyu doesn't leave her explanation at that.

"It's not a problem of individual strength or ability. It becomes *impossible for a solo adventurer* to dispose of every monster. That's the kind of place the middle levels are. While I'm unfamiliar with the level of support Ms. Erde can provide, I'm afraid that Mr. Cranell will be unable to deal with the monsters and the Dungeon layout on his own."

"So then, Miss Lyu is saying…"

"Yes. You should add additional members to your battle party."

A three-man cell is the most basic party formation for dungeon crawling. At the very least, that's what the Guild suggests.

The three-man cell—a formation that allows for attack, defense, and support roles.

One member focuses on attacking the front line while another member covers him or her from monster counterattacks. The third member stays at long range, sometimes assisting the front line with a ranged weapon, spells, or healing items when necessary.

The same holds true when attacked from behind. If the person in the supporting role also has the ability to hold their own against monsters, then it's possible to withstand wave after wave of attacks until the table turns into their favor.

It's easy to get surrounded when working in a two-man cell, not to mention solo. Conquering the deeper floors of the Dungeon will be extremely difficult for us without at least one more party member to turn the tide in a pinch.

Adding a third person won't have much impact on our individual strength, but it will make our unit exponentially stronger.

Knowing all of this, Lyu probably thinks that our two-man cell party wouldn't be strong enough to survive in the middle levels.

"But wait a minute, Lyu. Wouldn't it be easier for them to run away if it's just Bell and Lilly? The more people there are, the more likely someone is to be left behind, right?"

"While your reasoning is not flawed, Syr, the only time adventurers consider retreat is after being cornered. It is much more practical for adventurers to avoid those situations rather than plan their escape."

An awestruck sound comes out of my mouth.

Since she was once an adventurer herself, Lyu's calculated words carry a lot of weight.

"You must prepare for everything. Find someone worthy of your trust and add them to your battle party."

I get what she's saying. I see Lilly nod out of the corner of my eye and start thinking.

But...I don't know anyone like that who I could invite to join us. If I did I would have already asked them. I suppose that's why she told me to find someone...

I would ask her, but I'm sure Lyu has some circumstances. The only other person who would be an option would be Nahza, in *Miach Familia*. But no, she's no good, either. I don't want to take anyone suffering from monster trauma into the Dungeon with me.

Would scouting out someone to join my *Familia* be the best option?

I start massaging my temples.

"Ha-ha! Having some party problems there, 'Little Rookie'?!"

"Wha?" I'm so shocked by a sudden loud voice that I can't respond right away.

While I recover from the surprise, the customer—a male adventurer, followed by two of his friends—comes up to our table. They stop directly across from me, and right behind Lyu's chair.

These guys are...huge.

Their square faces are covered in scars...Enough to make me cringe.

"We heard your troubles! You need allies, yeah? Then why don't you join *us*, you little bastard?"

"Eh?!"

Okay, now I'm surprised.

Who would've expected a square-shouldered, red-faced man I've never met before to invite me into his own battle party?

"E-excuse me?"

"This ain't that hard. It's quite easy, actually. One of my fellow adventurers has a problem, and so out of the kindness of my huge heart, I'm gonna help you out. Hee-hee, doesn't that sound good to you?"

"W-well, I wasn't really..."

"Of course it does! It's called havin' your back, havin' your back! And considerin' it's you, we don't mind at all if you join us...Yeah!"

"Uggh...?!"

How much ale did this guy drink?!

A wall of alcoholic stench assaults me from across the table. Syr is grimacing next to me, and Lilly has a look of absolute loathing on her face. Oh yeah, that's right, she's allergic to adventurers...

Lyu is the closest one to them, so she should be the hardest hit by that smell. But she is just calmly sitting in her chair. Her stoic face hasn't changed a bit.

"So here's the deal! We'll take you to the middle levels, and in exchange..."

...Huh?

Is this situation getting worse?

"Let us have these ladies for a while?! I'm takin' this cute little fairy of an elf for myself!"

…Whoah. *Whoah.*

"I'd like to have an elf fill my jug, if you get my drift. Don't know how much you're spendin', but we scratch your back, you scratch ours. That's the basics, don't you think?"

Sure, I'll end up spending a lot of money tonight…But what does that have to do with anything?

The man in the middle is looking down at Lyu, and his buddies are eyeing Syr and Lilly. They look strange, like they're imagining something extremely perverted. I've never seen Lilly look so angry.

…This is not good, not good at all.

I will never shake hands with someone who looks at women like that.

I'm not good at this kind of thing, but I have to be the "man" here. I can't let anything happen to my friends…!

I start building the refusal in my head.

"That is not necessary. He does not need you."

However, before I can open my mouth—

Lyu suddenly speaks up out of the blue.

"…Ohhh? What was that, little fairy? Are you insinuatin' that we can't protect that kid?"

"Precisely. Now leave."

"Hi-hi, you guys, you hear that? She's sayin' we'd hold the rookie back! Not the other way around, ha-ha-ha!"

All three of the men laugh out loud. Not only have I lost my chance to stand up, I'm lost for words, too.

I'm already halfway out of my chair, but I don't know if I should get all the way up or sit back down.

"Listen, girly, we've been in and out of the middle levels for years now."

"Is that so?"

"That's right, Level Two. The lot of us, yeah."

"Thank you for the information. Now, begone. The likes of you are not worthy of him."

Silence. The men who had been laughing up until now go quiet, their faces contorting in anger.

Their grins come back a moment later. But their eyes…They're like the dark, dead eyes of a mask.

Even I can tell the tension around the table has shot way up.

"Girly, what are you tryin' to say? That we're trash, lower than that punk-ass kid?"

The man takes a step forward and reaches out to put a hand on Lyu's shoulder.

Ah! I'm about to jump to my feet when I remember something someone told me not too long ago:

—*Elves do not allow someone they don't trust to touch their skin.*

"Hands off."

Lyu's next movements are all a blur.

She reaches out and grabs my nearly full ale jug with lightning speed, and slams it back over her shoulder toward the oncoming hand.

A heartbeat later, *THUNK!*

The man's hand is now crammed into the sturdy jug, his eyes wide in shock. A soft "Eh?" comes out of his mouth.

Lyu turns around and jumps to her feet, twisting the jug in the process.

"Ow-ow-ow-OOOWWWWWWWW!!"

The man screams at the top of his lungs; his elbow points out at an impossible angle.

"I apologize. It appears that my reasoning was much more self-ish than I originally thought. I don't want Mr. Cranell to join your battle party."

Her words were like whips slicing through the air, the man writhing in pain beneath her.

"And I will not allow you to look down on him. He is my good friend."

She zeroes in her icy glare on him and gives the jug yet another twist.

The man's scream goes up an octave. His buddies rush to his aid and start pulling.

POP! PLUNK! The man's hand finally comes out of the jug and he lands flat on his ass.

"…You BITCH!"

"Frickin' girl!"

"The hell are you doin'?!"

Did Lyu just really say that about me? A warm feeling grows in my chest as the enraged men converge on her.

In no time at all, Lyu has a small sword in her grasp. All three of the adventurers move to attack her together. But before they can—

SMASH! BANG! Two loud cracks erupt from behind his buddies' heads.

""Ghaaah?!""

Both of the men fall to the floor with a dull thud.

Two cat people are standing behind where the adventurers once were, holding broken chairs over their shoulders.

"—Nyfufufu. Gotta watch yer *back*, meow!"

"Men are such a pain, meow—"

Chloe is laughing like she's one of the gods herself, while Ahnya's ears are twitching back and forth out of annoyance.

I know the girls snuck up behind them but…down in one hit?! Those guys were Level 2!

"Sir. Our elf tends to be rather violent. Backing down now would be a good idea."

Runoa calmly walks past the scene, carrying a ton of dirty dishes in her arms, and gives the man a friendly warning.

He's completely outnumbered in a small space, but he looks like he's itching for a fight. Am I seeing this right?

"Ah—ah, there they go." I can feel the eyes again, and many people are saying things. But they're not scared, it's like they knew this was going to happen. Their stares move past me and onto the man. He's on his own little island now, and the center of attention.

"…Wh-what the hell are you people?!"

Bathed in a magic-stone lamp spotlight, the man reaches behind his back and draws a white blade.

It's a shortsword. He's consumed with rage, his body shaking. There's no way to tell when he'll make his move.

The staff of The Benevolent Mistress all have their eyes locked on him.

Zing! A shiver shoots down my spine.

I have a feeling things won't end well for this guy. Just then—

An *explosion* comes from a different direction.

What is it this time?!

Every head in the room snaps in the new direction with blinding speed…And now I'm really lost for words.

The counter…It was waist height just a moment ago, but now it's in the shape of a large *V*. The poor customers sitting at the counter… Their mouths are hanging open in shock.

And standing at the base of the *V* is Mia, her outstretched fist right in the center.

Runoa and all the other waitresses suddenly shiver with fright.

"If you wanna brawl, take it outside. This place is for eatin' and drinkin'."

Silence falls over the entire bar. All the waitresses immediately break eye contact with Mia and go back to work.

Finally, Mia stands up straight and squares her shoulders directly at the adventurer himself.

"And you, ya blockhead. Be sure an' take those idiot lumps on the floor out with ya. If ya try an' cause any more ruckus—y'all will wind up six feet below my bar."

*Doesn't that mean he'll be…*A bead of sweat rolls down my face as the adventurer silently nods up and down.

Lifting his fallen comrades up by their shoulders, he makes for the door with his buddies' feet dragging behind him.

"Hey, crap-fer-brains! You gotta pay first!!"

"Y-yes, ma'am!!"

The man drops what looks to be all his money onto the floor in fear of Mia's rage. A bag full of coins clinks as it hit the ground at her feet.

After the three of them practically fall through the door, the usual din of the bar starts back up again. Prums start drinking and singing as if nothing ever happened, their voices echoing through the building.

A bar where Level 2 parties run away in fright...

All I could do was watch...

"My apologies, I have destroyed the atmosphere on your special night."

"N-no, don't worry about it..."

"Hee-hee, Miss Lyu really is very strong...Lilly's lower back is still tingling."

I'm still trying to shake off the panic that overtook me, and here's Lilly teasing Lyu about her apology.

Am I the only one here who's not used to something like this...?

Tension is still in the air from what just happened when Syr suddenly claps her hands together and stands up.

"Well, shall we try this again from the start?"

...She's pretty strong, too.

She orders a new round of drinks for all of us and a moment later we're clinking glasses again. I can't help but smile as I watch her work.

Once again I've been reminded of what the staff of The Benevolent Mistress is capable of doing.

After that, we enjoy good food and ale well into the night.

Beautiful blue skies and a light breeze in my face.

It's the morning after my party at the bar.

Using my hand to shield my eyes from the sun, I look up at the massive structure in front of me.

A white tower, Babel.

I've decided to go to *Hephaistos Familia*'s weapon shop to find the equipment I need.

I don't have to worry about the quality of weapons and armor sold here. Considering I don't know how to tell the good stuff from the bad, there's no reason for me to look anywhere else. But above all, Eina brought me here before, so I don't feel nervous going in.

I'm not concerned about money today, either. I've been able to save up quite a bit recently…Not to mention the Minotaur's magic stone was worth 50,000 vals. Lilly told me that even the clerk at the Exchange was surprised, so I'm pretty sure that Minotaur was something special…It was wielding a sword, after all.

Anyway, I have more than 100,000 vals on me right now. I walk through Babel's main gates with a smile on my face.

Rather than riding the elevator, I take the stairs all the way to the eighth floor.

The best part about the stairwell is definitely the view out of the windows. The blue sky is absolutely stunning today.

Ah, here it is.

The eighth floor.

The layout is like a big doughnut, with a hole in the middle for the elevator to go through. The shops are built on both sides of the circular hallway. Each shop has its own combination of swords, spears, and the like outside its entrance or on its sign as decoration.

Stopping to take a look at some of the tenants along my way, I arrive at my destination.

Since the thing that protects my body, my light armor, was completely destroyed, coming here first makes the most sense.

Just like before, it's like a forest of armor in here. Most of it is designed to protect the torso, but the color schemes are a lot plainer than the last time I was here. There's a lot of black and gray.

As long as I stay on this floor, I should be able to buy…pretty much anything?

I take a look at the price tags on the armor closest to me…21,000, 35,000, 46,000…Yeah, I should be okay. I can't splurge, though. Armor isn't the only thing on my list.

To think that a day like today would come…Even a few weeks ago I couldn't even imagine it.

…Are they not selling it anymore?

From the very sturdy to the downright gaudy, this shop has a wide selection of expensive armor on display. But I'm looking for the work of one particular smith.

I wore his work every day until it was destroyed by the Minotaur. Its name was rather…strange—"Pyonkichi"—But it was light, strong, and fit my body like a glove.

I walk all around the store before swinging by the corner where boxes of parts of armor not on display are kept and have a look. This is where I found the smith's work before.

And they have…nothing.

"…"

I can feel a knot of disappointment growing in the pit of my stomach. There's no reason I have to buy something *he* made, but still.

Welf Crozzo…

…Well, I might as well ask.

Feeling defeated, I drag my feet toward the customer service counter.

There should be a ton of armor that's as good as or better than my old stuff in this shop, but I can't bring myself to take a look.

When did I become this guy's fan?

"Why such…horrible…!"

"?"

Just as I'm getting close to the front of the store, an angry voice shoots out from beside the counter.

There are actually two counters at the front of the shop, and a customer seems to be having a very heated argument with a *Hephaistos Familia* clerk.

"Why always…the middle of nowhere…! You have something against me…!"

The closer I get, the more words I can make out.

There's a young man, a human, exchanging words with an extremely exhausted store employee. He's wearing what looks like a long black coat…but it's in really rough shape, almost like rags.

He's got a head full of flaming red hair, and he looks a little bit older than I am. Maybe a little taller, too, and muscular but not beefy.

I can see his face as I step up to the counter. But the front of his hair looks rather strange. It's like his short-cut hair had grown out, but he took scissors to his bangs because they were getting in his eyes.

There's a box of light armor parts on the counter in front of him. Judging by his choice of words and angry demeanor, my best guess is he's also an adventurer. Maybe the armor he bought was defective?

"This is my lifeblood, you hear me? At least treat me like everyone else!"

"This was a decision made by management...It needs to sell, and without that..."

"Oh, so you're going to bring that up, huh?! Well then, I've got a few things to say—!!"

The adventurer in the black body-length jacket is refusing to back down, his rage building.

The clerk behind the second counter watches the argument with a slightly annoyed look on her face until she realizes I'm standing in front of her. "Welcome!" she says with a smile.

Doing my best to ignore what's going on next to me, I rest my hands on the counter and prepare to ask my question.

"Can I help you with something?"

"Yes. Do you have anything made by Welf Crozzo...?"

—Silence. The argument stops on a dime.

The clerk's eyes go wide, and the two people at the other counter slowly turn to face me.

Huh...wh-what?

Three sets of eyes are locked right on me; this is so awkward.

"...U-um, are you looking for Welf Crozzo's work...?"

"Y-yes. I want to buy armor made by Welf Crozzo..."

I've never heard someone so scared to ask a question in my life. Just responding felt like something bad would happen if I said something wrong.

But the first person to react isn't the clerk in front of me but the young man who had been arguing at the other counter just a few moments ago.

"Hee...ah-ha-ha-ha-ha-ha-ha-ha-ha! Would you look at that! There is at least *one* name on my list of clients!!"

After laughing at the top of his lungs, the young man turns to face the clerk before slamming his hand down on the counter.

The clerk can't respond, he just stands there doing his best to avoid making eye contact.

I am so confused right now...The young man must have noticed the look on my face because now he's looking this way.

"Yessir, adventurer, if you're looking for Welf Crozzo armor..."

"Eh?!"

"Right here."

Swish. He picks up the box and slides it onto the counter in front of me.

Inside is a full set of shiny, white light armor.

The shape is a little different from what I was using before...but there's no mistaking it, this is his work!

"So how 'bout it? Will you try it out?"

"Eh? Umm, isn't this yours...?"

Is that a strange question? Because as soon as I finish speaking, he blinks a few times before smiling like a kid in a toy store.

He looks me square in the eyes before saying, "Yep, it's mine, all right...I forged it, you see."

"—Huh?"

"Please allow me to introduce myself, fan number one. The name's Welf Crozzo, currently a low-level smith belonging to *Hephaistos Familia*. Want an autograph?" he says with a genuine smile on his face. He has a very brotherly aura about him...Mr. Crozzo gazes at me for a moment as I try to collect my thoughts.

"Seriously? You're Little Rookie?! The new record holder!"

"N-not so loud...What you mean by 'record holder'?"

I have no idea what he's talking about, so what else could I say?

There is a small rest area on the eighth floor of Babel Tower, right next to the elevator entrance. Mr. Crozzo and I are having a conversation on chairs just inside the rest area.

After we met in the shop, he asked to talk to me in private and led me out here.

I guess he wants to talk to me because apparently he's sold only two pieces of his work in the past, and I'm the only one who's come back looking for more.

Everything that's happened to him up to this point...doing everything he can to get a good reputation from the store and yet being treated like trash, the first item of his that sold was returned to the store, the underhanded tricks that his fellow smiths in *Hephaistos Familia* had used to get their way...He told me quite a bit.

He seems to have lost himself in the excitement that someone wanted to buy his work. Sure, he looks rather grown-up and mature, but every so often he starts laughing. I know I just met him, but he strikes me as a good-natured, wear-his-heart-on-his-sleeve kind of smith.

"You really are younger than me. Then again, age doesn't matter much to adventurers, does it?"

The moment I finish introducing myself, Mr. Crozzo lightly tilts his head to the side. His red hair swishes slightly at the same time.

He has a very masculine face and speaks with a lot of confidence— like an honest worker who would never go back on his word, always sitting up straight and facing forward. I know this is coming from someone who can only roll with the punches, but he looks really cool.

His build isn't all that robust—actually, he's rather thin—but I can see the bulging muscles around his shoulders and chest because the collar on his robe-like jacket is very loose. There is no doubt in my mind that they were built up over many hours of hard work in a forge.

"Um, Mr. Crozzo, can I ask how old you are...?"

"Nineteen this year. One other thing: Could you stop calling me Mr. Crozzo? I'm not particularly fond of my family name."

That's a strange thing to say right in the middle of a conversation.

He tells me to call him by his first name. But, not only is he older than me, he made an armor that I really liked. I should show him more respect...but since he insists...

"Well, um...Mr. Welf? You said you wanted to talk to me about something...?"

"Hey, hey, what's with the 'Mister'?...Eh, not important now. Okay, here's the deal."

He stands up from his chair and looks down on me from above.

The box of armor parts from the shop is at his feet. "I made them, so it's no problem if I take them, right?" He had said that to the clerk, took the box off the counter, and brought it out here when we left.

"To be completely honest, I don't want to lose you."

"?"

"Doesn't matter if it's weapons or armor, my stuff doesn't sell. I don't want to sound too full of myself, but I know I'm making good, high-quality pieces. The only other thing I've sold was returned almost immediately. I can't figure it out."

"..."

Pyonkichi...I want to tell him maybe the problem is the names he gives to his finished pieces, but I can't bring myself to say it to his face.

"Despite all that, here you are. An adventurer who recognizes the value of my work."

"And that means...?"

"You came to buy my armor again, my work. That makes you my customer, my client. Am I wrong?"

Well, when he puts it like that...it sure sounds like it.

Even when I was wading through the forest of armor, I never considered anything else but Mr. Welf's work.

"Truth is, lower-level smiths like me have to fight over clients, steal them from each other. Once one of us gets famous, everyone and their mother will go to them, asking for weapons and armor.

The same is not true for the unknowns. We fight tooth and nail to talk with adventurers, get their advice, and sell our work. That's the world we live in. You with me so far?" he asks.

I struggle to nod.

Fighting over clients...They have to figure out if someone will be a loyal customer or not. It's the most basic part of the business world. Also, should an adventurer become famous, the maker of the weapons he or she uses would also become well known. Their name would become famous even if that smith lived in obscurity until that point.

I wouldn't say adventurers become walking advertisements...but it looks like the connection between smiths and adventurers is far more important than I originally thought.

"Oh, it's important, all right, when a smith's work is recognized by an adventurer. Like I said before, you recognized my armor. There is nothing that could make a smith happier than that. You're my first, so I don't want to let you get away...I can't let that happen."

Despite his rather coarse choice of words, he always keeps that same brotherly smile on his face.

He may be a little overbearing at times, but I can't help but like and respect Mr. Welf as a person.

He's a good man, a good smith.

"So then, you would like me to continue to be your customer?"

"While you're right about that...I'm after something a little bit more permanent."

Mr. Welf's face turns from a warm smile to a shrewd grin.

"Would you sign a direct contract with me, Bell Cranell?"

—A direct contract?

Seeing the look of confusion on my face, Mr. Welf sums it up for me.

It's a contract that binds individual smiths and adventurers together in a mutually beneficial relationship.

Adventurers bring drop items back from the Dungeon for the smiths, who in turn use them to make strong weapons for the adventurers at a reduced price.

Mutual benefit. Smiths and adventurers helping each other out.

And the icing on the cake: Weapons tend to have stronger characteristics when they're made for a specific person rather than for general sale.

So that's what Eina had been talking about.

"Are...are you sure it's okay?!"

"Hey, hey, that's my line. You're already Level Two, and I'm a no-name, low-level smith who hasn't even learned the Forge Ability yet. When you think about it, this isn't that fair, is it?"

I'm about to say that's not true at all, but when I think about it again, he has a point.

If I try to tell Mr. Welf otherwise, it will sound less like modesty and more like sarcasm to him.

It takes a great deal of effort, but I manage to stop myself from speaking and close my mouth.

At the same time that I'm thinking, Mr. Welf leans over and wraps his arm around my neck, pointing my head in the direction of other shops. I can see a smile on his face out of the corner of my eye.

"Have a look over there, past all the swords, axes, and shields, to those guys standing there. They're staring right at us."

"Y-yes..."

The gazes of many humans and demi-humans meet right where we are.

It's almost like they're expecting something to happen...

"All of those guys, they're after you. They want to sign a contract with you, just like me."

"Huh?"

"Not just you. For better or worse, all adventurers who level up to Level Two are targeted. That's the difference between lower and upper class, my friend."

S-seriously...?

My head still locked firmly in place, I shift my eyes to look at Mr. Welf's face.

He's sending all of the other smiths a very smug look, as if he's already won. "Well, that's how it is," he says with a grin and releases me.

"I want to be your go-to guy for smithing. If I sit back and twiddle my thumbs, some other smith is gonna sign you, and I'll lose my first customer. So I have to pull out all the stops to get you first.

"And it's really good for my rep if I can sign an adventurer with a lot of potential like you," he adds with another laugh.

"...On a bit more of a personal note, your Level doesn't really matter to me, believe it or not. Never thought there would come a day that someone would say they want my work, after looking at all the other options out there...You get it?"

"..."

"It's like, this awesome feeling inside me just piling up, you know? It's a smith's badge of honor," he adds shyly.

Finally able to read between the lines, I'm not happy that he's after a direct contract from the start.

He went a little overboard putting on this show. But the thought of the two of us novices working together warms me to the idea.

I don't really understand it myself...but I think it's a good sign.

"...All right, then. I'll sign a direct contract with you, Mr. Welf."

"That settles it! Don't know what I would've done if you'd said no!"

I stand up and take his outstretched hand.

"Looking forward to working with you, Bell," he says, his face beaming with enthusiasm.

Not only is his hand bigger than mine, it's as hot as a furnace.

"We'll worry about the official contract later, but for right now..."

He vigorously shakes my hand up and down as he speaks.

The other smiths who were watching us droop their shoulders and turn to leave. Mr. Welf is putting on another show to let them know he won.

After watching the last one go, Mr. Welf immediately releases my hand and drops his head in apology.

"I know this is a little early...but would you be willing to do me a favor?"

My eyes pop open as I look back at him.

"Of course, I'm not expecting you to help me for nothing. I'll make any and all equipment you need for free."

"HUH?!"

"Don't be so surprised. It's common sense that adventurers want items from smiths, right?"

Not even in my wildest dreams did I think that I'd ever get a new set of equipment for free.

If what he's saying is true, then I don't need to replace anything else that was broken…

All of the muscles in my face suddenly let go; I'm sure I look like a dumbfounded idiot right now.

"Here it is. You ready?"

"…"

I hold my breath and wait for his next words.

"Let me join your battle party."

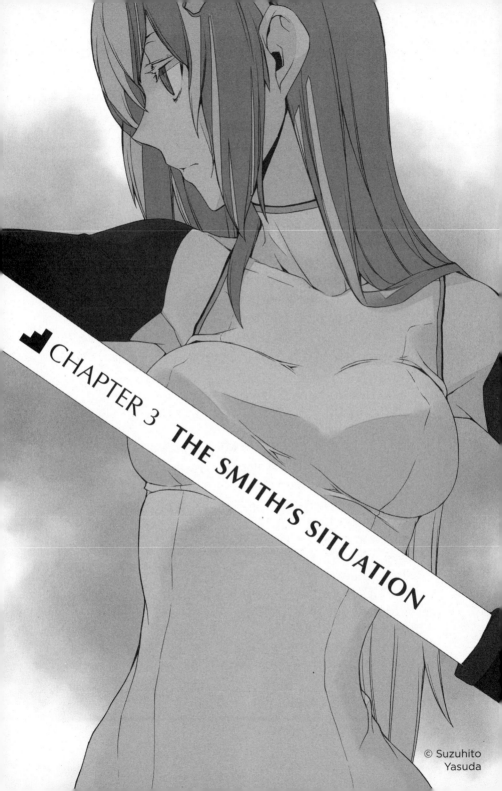

CHAPTER 3 THE SMITH'S SITUATION

© Suzuhito
Yasuda

"Finally, the eleventh floor!"

Mr. Welf pats his lower back a few times, his weapon over his shoulder as he announces our arrival to no one in particular.

Just like he so vigorously said a moment ago, we're on the eleventh floor of the Dungeon.

We've just stepped off of a very wide stairwell and into the room that serves as the starting point for this floor. Just like the tenth above it, a thick fog fills every room on this floor except for this one.

With nothing to block my vision, I can see that the floor in here is covered in ankle-high grass just tall enough to hide my boots. There are also several dead trees scattered throughout the room. Monsters can use these landforms as weapons.

"Didn't you say this is the lowest you've ever been, Mr. Welf?"

"Yep, that's right. Sorry about this, Bell. I've thrown a lot of information at you since we met."

At first I was really surprised when he asked to join my battle party yesterday, but after hearing why, I invited him right away.

We'd already agreed on a direct contract so there was no reason to refuse him. I was looking for another battle party member, too, so I'd call it a win-win.

"Don't worry about it. And this is all to get Forge, so I'm already involved as it is..."

"Glad to hear you put it like that."

Mr. Welf's request was to help him level up so he could acquire the Advanced Ability called Forge.

That ability is a complete game-changer for the smiths who acquire it. It wouldn't be an overstatement to say it can make or break the future for a smith. Mr. Welf explained with a very sad look in his eyes exactly how much more his fellow smiths in *Hephaistos Familia* could do as soon as they leveled up.

Normally, whenever a member of any *Familia* goes into the Dungeon, they form a party with other members of the same group...

"It's a little embarrassing to say this myself...but what's their deal?! Whenever a battle party goes into the Dungeon, I'm always left out! Can you believe that?"

...So, that's what's going on.

Mr. Welf needs high-quality excelia in order to level up, but since his allies always kick him out, he's had to work solo. Therefore, going deeper than the top few levels is impossible—no one can make it out in one piece. So he started looking to join battle parties with members of other *Familias* as a last resort.

It sounds like the members—smiths of *Hephaistos Familia*—have to overcome many obstacles on their own, as well as engage in friendly competition with other smiths in order to improve. But the Forge ability—in other words, leveling up—is the equivalent of life and death for a smith. Since they're all in the same boat, most form deep friendships as they fight their way through the Dungeon...

I asked Mr. Welf why he was always left behind, but all he said was, "They're just jealous of my hidden talents," in a really sullen voice. I wonder what's really going on...

Mr. Welf must have noticed me looking at him as he scratches his head. He drops his shoulders and flashes a warm smile.

"In any case, I'm grateful, Bell. *Familias* tend to be picky about who they work with, but I'm glad you could throw that way of thinking out the window."

"W-well, um...I couldn't exactly refuse, not after receiving all of this..."

Mr. Welf smiles at me again. I take another look at my new equipment before smiling back at him. It can't be helped.

The armor on my chest sparkles like new, even in the dim light.

"...Lilly heard that we had a new friend, but what's this? Mr. Bell's trust was bought by such simple things?"

A very annoyed voice cuts into a pause in our conversation.

A bead of sweat rolls down my cheek. Lilly's disapproval of the arrangement came across loud and clear. I look over my shoulder to see her a few paces behind, hands clamped firmly on the straps of her backpack and a very irritated look in her eyes.

I tell her there's a misunderstanding, but from her point of view, it really might look like I was bribed.

At this moment, I'm wearing the new light armor set that Mr. Welf made for me.

The set isn't all that different from my old equipment. It's a plate of armor over each knee and a breastplate, along with two ruby-encrusted wrist guards that cover my forearms all the way up to my elbows. A little fancier than before.

It's just as light as the last one. Mr. Welf said that the material is a little thicker, but I can't feel that much of a difference. It takes time to adjust to a new set of armor, but it feels like I've been wearing this for years.

It's not that I didn't want an armor that my body was used to… but, yeah, I'd be lying if I said it wasn't a factor.

The pressure from Lilly's half-eyed gaze is so strong that I can't even crack a grin.

"Oh, Lilly's sad. Very, very sad. It was supposed to be a nice, easy shopping trip, but Lilly's hopes were completely dashed and now we're stuck with a problem…Mr. Bell's kindness is making Lilly cry."

The sheer sarcasm in her voice is like a body blow. But Mr. Welf's armor can't block that…!

But what does she mean by "problem"…?

"Isn't that going a little too far, Lilly?! Mr. Welf's not trying to do anything bad…There's no problem, just a misunderstanding!"

"—What is Lilly misunderstanding?! 'Until an ability is acquired'? He's just taking advantage of us! And isn't this too-perfect timing to find a party member?! As soon as this no-name smith meets his goal, he'll leave and we'll be back to where we were before! One step forward, one step back! This is a complete waste! There's no light at the end of this tunnel!!"

Her eyebrows sink lower with every word, her eyes sharpening like daggers.

Her relentless barrage attacks me from every angle, a swarm of verbal bees coming out to protect the hive. At this rate, she'll break me in half!

The way Mr. Welf is looking at me…It's too pathetic…!

"Why didn't Mr. Bell talk with Lilly before adding someone to our party?! Why, Mr. Bell?!"

"Was…Was that bad…?"

"Not bad, no, not bad, but if Mr. Bell doesn't talk with Lilly first, Lilly might get in trouble! Lady Hestia entrusted Lilly with making sure Mr. Bell is safe!"

R-really? The goddess asked her to do that…I guess that's how little she trusts me.

I can feel my head drooping as I look back over at a still very hostile Lilly. I get the feeling that the real reason she's angry has nothing to do with Mr. Welf.

Maybe she's trying to take care of me…No, that can't be right.

She must think it's dangerous for me to be doing things on my own and wants to keep me under her thumb. Probably.

"Oh, am I getting in the way, Small Fry?"

Mr. Welf had been watching us talk in silence but chooses this moment to jump in.

Lilly isn't too fond of Mr. Welf already, but her chestnut-colored eyes went ablaze after being called "Small Fry."

"Lilly is not Small Fry! Lilly's name is Lilliluka Erde!"

"Okay, pleasure to meet'cha, Li'l E."

"…Lilly doesn't care anymore. It's pointless!"

Mr. Welf bends over and sticks his toothy grin in Lilly's face like he's making fun of her, which I'm pretty sure he is. Lilly lets out a small "Humph" and looks the other way.

He doesn't seem to mind Lilly's reaction; on the contrary, he looks like he's enjoying it…I don't have a good feeling about these two from here on out.

"…Well, um, Lilly. I know it's a little late, but I'll introduce him. This is Mr. Welf Crozzo. He's a smith belonging to *Hephaistos Familia*."

Lilly should at least know Mr. Welf's full name, so I tell her. I wanted to tell her earlier this morning when we were on our way to meet up with him, but her mood was so bad it just didn't seem like the right time.

And Mr. Welf already knows Lilly's full name, so there shouldn't be a problem.

I wasn't expecting any kind of response, and Lilly is looking the other way anyway—

"Crozzo?"

Lilly's body shakes as if she'd been slapped in the face the moment she hears Mr. Welf's family name.

"Huh?" The sound escapes my mouth before I knew it. What's with that reaction?

"The cursed house of magic swordsmiths? The noble family of smiths that fell into ruin?"

Magic swordsmiths…?

Even more than that, what does she mean by "noble family of smiths"?

I turn to Mr. Welf in confusion and look for answers.

His playful grin is gone; a sour face has taken over.

"Ah, um…Crozzo?"

My eyes jump back and forth between them, Lilly in shock and Mr. Welf with an irritated twitch in his eye. I have to break this uncomfortable silence, so I ask him about his family name. Lilly's eyes go wide as her face snaps right to me in surprise.

"Do you not know about them, Mr. Bell…?"

"Eh, well…No, I don't."

What reason is there to say anything else? I shake my head no.

"Long ago, the Crozzo family was granted noble status by a king for the magic swords they forged. It's said that the only thing they made was magic swords…tens, hundreds of thousands of them."

"So that means…?!"

"They were the masters of the magic sword, the symbol of their time. Some claim that their magic swords were so powerful that they could 'set fire to the ocean'…"

Lilly pauses for a moment and looks up at Mr. Welf.

Her fingers curl; she looks like she's building up courage to say something difficult.

"…But one day they fell out of favor with the king. They lost their noble status and their house fell into ruin…"

Lilly speaks as quickly as she can. What kind of face am I supposed to make now? I try to keep my expression as neutral as possible as I look over to Mr. Welf.

He scratches the back of his head for a few seconds, his hair wavering back and forth. Then he lowers his hand and waves, a forced smile on his face.

"…Well, that's not important right now, is it? We're here to crawl the Dungeon, aren't we? Right?"

"Ah…y-yes."

Mr. Welf's slightly higher gaze falls on me as he tries his best to change the subject.

He takes the weapon resting on his shoulder, a surprisingly wide-bladed longsword with incredible reach, and thrusts it into the ground.

I give him a quick nod as Lilly takes a step back, like she's waiting for something to happen. She looks up at him, her penetrating gaze looking for anything unusual.

"—?"

"Hm?"

Crack! All of us hear it at the same time.

We freeze for a moment. The three of us have spent enough time in the Dungeon to know exactly what that sound means.

A monster is being born from the dungeon wall.

"W-woah…!"

"…Big one."

"An orc, for sure."

All of us respond as our eyes seek out the source of the noise. It doesn't take me long to find a massive crack in the wall.

Another series of cracks echoes through the room as a thick brown arm forces its way out.

Pieces of the dungeon wall fall to the ground like bits of a broken eggshell. A huge chunk crashes to the ground as the monster's right arm blasts through, followed closely by the beast's head and torso.

"BUGGIII...ooOOOHHHH...!"

Announcing its birth to the world, the orc fully emerges.

I've never seen an orc birth before...

I clear my throat to steady myself. Large-category monster births are quite a sight.

The only word I have for seeing the dungeon wall crumble like that is "overwhelming."

The monster falls onto all fours as it lands with a loud crash. Slowly but steadily, it climbs to its feet.

"...It ain't over. This is why the Dungeon is so scary from the tenth on down."

Crack, crack, crack! Sounds keep coming from the dungeon walls. Now the sounds are echoing from every direction in the room, and monsters are right behind them.

Many adventurers have reported that monsters will suddenly emerge in large numbers in the same room, starting around the tenth floor of the Dungeon.

The walls basically fall apart as the room is inundated with monsters. A "monster party," that's what this is called.

They are, of course, very dangerous. Especially if you happen to be in the middle of the room when it happens, since you'll be surrounded in no time flat. I take a step back, a dumbfounded smile on my face.

"There is no reason to panic. There is no fog in this room and it is very wide. There's little chance of being surrounded and we can retreat to the tenth if necessary."

Lilly speaks calmly as she adjusts her backpack with a small sigh.

She has traveled with many battle parties, and this isn't her first trip to the eleventh floor. Her Status might be far below ours, but she knows what she's doing.

I take a quick look behind me and see the stairwell right there, just as Lilly had said. A little of the tension gone, I take a deep breath and survey the room.

"All right, I got dibs on the orc."

"Eh, are you sure?" My eyes pop open at Mr. Welf's declaration.

Orcs are extremely strong. If a Level 1 adventurer, or even a Level 2, takes a direct hit from one of these monsters, that person won't be getting up for a long time.

Mr. Welf's eyebrows sink, a grin back on his lips as he looks at the surprise on my face.

"Should be great news, yeah? The things are slow and stupid. Even I'm more than a match for them."

Oh, so people can think like that…

Whether I'm still a novice or Mr. Welf is a daredevil, I'm not sure. But in any case, he seems to believe that an orc will be no problem. He takes a step forward, jerking his jaw in the direction of the beast.

Hephaistos Familia might be a group of smiths, but they're also very powerful. Warrior smiths, if you will. And Mr. Welf is no exception—although he claims it's all just to get the Advanced Ability Forge. From what I've seen of his fighting style so far and what he did on the lower tenth floor, he won't hold us back. He may be a Level 1 adventurer, but there's no doubt he's one of the most powerful.

"Mr. Bell, please fight as you like. Lilly will support the smith from behind. To be honest, Lilly would appreciate Mr. Bell checking on us from time to time."

"Oh? What's this? I thought you hated my guts, Lilly?"

"Of course Lilly does. But Lilly doesn't want you to get in Mr. Bell's way."

Lilly grins at him, her eyes sparkling. I can only grimace at the look on her face.

She's probably made this suggestion to give me a chance to try out my new Level 2 abilities. She's determined that I'll be okay on my own in this situation.

I'm not going to argue with her.

…And also, it might be a little reckless, but…

I want to test myself.

"Let's get cracking! Before the imps swarm in, yeah?"

"You don't have to tell Lilly twice. Mr. Bell. Lilly thinks Mr. Bell knows, but…"

"Yes, don't worry. I won't let my guard down."

A chorus of sliding metal and snapping sounds surrounds us as we each arm ourselves for battle.

I do a few quick stretches, take a deep breath to focus, and charge into the fray.

"Hyyeeh!" "Hyyeegii!"

I race across the open plain, a swarm of imps heading right for me.

Mr. Welf has taken care of the monsters that we encountered on the way down to the lower eleventh floor. This will be my first actual combat today.

A small group peels off from the swarm and swoops down at me, all of them shrieking at the top of their lungs. It's five on one for now.

I have no clue how many monsters are emerging from the dungeon walls. Loud cracks are still echoing through the room, and the imp swarm is growing larger by the second.

—For the first time ever, I dash toward them at full speed.

I lean forward while on the move.

The distance between us rapidly disappearing, I slam my foot into the ground and push off.

Dirt goes flying in my wake.

"—Hye?"

The imp flies up to my face.

No.

I closed the distance.

This speed is no joke. The wind is whistling in my ears.

Even though I'm flying through the air faster than ever before, my senses are keeping up.

I take a swing at the imp in front of my face with the Divine Knife.

SHING!

"?!"

The imp's head leaves its body and flies toward the ceiling.

About half of the accompanying imp swarm is distracted by their comrade's flying head and by the arc of purple light that took it off.

Their surprise at the sudden turn of events opens the window I need to keep going forward and take on the rest.

Downward slash.

My body light as a feather, I weave my way from imp to imp like a lightning bolt through the sky. One of the monsters drops to the ground in pieces with every hit. I'm on to the next before they even knew what hit them.

It only takes one hit. Armed with my dagger and the Divine Knife, my black and white fangs, I tear through the imp swarm and leave a trail of bodies in my dust.

They're so slow... Wait—

I'm taking the first strike. None of them have even tried to counterattack.

My enemies aren't slow.

I've become so fast that—

They can't counterattack!

I've changed. I've completely changed. Nothing's the same as before!

So this is the true meaning of leveling up!

The goddess's blessing!

"AAAAHHHHHHH!!"

"GAHII?!"

I land one of Aiz's spin kicks square into the chest of an oncoming imp. It's launched with the speed of an arrow off of my foot and straight into the dirt. After bouncing and tumbling a few times, it comes to a dead standstill and doesn't move.

An imp swarm that once contained more than ten individuals is now completely wiped out.

"RWOOOOOO!!"

"！"

A new monster appears in front of me, howling.

It's about as tall as I am. It stands on two short, stubby legs, but its two long arms end in a very deadly looking set of claws. Its back and arms are completely covered by a series of shells, almost like it's wearing a suit of armor. The shell on its head comes to a point in front of its eyes, like it's wearing a battle helmet.

Another one of the armadillo-like monsters emerges. The two of them advance on my position.

"Hard Armoreds." They first appear on the eleventh floor.

I've never seen one before, but luckily I've got a monster encyclopedia in my head courtesy of Eina's aggressive lectures. What did she have to say about these guys again?

Much like the killer ant, Hard Armoreds have very strong defense courtesy of their thick shell-like armor. However, their unprotected underbelly is very vulnerable to attack. Compared to the killer ant's full-body protection, it's easy to see where to strike…However, their Defense is by far the better of the two.

Out of all the monsters on the lower eleventh and twelfth floors, their Defense is second to none. In other words, when it comes to taking a hit, they can withstand more damage than anything else in the upper levels.

A Hard Armored is basically a walking iron fortress that can repel a dwarf's attack with ease. It has often been said that a Level 1 adventurer doesn't stand a chance against one of them in hand-to-hand combat.

It wouldn't be an exaggeration to say that adventurers need Basic Ability levels ranging from *B* to *S*, in order to survive on the lower eleventh and twelfth because of Hard Armoreds.

"—HEH!"

Time stands still for a moment as we size each other up. The instant our eyes meet, we charge.

My powerful legs burst forward.

One of the Hard Armoreds curls his body into a ball and rolls at me with blinding speed.

That thick shell on his back is a very sturdy defense, but it can be a powerful weapon at the same time. One of these attacks has enough power to plow through entire battle parties and send them flying. Nothing short of a powerful blow will bring them to a stop.

The rolling beast is practically a man-size boulder careening toward me. Covering the area between us in no time flat, I barely avoid an impact that would have sent me reeling for days.

I set my sights on the other one.

It's still on its feet, so if I take care of this one first, then I can focus on the roller without having to watch my back.

"OOAAAHHH!!"

The beast charges at me, claws drawn and ready.

I bring my blades forward and hold my ground until the last possible moment—before jumping up and to the side.

"?!"

My body arcs just in front of the monster's nose and eyes.

Unable to follow my movement, I completely disappear from its line of sight.

I'm in its blind spot, diagonally behind its head.

Bringing my knees up and flipping forward with the Divine Knife upside down in my grip, I slash downward.

"—GAAhhh?!"

The Hard Armored's shell splits cleanly in two under the force of my attack.

—An opening!

The best Defense in the upper levels is breakable.

Rotating in midair, I catch a glimpse of the amount of damage I inflicted on the creature's body and tighten my grip on the knife.

"ROOOOOOAAHHH!!"

The remaining Hard Armored has regained its balance and is rolling at me at full speed.

I curl my head under my shoulders and roll over my back as I land. The instant my foot hits the dirt, I raise my right arm and spin around to face the oncoming monster.

"Firebolt!"

An electric inferno roars to life.

Each bolt is louder, faster, and thicker than ever before. Violet light flashes over the beast just before the flames tear into it.

KABOOM!

The shock wave from the explosion blows past me, the Hard Armored's burned body emerging from the smoke a moment later. Part of the shell on its back is completely gone. Other pieces fall off as its lifeless body collapses to the ground.

The completely exposed Hard Armored's smoldering remains lie in silence, smoke pouring out from its mouth.

Even my Magic is stronger...

Watching the remaining sparks fizzle out, I bring my arm in front of my chest.

My power is on a whole other level. The scale is completely different.

It's not just my Firebolt; I can't deny that I feel like I don't have full control of this power yet, but...

I'm getting closer, for sure!

I can see her in the back of my mind, one female knight.

The place I want to be off in the distance, behind that long, flowing blond hair, I'm closing in.

My heart is racing, pounding in my ears. I use all of my might to force myself to calm down.

"—ooOOHH!"

The roar of an orc caught me off guard and brought me back into the present.

Suddenly, Lilly's words run through my head and I look in that direction. The noise leads my eyes to the spot where Mr. Welf and an orc are preparing for combat.

"Now that's speed..."

Welf muttered under his breath.

He caught flashes of Bell's attacks out of the corner of his eye.

Bell's movements, reflexes, attacks, and Magic were all extremely fast to his eyes.

While he didn't know where it came from, Welf realized why Bell had been described as a "rabbit."

"Heh-heh-heh, don't get flattened into a pancake by getting distracted. Mr. Bell will be very sad."

"Li'l E, I've figured you out."

Welf responded to Lilly's words and gave a big nod to the girl directly behind him.

He didn't turn around to face her, the reason being there was a large orc howling an ugly howl and charging right for them. It would be on top of them in moments.

Noticing Bell's gaze, Welf flipped up his chin and grinned as if to say, "Quit checking on me."

"All righty, then. Big piggy number two."

His back to the body of the first orc that lay motionless next to Lilly, Welf swung his longsword up to rest on his shoulder.

"OOoooOOOOO!!"

Slam, slam, slam! The orc took clumsy but powerful strides as it advanced.

The edges of Welf's mouth curled upward as he took a few bold steps toward the monster.

"BUGURUAAA!!"

Seeing that its prey was in range, the empty-handed orc swung its meaty arm forward with all of its might.

Welf ducked under the reckless sideswipe without any hesitation.

Squatting as low as possible, left hand on the ground and right hand holding his sword against his right shoulder, Welf had the eyes of a beast not unlike the one he was about to strike.

Seeing an opening the moment the massive arm passed by him, Welf sprang forward and swung his thick blade at his target.

"—RAAA!"

The sound of steel through flesh. The blade hit its mark, slicing straight through the orc's exposed stomach.

A dark greenish blood spraying from its wound, the sheer force of the blow threw the monster off-balance. It fell backward, slamming its head against the dirt.

"How'd you like that!"

Welf ran forward and jumped to the side of the orc's head.

Grabbing hold of his longsword with both hands, Welf's unblinking eyes locked onto the monster's neck before he brought the weapon down in one fell swoop.

SHING-THUD! The sound of the impact reverberated throughout the room.

"Li'l E! Next!"

"Already here!"

Leaving the headless monster behind, Welf turned in the direction that Lilly was pointing.

What greeted his eyes was the silhouette of another orc—this one carrying a landform tree club in its right hand. The beast was already dashing toward them. Welf clicked his tongue in frustration, but with his usual smirk still on his face.

"Well, isn't that a pain in the ass!"

"Lilly is aware!"

Lilly circled around the dead bodies on the ground to get a different angle on the new orc.

She reached inside the sleeve of her robe and withdrew a bowgun, taking aim with her slender arms.

PING! Her golden arrow pierced the beast's shoulder.

"!"

The orc stopped in its tracks to nurse its injured shoulder. The eyes of its pig head narrowed, forgetting its original target—Welf—and finding a new one: Lilly.

There was a momentary pause.

Seeing an opportunity to attack the distracted orc, Welf took a step forward and planted his left foot firmly into the dirt.

His black coat rustling like smoke in the wind, Welf's boot carved a new divot into the dungeon floor as he took another step forward.

"EAT THIS!"

The blade that had been resting on his shoulder carved a massive arc through the air.

All of the strength Welf possessed was focused through his right arm and into this single strike. It slammed into the monster's body at full force.

The longsword hit the orc with enough force to slice it clean in half. The orc's body flinched, but it was unable to cry out in pain due to the blood spewing from its mouth. The beast's bloodshot eyes caught one last glimpse of its attacker before its body dissolved into ash on the spot.

Welf's attack had cut through and destroyed the magic stone buried deep in the monster's chest.

"Mr. Crozzo, we're going to have a problem if you keep breaking magic stones! Mr. Bell and Lilly will make less money!"

"What's done is done. Can't be helped. Oh, and don't call me that."

He turned to face the girl who stood a good distance away with a slightly annoyed look on his face. She was always complaining about something.

"And what about my share, huh?" Welf retorted with a verbal jab at the prum.

Only specs of purplish ash remained on the grassy dungeon floor.

"...Mr. Crozzo!"

"What did I just say about that na—ahh..."

Just when Welf opened his mouth to yell at her, he realized why Lilly had screamed in the first place.

Two new monsters, smaller than orcs, had quietly snuck up behind Welf.

"Silverbacks."

Muscular bodies covered in thick white fur, these monsters looked like massive wild gorillas. Their name came from a silver mane around their necks and the thick stripe of silver fur running all the way down their backs. The fur on their lower backs was long enough to look like a short silver tail.

Not too long ago, Bell fought one of these beasts during Monsterphilia. Along with the Hard Armoreds, they made the lower eleventh floor of the Dungeon an extremely dangerous place for Level 1 adventurers. While they didn't have the orc's size, they more than made up for it with power and agility. Fangs bared and muscles bulging, there was only one way to describe them: strong.

Welf turned to face these new attackers when suddenly, *THUMP*. A third silverback jumped down from a particularly large dead tree and landed between him and Lilly.

"…"

"Geeeh……"

"Shit," he spat almost like a reflex.

They were ganging up on him. This was one situation that adventurers want to avoid at all costs in the Dungeon.

Fantastic…Like I'm solo all over again.

Feeling the sweat dripping down his brow, Welf took a defensive stance and looked at all three beasts in turn.

After being left out of other battle parties, he had equipped himself with as many potions as he could carry and ventured out into the lower tenth on his own…All the moments when he nearly died flashed before his eyes as he stared down the silverbacks.

I have to run, now…Dammit, I'm pinned down!

His body getting impatient as the monsters started closing in, Welf's mind raced to find an escape route.

He estimated as he sized up his opponents that he was slightly more powerful than one silverback. However, that meant the moment he engaged one in combat, he would be wide open for the others to attack from behind. Catching a glimpse of Lilly's startled face, he knew in an instant he couldn't count on the supporter for any help.

I'm toast, was the only conclusion he could come up with, but Welf chose to ignore it. Swinging his longsword in a wide arc, he brought it to rest on his shoulder before taking a step toward the closest silverback.

He decided to break through a point of their net. A strange pinging sound filled his ears. He would never get used to the tension that came from being surrounded by enemies in the Dungeon, no matter how many times it happened. He braced his body for battle.

A perilous ambience surrounded them.

The silverback Welf was staring down glared right back at him, its eyes glistening in anticipation.

The monsters made their move as one.

A heartbeat later...

"—One, two, anddd!!"

"GehGOOH?!"

"?!"

Something incredibly forceful flew in from outside the net.

Bell had launched himself like a javelin, his fearsome kick catching the jaw of one of the silverbacks. Caught completely off guard, the beast's head spun to a gruesome angle as it plowed into another silverback.

Welf and the other beasts stood in stunned silence at the sudden turn of events. Bell, however, drew his dagger from its sheath while still in midair.

"Mr. Welf!"

Ruby-red eyes meeting his gaze, Welf realized it was about to happen.

He leaned back as quickly as he could to get out of the way.

Not wasting any movement or momentum, Bell threw the dagger in his right hand with all of his might.

"GEH?!"

"—!!"

The dagger whizzed past Welf's face and straight into the eye of the silverback behind him.

The beast reared back, screaming in pain. Taking that as his cue, Welf spun in place as he brought his own blade to bear.

The longsword cut a deep gash into the monster's body.

"..."

The limp monster fell to its knees. Welf had come to a stop, blade still at the top of its cutting arc. Keeping the same pose, he looked back over his shoulder toward Bell.

Bell had just slain the second silverback and stood over their bloody, motionless bodies.

Welf stared at Bell's back for a moment before grinning and returning his sword to his shoulder.

"I could really get used to this battle-party thing."

The white-haired boy turned toward him, nodding in agreement with a big smile on his face.

"You are one fast dude, you know that? I didn't even see you fly in."

"I-I'm not exactly sure when I did myself..."

Our battle against the monster party finally over, the three of us are now taking a short break.

We're still in the same room on the lower eleventh floor. The aftermath of our skirmish is scattered all around. Uprooted dead trees, divots in the ground, ash left behind by monsters' bodies, even pieces of the dungeon wall are everywhere I look. It's an absolute mess in here.

Mr. Welf's longsword is back in its sheath and strapped to his back. He's standing next to me with his arms folded across his chest as we talk about what just happened.

"This dungeon-crawling thing sure is easier when you've got a strong ally with you. 'Course I can't rely on you always saving my ass."

"I have a feeling that I didn't slay as many monsters as I usually do."

"That's the good thing about being in a battle party. Your mind and body don't have to work as hard, and you're free to move however you want. Your allies cover your blind side."

Mr. Welf is making some good points. Since he has more experience working in the Dungeon with a party than I do, I'm listening to every word.

"I thought we did pretty well, considering today's our first day as a group. We're not exactly reading each other's minds, but our movements meshed...That's all thanks to Li'l E."

"Thanks to Lilly?"

"Yeah. Her actions seem minor, but she had a big influence. Alerting us to new monsters, keeping us from running into each other, she did a great job coordinating us."

While that is a strange way to say it, simply put, Lilly was guiding us.

It might be better to say she was steering us in the right direction. She could see the whole battlefield from her vantage point, so she knew exactly when and how to assist us. That included keeping us apart.

I hear Mr. Welf say, "She knows how adventurers move."

I slowly nod as his words click and say, "Ah, that makes sense." Considering all of Lilly's experience as a supporter and as a thief, I bet she knows the way adventurers think like the back of her hand.

"She really is something else, Li'l E."

"It's times like these when you really can't think of anything bad to say about supporters…"

"You can say that again," replies Mr. Welf as he looks over his shoulder at Lilly. She's in a deeper corner of the room, collecting magic stones and drop items with amazing speed and efficiency.

The two of us had slain a lot of monsters, so naturally there was a lot of work to be done. We offered to help, but she turned us away immediately. "This is Lilly's job, rest while there's time," she had said as she pushed us away from the monsters' remains.

She said she wanted to do her share.

"Well, whadda you know, we've got even more company. Should we head somewhere else?"

"Hmm, we could do that…"

There are a few groups of adventurers in the room now who weren't here when we arrived.

Many adventurers pass through here, since this room connects to the floor above. Quite a few battle parties use this room as a staging area because there's no fog. Needless to say, it's difficult to find any monsters to slay in this spot.

It would be miserable to have to compete with them for loot, and even worse to have something happen that causes problems between *Familias*. Actually, there were a few parties that edged around the room while we were in combat. It's an unwritten rule among adventurers: We stay out of one another's way as much as possible while in the Dungeon.

...Now that I think about it, Lilly was the first one to realize that other adventurers were here. She immediately gathered the bodies of slain monsters in one spot to protect our loot. Kind of like, "These are ours, don't get any ideas."

I don't know if she's just got an eye for details, but that's something that only an experienced supporter can do for their party.

"...Since we're already here, why don't we eat lunch? There are a lot of people in here, so we shouldn't need to worry about monsters sneaking up on us."

"Good point. Plus, it'd be a real pain to give up this spot. Let's take advantage of the situation. Lunch sounds good."

His reasoning sounds a bit pushy, but at least he agrees with me.

We'll start eating as soon as Lilly gets back.

All these people...I know it's the lower eleventh, but each party looks insanely powerful...

Even the air around each group exudes strength and experience.

The same goes for their armor and weapons. Sharp, sturdy...The list of words that comes to my mind just looking at them goes on and on.

An animal person with a robust bow strapped to his back, an Amazon leaning on a particularly large battle ax, a majestic elf wearing a silver white cloak and carrying a staff...They're a mix of races of humans and demi-humans, with a few interesting quirks.

How many of them have leveled up...?

By and large, the parties that crawl the eleventh and twelfth floors are preparing to venture forth into the middle levels. So there have to be quite a few Level 2 adventurers in here right now.

...Am I really on par with any of these people?

I'm Level 2, so we're equal at least on paper...but looking at the huge muscles on that dwarf makes me want to make myself as small as possible. My goal is much, much higher, so it's not a good sign that I'm getting intimidated so easily.

I'm sure all of them have some impressive Magic and Skills...

Wait a minute, I have a Skill, too...

Can't believe it took me this long to remember that I learned one, too.

"Heroic Desire, Argonaut." I completely forgot about it up until now, so I wasn't exactly trying to test it out...

I fought like normal, nothing strange happened...did it?

I'm faster and stronger than before, but that's because I leveled up. I don't think a Skill will have any effect on that.

"Active Action. Choose to move. Attack, not counterattack."

I tilt my head to the side as I remember the goddess's words. "Hmmm..."

I have no idea what she was talking about. Choosing to move, attacking and all that...That's normal to me. And yet nothing unusual has happened. Maybe it takes more than movement to trigger it?

Magic needs spells to activate, so maybe this Skill does, too?

How did I...

...Learn a skill called Argonaut in the first place?

Because I leveled up?

Because I slew that monster, the Minotaur?

Because I wished from the bottom of my heart that Aiz wouldn't see me in another embarrassing situation?

...At that moment, I...

I want to be—

"—a hero!"

That's what I wished for.

"..."

Just like the heroes in fairy tales.

Just like the men who could face down powerful enemies without fear.

Just like the women who risk everything to save lives.

To become that, to be one step closer, that was my desire.

Heroic desire.

"...Hey, Bell. What's that?"

"!"

A voice drags me out of the depths of my memories and back into the present in the blink of an eye.

Welf is standing in front of me, eyebrows cocked in confusion.

I'm about to ask him what's wrong, but I follow his gaze to my right arm first.

Small specs of light are shimmering around my arm.

"...Eh?"

My eyes go wide as a dumbfounded sound rolls off my tongue.

The small lights are spinning around my forearm, their white light softly pulsing.

The lights are smaller than a snowflake, about the size of a grain of sand. They disappear as they rotate toward my arm, only for new ones to appear in their place in an endless cycle.

Sparkle, converge, dim, and repeat.

It's as if my arm is stuck in a whirlpool of sparkling white light.

Ping, ping. The lights are making sounds as they glisten.

All like little chimes.

"..."

"..."

Mr. Welf and I look at each other.

He looks just as surprised and confused as I am. I don't think I could give him any answers even if he asked me.

What...what is this...?

My eyes are focused so hard on my right hand, and I'm surprised it hasn't fallen off yet.

I can see Mr. Welf's gaze going from my face to my arm over and over again. Just as he's opening his mouth to speak—it happens.

"—oooOOOOOOOOOOOOOO!!"

A ferocious roar stampedes through the room, making my ears scream in pain.

"?!"

Mr. Welf and I flip around to look in that direction. No, not just us. Every other person in the room is looking that way, their eyes wide with terror.

It's in the room's entrance. Amber-colored scales emerge from the fog flowing in from the next room.

Not only scales, there is a long tail, sharp claws, and a ton of fangs as well.

It's only about 150 celch at its tallest, but it looks like it's more than 4 meders long—a small dragon.

"An infant dragon...?!"

The voice of an adventurer I've never met rings out.

This four-legged beast is a species of dragon, said to be the most powerful type of all the monsters in the Dungeon. While it doesn't have wings, its muscular body is covered in thick amber scales. I can tell just by looking at this thing that it has the potential to overpower an orc. Its head twists from side to side as it scans the room with red eyes the size of dinner plates.

Infant dragon.

It's a rare monster that only appears on the lower eleventh and twelfth floors of the Dungeon.

Considering that only four or five of these things roam the Dungeon at a time, it takes a considerable amount of luck to encounter one of them. Then again, infant dragons have annihilated entire parties of Level 1 adventurers. So they weren't all that lucky...

There is no "Monster Rex" on these floors, so it's safe to say that infant dragons are the bosses of the upper levels.

"—!!"

The dragon springs into action the instant the man screams, as though the cry is an opening bell. Flinging its long tail around like a whip, it hits an elf who happened to be close by and sends him flying. He slams into a wall in a heartbeat, eyes wide. He falls to the floor like a puppet whose strings have been cut, head limp. A chorus of new screams erupts throughout the room a second later.

It may not be as strong as that Minotaur, but I wouldn't be

surprised if this beast is also categorized as Level 2. Now is the time to ignore the adventurers' unwritten law, and everyone else realizes it. All battle parties act as one. Numerous spell incantations start as Amazons and dwarves charge forward with swords and axes drawn.

"Li'l E! GET OUT OF THERE!!"

Mr. Welf's scream cuts through the chaos.

Even in my state of stunned silence, I can see everything unfold in front of me.

The dragon is charging toward Lilly, who is still in the corner of the room collecting magic stones.

I see her stand and turn to face the monster. Suddenly, my body starts moving on its own.

My still-sparkling right arm thrusts forward as the muscles in my throat tighten to yell:

"FIREBOLT!!"

Half a moment later.

Everything goes silent.

"___"

A beam of pure white light.

The entire room is bathed in a flash as a sound rivaling the dragon's roar rings in my ears.

Flaming bolts of lightning explode from within the white light surrounding my right arm. Firebolt.

But it's completely different. The usual scarlet bolts of my Magic are surrounded by white shards of light and are so thick that they could swallow a person whole. The flames are headed toward the infant dragon.

Engulfing the beast in plasma, the Firebolt continues past the dragon and smashes into the wall beyond.

A massive explosion.

"...GAH, ahh..."

Those amber scales that looked so sturdy a moment ago flake off like ash in the wind.

The infant dragon leaves behind a soft moan of pain before collapsing to the ground, a victim of the electric inferno. I've heard that dragons have a natural resistance to flame, but its exposed skin is burning away amid the smoldering remains of everything around it.

All that's left in the corner of the room now is the burned remains of the dragon dissolving into the air. The wall that took the blast is heavily damaged. Covered in cracks, more and more pieces fall to the ground every moment.

CRICK CRASH! A large segment collapses to the floor like an afterthought.

"..."

An uneasy stillness descends on the room.

All of the other adventurers have stopped moving and are looking at me. Lilly and Mr. Welf, too.

Shock, shudders, and...hostility. I don't react to any of the emotions being slung at me. Coming back to myself, I pull my right arm down and toward my chest. The glimmering specks of light are gone, and my arm looks like nothing ever happened.

"......oww."

I push my head through the opening in my shirt. Every part of my body aches, and every movement is painful.

Now fully dressed, I open the door and leave the shower room.

The goddess, already changed, is sitting on the purple sofa.

"Bell, if you're tired, go ahead and get some rest. I can make dinner on my own."

"No, I'm fine. I'll help!"

"Heh-heh, is that so? All right, we'll make it together."

It's been a long day at work and a very long day of dungeon crawling. Both of us were late getting home that night, so I don't want her to do everything by herself. It's already late evening.

We do most things around our home together as much as possible; I know that's what the goddess wants. I shouldn't let her do so much, but every time I try to do something on my own, she always says something like, "Aren't we in this together, Bell?"

But in the end, it really does feel strange…

"…Um, Bell? Can I ask you something?"

"What is it?"

I've just started washing vegetables in our small excuse for a kitchen when the goddess, who was cutting meat, suddenly asks me a question.

I turn to face her, our eyes level because she's standing on a small stool.

"Have you ever met Freya…Ah, a silver-haired goddess?"

"A goddess with silver hair? No, I don't think I have…"

I think hard as I answer.

I can count the number of times I've seen goddesses other than Lady Hestia since I came to Orario on one hand. I should be able to remember if any of them had silver hair.

"Hmm, yes, I suppose that's right…"

The goddess mumbles as she looks toward the ceiling. Did something happen?

I feel like the goddess has had her head on a swivel ever since the Denatus ended. I've asked her about it a few times, but all she does is shake her head and say, "Nope, it's nothing at all."

I'm a little worried about it, but I've got food to make. In what feels like no time at all, everything is ready and I'm sitting at the table with the goddess.

"Ohh? So then, that smith is a good one?"

"Yes. He's very open about what he's thinking and I feel like I can depend on him. I'm a little bit concerned about him and Lilly, though. I don't think they like each other too much…"

"Ha-ha-ha-ha!"

I laugh with the goddess in the late evening hours while we eat dinner.

Recently, our dinners have gotten a lot fancier. There's a lot less of the most basic food, anyway.

It's normal for us to each have a slice of bread, and typical to have pieces of meat mixed in with our salad, and it's become our tradition to have a small mountain of crispy potato puffs in the evening.

It didn't take much time to get to this point, but it feels like it did. Dirt-poor, that's what we were a little more than a month ago. I'm pretty sure we've escaped that label by now.

"Well, if *he's* that kind of person, I don't see a problem. I'm all for it and I'll raise a glass to him. You better not let him get away, Bell."

"I think so, too. Mr. Welf is a smith and with him around, we can make a three-man cell. I've heard it's much safer to crawl the Dungeon with three! I'd like him to stick around for a long time, but..."

"You should make sure *he* stays. It's much too dangerous for you and the supporter to be *alone* in the Dungeon. *Much, much too dangerous.*"

A refreshing smile grows on the goddess's lips when I eagerly nod in agreement.

Even the goddess's twin black ponytails look like they're in a good mood, swinging back and forth like that. She must've been really worried about us.

It's also become a routine by this point, but I've been telling the goddess about everything that happened that day.

First, I told her about Mr. Welf. I told her about the direct contract and all that yesterday, so today I tell her about my impressions of him as a party member.

"I still can't believe that you would form a battle party with one of Hephaistos's group members...hee-hee, maybe it was fate, since you entered my *Familia*."

The goddess grins from ear to ear.

Lady Hestia and Lady Hephaistos have spent a lot of time together, dating back to their days in Tenkai, so it makes sense that they would be friends down here on Earth. However, I've heard that a lot happened in the time between coming to Orario and before the goddess started this *Familia*. Now it's difficult for them to casually meet up anymore.

The goddess seems to find this unbreakable bond rather amusing. She's giggling hard enough to make her shoulders shake.

"...Um, Goddess? Mr. Welf's last name is Crozzo. Have you heard anything about them?"

Seeing an opening, I decide to ask her what has been on my mind since earlier today.

Lilly's story about the Crozzo family and magic swords.

I feel a little bad about looking into his family history behind his back, but I'm unable to control my curiosity.

"Crozzo's Magic Swords, right...? I've heard a little about them, too, but...I don't think I know any more about them than you do, Bell."

"I see..."

I've heard that the goddess hasn't been on Earth very long. It can't be helped that she knows about as much as I do concerning what happened on Gekai—Earth—long ago.

Looks like Mr. Welf is going to remain a mystery for a while......

"...While I don't know much about the Crozzo family, I might have heard a few things about the smith, Welf Crozzo."

"Huh?"

"Hee-hee-hee. Bell, don't tell me you've forgotten where I work?"

OH! So that's what she's talking about.

The goddess works for a shop owned by *Hephaistos Familia*, the same *Familia* that Mr. Welf belongs to. I'm sure just by working there, she's heard a few things about him.

"So how about it, Bell!" she says, puffing out her generous chest a little too much. I respond with a quick "Please" as my face turns red. It takes everything I have to force a smile so that the goddess will start talking.

Apparently, when she heard Mr. Welf's name yesterday, she started collecting information on her own.

"He's actually a pretty good smith. The boy's still got a lot of growing to do, but Hephaistos talks about him all the time. I'm sure of that."

"L-Lady Hephaistos talks about Mr. Welf?"

"Yep. I heard this when she was drunk, but that boy has a lot of hidden talent, and he could be so much more."

To think that in a *Familia* known for highly skilled smiths, Lady Hephaistos would take note of Mr. Welf. Is he some kind of prodigy within the *Familia*?

"Oh, Hephaistos has an eye on him, all right. She's given him a once-over and found that he has a special glow about him...But, she did say that he's quite a disappointment, in terms of sensibility."

"..."

"Pyonkichi," the name of my armor, quickly comes to mind.

By the way, my current armor was given the same name as its predecessor. The current model is the MK-III.

"And now the juicy part. Hephaistos is extremely harsh on him inside the *Familia*, completely the opposite of how she talked about him when drunk."

"Huh? What do you mean?"

That was completely out of the blue. I ask her for more information and she nods with a soft "Sure.

"To get straight to the point, he can already make magic swords."

"...!"

"Not some cheap imitation, but the real thing. He can produce magic swords that are strong enough to outdo the work of the High Smiths inside *Hephaistos Familia*. Magic swords worthy of the name Crozzo."

—Magic swordsmiths.

I've heard those words before. I take a moment to chew things over in my head.

"But, wait a minute...That can't be right. Smiths can't make magic swords without the Advanced Ability Forge...right?"

That's it. Eina told me as much on the day that we first visited that *Hephaistos Familia* shop in Babel Tower. I'm sure of it.

Only high-level smiths who have mastered the Forge ability to a certain degree can make them.

"Even I don't know the reason why, but he can. Hephaistos herself confirmed it."

"That means..."

"Yeah, the Crozzo family is the real deal. And he has their blood running through his veins."

I feel like my brain just hit a wall.

Mr. Welf really is a member of a noble family of smiths that fell into ruin.

And he really can make magic swords without the ability Forge.

...A Skill?

That's the only thing that comes to mind. Maybe he has some special Skill that allows him to make that kind of weapon without Forge.

Then again, Lilly said that the Crozzo family could all make magic swords...Did they all have the same Skill?

Hmmm, that seems a bit...I rub the sides of my head.

It's no use. Random guesses aren't going to solve anything.

Doing my best to cool off the burning questions within me, I focus on the goddess's story.

"However, he doesn't make them."

"...eh?"

"For some reason, he doesn't even try. If he did, his name would be famous and clients would be knocking at his door, but he doesn't. He's so stubborn that he's turned down a chair at the High Smiths' table."

He can make magic swords, but he refuses?

A blade with the ability to unleash magic—or something very similar—with just one swing is extremely strong. While they do have a limit, magic swords make it possible for anyone to wield the blessing of Magic. It's as easy as swinging your arm.

That kind of weapon can save hundreds of lives.

Not to mention the money he would earn, all the customers he would have, if he would just make them.

Despite all that, Mr. Welf doesn't want to...?

"He's referred to as the 'Rotten Treasure' at the shop I'm working at. Members of his own *Familia* call him 'Crozzo the Defective' and other kinds of cruel names."

The goddess goes on to say that no one ever says these things publicly.

…People understand these kinds of things without hearing them directly.

"Rotten Treasure"…A shop would say that, thinking about all the money they could be making. As for the members of his *Familia*— they're smiths just like Mr. Welf, and they're very jealous.

He has the potential to easily join the High Smiths and make all the money he wants just because he's a descendant of the Crozzo family.

I can see why he's always left out of their battle parties.

"He has the ability, but for some reason…That's the smith you signed a direct contract with, Bell."

"…"

He has a reason…

It's probably the reason why Mr. Welf never told me he could make magic swords.

No one tells their secrets to a person they just met two days earlier, so I'm sure that Mr. Welf wasn't trying to hide anything.

Thinking back to how he reacted when Lilly was talking earlier today, it makes a lot more sense now.

"Bell, you have to be able to accept a secret or two with a smile. Even the gods have things they don't want others to know. Please welcome him with open arms."

"Goddess…"

She speaks with a very soothing tone in her voice, like she's watching over me, guiding me.

Both of her elbows are on the table, her head in her hands as her eyes meet mine. My shoulders relax and a smile grows on my face before I know it.

The goddess giggles at my weird expression.

"We've been talking quite a while. We should dig in to dinner. Or is there something else you'd like to talk to me about?"

The goddess asks me with her eyes on our already cold dinner. I think about it for a moment, and I decide to ask one last thing.

About that Skill.

"So, you activated it? That Skill of yours."

"Yes..."

I tell her that it came to life when I thought about the people I admire, heroes.

It starts with tiny specks of white light swirling around a part of my body. Then, incredible power is unleashed from that spot... That's the effect of Active Action: My strength flies off the charts.

More than likely, it needs to charge before releasing energy.

I tell the goddess everything I can think of about my Skill, based on what happened today.

"...Bell, would you stand up for a moment and show me your Status?"

"Ah, yes, sure."

Her serious gaze catches me off guard.

Plunk. The goddess hops off her chair and walks over to me as I take off my undershirt.

I turn my back to her and feel her eyes skimming the hieroglyphs on my skin.

"...Hmmm."

Her warm fingertips graze over my back.

Then her fingers come to a sudden stop. The hieroglyphs under her soft hand start to heat up.

I shouldn't be able to see them, but for some reason it feels like the symbols are written inside my head.

Not just symbols...The story of "Argonaut" written on one massive stone tablet.

"That's enough."

I slowly turn around.

The goddess picks up my undershirt that was draped over the chair and hands it to me.

"I'm going to go ahead and give you my personal assessment. That Skill is the power to turn the tables."

That's what she tells me.

Her arm is still outstretched, her voice so quiet I have to focus to hear her.

"It gives you the power to defeat enemies stronger than you are… The ability to come back from the most hopeless of situations. At the very least, it gives you the capacity to do so."

I can see my reflection in the goddess's large, mystical eyes.

"This Skill is a key that only children obsessed with being a hero can receive—a key that unlocks the hero within you."

—Argonaut.

A story about a boy who aspired to be a hero.

And the path he took, his head in the clouds.

The path to heroism.

"When you bet everything on one strike, this Skill drastically increases your strength. Even in the face of overwhelming odds, it gives you a chance to punch through and turn the tide."

Just as heroes have done many times before.

The goddess adds one last thing.

"You've acquired a 'heroic strike.'"

With those words, the entire room falls silent.

It takes me a few moments to realize that our eyes are locked on each other. I only notice that we're looking deep into each other's eyes when the goddess hits my shoulder a few times with my shirt.

I grab it and ram my head through, my ears turning bright red. I can still feel her watching me as I wiggle and squirm my way back into my clothes.

Then she smiles.

But I've never seen her smile like this before. It's like she's looking down from a place far away, a place that I can't reach.

A smile that a loving angel sends down to the child she's protecting from high above the clouds.

This is the first time.

The first time the goddess has taken away my senses and robbed me of my thoughts.

I stand in awe of her, in complete silence, as I hear her say, "Remember this well."

"GWAAARRRRRAAAAAHHHHH!!"

A ferocious roar echoed.

A shockingly swift kick hit a silent monster square in the face, shattering its skull.

Long, golden boots were splattered with fresh blood. Despite delivering the finishing blow to hundreds of monsters up to this point and being covered in molten lava, their golden sheen has not diminished in the slightest.

These metal boots were not designed to protect the feet of the wearer. They were weapons, plain and simple. Tearing through the air with extreme velocity, they mow down everything in their path.

"Out of the way, Bete! It's not my fault if you get smashed to a pulp!"

"Who the hell would get hit by a crappy weapon like that?!"

"Tione! Wolf soup for dinner tonight! Eww! Nasty!"

"I'll frickin' kill you!"

"...Idiots."

The forty-fourth floor.

A stage of the Dungeon's lower levels filled with sweltering heat.

The crimson floor looked like it was always burning, with oddly shaped rocks jutting out all over the place. There were many cracks in the scorched walls, white-gray ash peeling off the Dungeon itself. A deep red light glowed from within the cracks, as if something inside was ready to burst forth.

Loki Familia's expedition was in full swing, with several adventurers having engaged a group of monsters called Flaming Rocks in combat within what looked like the belly of a volcano.

"What's got their britches in a bunch?"

"Gareth."

A surprised but low, growling voice reached the ears of *Loki Familia*'s field general, Fynn.

A dwarf walked up to him from behind.

A long beard flowed over his thick chest plate; muscles like steel bulged out from between the gaps in his imposing armor. A cape around his back, spinning an enormous ax lightly in his hand, the dwarf exuded a powerful warrior's aura.

The dwarf called Gareth watched in amazement as Bete and the other adventurers recklessly charged down monster after monster.

"Been pipin' hot since the middle levels, ya hear? The other youngsters can't grow like this. See there, Raul's in dire straits."

"Hmm. I don't like it much either, but there's no stopping them now."

It wasn't just Bete's small group that was engaging the monsters right now. Many members of *Loki Familia* had joined the fray. Most of them were Level 3, so they had to be careful to avoid the attacks of the higher-level adventurers as well as the monsters.

Bete, Tiona, Tione. The three of them slew more and more of the horde of monsters, taking the valuable excelia for themselves. Fynn watched them from his vantage point on top of a large boulder, an exhausted look on his face as he sighed under his breath.

"Even Tione's inner monster's breakin' loose...Fynn, what in blazes happened before our rendezvous?"

One of the Amazonian twins, who usually behaved herself in Fynn's presence, had a frighteningly calm look in her eyes but a telling grin on her lips. Grasping her set of Kukri knives, she hacked and slashed her way through the enemy ranks as her glossy black hair danced violently in her wake.

Gareth looked up at Fynn—who was still standing on top of the boulder—through the eyeholes of his helmet.

"They seem to have been inspired by an adventurer we ran into on our way down."

"Inspired, ya say? Anyone that good crawling the middle levels?"

"No, the upper levels."

"The hell?"

Loki Familia had followed the Guild's requirements for expeditions by splitting the group into two teams. Gareth had been in charge of the second group. Most of *Loki Familia*'s firepower had been in the first group to clear a path for the latter, leaving him as the only top-class adventurer on his team. The two groups had met up at a predetermined point in the Dungeon. Therefore, Gareth didn't know what Fynn's team had seen or experienced on their way down.

The dwarf's eyes went a little wider, his jaw slack in surprise.

"I think something was pulling the strings, but a Minotaur appeared on the ninth floor. A Level One adventurer encountered and slew it."

"A Minotaur done in by a Level One? No, hold up there, how do y'know the laddie was Level One?"

"The boy's Status was exposed and it was confirmed. Well, so long as Reveria can still read hieroglyphs, that is."

"What's this? Are you doubting my vision, Fynn?"

"Ahh, Reveria."

An elf walked up from behind them to join their conversation.

Her long jade hair sparkled in the crimson light. Even in this heat, there wasn't a bead of sweat anywhere on her silky white skin.

She wore an elegant blue dress that flowed like water as she came to a stop next to Fynn's boulder.

"Fynn, I would prefer to wear a robe next time. This Undine-made dress takes far too long to put on."

"Hmm. After all that Loki went through to get it for you, you should be able to put up with a little hassle."

"Aye. Y'wear it well."

"Just thinking about those eyes undressing me makes me want to set this wretched thing ablaze right here and now..."

The head of her *Familia*, Loki, had suddenly appeared a few days before the expedition and thrust this sheer blue dress at her and said, "Reveria, darlin', wear this, won'cha, please?" Reveria had accepted the dress with a cold, hard stare.

Fynn and Gareth had similar blue garments under their armor as well. Just like Reveria, neither of them felt the heat on this floor.

The material was enhanced with fairy magic and protected them from extreme temperatures.

"Back to the matter at hand, one other person can confirm the adventurer's level. Aiz also read Bell Cranell's Status."

Hearing the name of the adventurer for the first time, Gareth raised his shoulders as he looked at Reveria, before turning his body to cast his gaze at the ever-silent Aiz.

"...If what these ears have picked up be true, Aiz made for that monster like a moth to a flame. Or am I losing my wits?"

"Hmmm. That's very true. She's been so quiet I nearly forgot."

"Oh, give her some space. She always returns to her usual self."

Fynn looked down at Reveria with a very puzzled look, while the elf grimaced as she used her eyes to point something out to him.

Aiz stood in her line of vision. The girl was staring at the ground as if deep in thought.

She wore no particular expression, but every so often the group could hear a soft "Hmmmmm" coming from her direction.

"I still think you're puttin' me on...The laddie that impressive? What'd ya think, seein' 'im in action?"

"He was rather brash and very inexperienced...But, then again, I can understand why Bete and the others can't stand still. That boy reminded them that they are *adventurers*, just like him."

Fynn's golden hair swished from side to side as he looked at Gareth, an innocent smile on his childish face. Reveria nodded in agreement and opened her mouth to speak.

"As leaders of this *Familia*, we have endured many battles but have become too accustomed to combat. The chance that one of us will fall is extremely slim. However, witnessing a life-or-death battle firsthand was...breathtaking."

"...Sounds like ya found somethin' more precious than loot."

There was a twinge of remorse in his voice as Gareth stroked his mighty beard.

The three highest-ranking members of *Loki Familia*, always so careful to avoid careless actions, looked on as their younger allies fought tooth and nail against the horde of monsters.

"...Reveria."

"What is it, Aiz?"

Reveria responded to the hushed voice as if she'd known it was coming.

Aiz paused for a moment to gather her thoughts before continuing.

"How do you think someone…goes beyond the limits of Basic Abilities?"

Gareth's and Fynn's ears perked up, the question catching them off guard.

However, Fynn's eyes narrowed a moment later as he realized what she was asking, and he cast his gaze on the young girl.

"We are entering the realm of impossibility. While we can always try to hone our abilities, there's no way to go beyond them."

Reveria answered Aiz's question.

Using herself as an example, she explained that as an elf and magic user, a Magic ability ranking of *S* was obtainable. On the other hand, the physical limits of her body made it futile to try to improve her Strength and Defense abilities beyond a certain point. Just as every person had their individual strengths and weaknesses, be they mental or physical, the abilities of adventurers worked in the same way. There was a ceiling.

She finished her speech by saying that it was extremely difficult to maintain peak condition, but no one was able to go beyond the limits of a Status set by the gods.

"Do not concern yourself with such ridiculous ideas, Aiz. The absolute strongest we can become is determined by our Level."

"…Okay."

The girl once again fell silent under Reveria's harsh gaze.

Aiz took a step back, as if her mind had left her body for a moment—before she drew her saber.

The blade that emerged from her sheath whizzed around her, slicing through the heat with a crisp *swish*.

The others watched as she turned on her heel and stepped toward the battlefield.

"…Hey, Reveria."

"It's useless. Her spirit has been ignited."

Reveria sighed like a mother who had been putting up with her children too long, as she answered the dwarf standing beside her.

Aiz stepped forward with more and more resolve as she set a course for Bete's battle party. Her blond hair danced in the heat, but her golden eyes didn't waver from her target. Her expression was cold as ice, but her soul was on fire.

This was the other face of Aiz Wallenstein.

This was the Senki, the Princess of the Battlefield, as she had been called.

Summoning up all the power within her, she charged into combat.

...Stronger, I can get stronger.

The Dungeon's heat the least of her worries, Aiz's new target wasn't a monster but an impossibility.

She had seen with her own eyes the boy who broke the limits. His image was still burning in her soul.

Early morning.

The sun is just now peeking over the upper rim of the wall that surrounds the city.

Syr catches my attention in front of The Benevolent Mistress as I'm on my way to the Dungeon.

"I'm so sorry, can you wait just a little longer? Something went wrong when I was cooking this morning..."

"Um, Syr, you don't have to worry about it...You always give me a lunch, so one day isn't a big deal..."

"No, I will finish it! So please, take it with you!"

Shoop. I can almost hear her muscles tighten as her face becomes more and more frightening. "S-sure..." I say with a quick nod. I'm too scared to do anything else. Suddenly, her cheeks blush like she's shy and she runs back into the bar.

She makes a lunch for me every day. Sounds like something didn't go according to plan this morning. Normally she's very hard to read, but today she seems to be in a great mood…Oh no, what's going to show up in today's lunch? I break out in a cold sweat just thinking about it.

"Good morning to you, Mr. Cranell."

"Ah, Lyu. Good morning."

"I am deeply sorry for the lost time. Syr is working very hard…so please accept her lunch."

Just when I thought I'd be standing alone for a while, the front door opens with a creak.

Lyu steps out from behind it and greets me. She's trying to cover for Syr, so I tell her it's not a problem at all and smile at her.

She even put her duties as a Benevolent Mistress staff member on hold to talk with me for a little while.

"So, you have successfully found another battle party member."

"At least temporarily, yes…"

She asked me about finding another party member at our get-together the other night, so I start by telling her about what's happened since. She's wearing a white cardigan over her waitress uniform. After waiting for me to finish, Lyu asks me another question.

"Mr. Cranell, is this person worthy of your trust?"

"Eh? Well, um…"

"My apologies, it was not my intention to accuse you of anything. Circumstances change when adventurers from different *Familias* form a battle party."

Lyu looks at me with her sky-blue eyes and explains that we will have to be conscious of more than just personal issues, but inter-*Familial* affairs as well.

I know she's just looking out for me. After all that she did to protect me from those other adventurers the other night, I'm sure that she wants to make sure the person I found is the right man for the job.

I gather my thoughts to respond, Lyu's sincerity making me feel all warm and fuzzy.

"Since he's a member of *Hephaistos Familia*, I don't think there's going to be a problem. Our goddesses are on good terms, too."

Hephaistos Familia is filled with smiths who make many personal

contracts with many different adventurers, so they have a good reputation. I've heard horror stories about fighting between *Familias*
that all started with a mixed battle party, but I don't think that will
be a problem with them.

And I don't have any complaints about Mr. Welf...But there is
something.

I've been doing a lot of thinking after talking with the goddess last
night. I might as well see what Lyu has to say on the subject, so I tell
her Mr. Welf's full name and that he is a very talented smith.

Wow, I really am talking behind his back a lot...

"Crozzo..."

She freezes in place after hearing Mr. Welf's family name. The
name practically fell from her lips.

She normally doesn't react to anything like this. It's making me a
little nervous.

"D-do you know anything about him...?"

"No, nothing about him personally...However, Crozzo is a name
that is impossible for elves to ignore."

E-elves can't ignore it?

I never expected to get information about the Crozzo family here.

"If you don't mind, could you tell me why? I want to know as much
about Mr. Welf as I can..."

"...Very well. I would like to caution you that this is most likely
not the information you're seeking."

She jumps into her story after giving me that short disclaimer.

"I believe you have heard about their magic swords, but are you
familiar with where those blacksmiths resided?"

"No, I'm not."

"A kingdom called Rakia. Of all the countries in the world, that
kingdom is relatively close to Orario."

Rakia...I think I heard that name a few times in my hometown
before coming to Orario.

Things like "That country's starting a war again," or "They're sending expeditions all over the place," and others.

"The country itself is governed by one god who declared himself king using his *Familia*. The Crozzo family offered their services in exchange for nobility. Those services were, of course, producing a large supply of magic swords."

Everything she said so far matches up with Lilly's telling very well. I nod and Lyu continues.

"Perhaps due to the fact that its ruler considered himself a god of war, Rakia was an extremely aggressive nation. That is still accurate to this day. Whenever a neighboring country or city shows weakness, Rakia moves to invade."

So the rumors are true...

"Within that country's long history of repetitive wars, the full power of Crozzo's Magic Swords was unleashed many times."

She's about to get to the point, I can feel it. I'm on the edge of my seat, or at least I would be if I were sitting down.

"An army of common soldiers armed with magic swords—can you picture that, Mr. Cranell?"

"...Don't tell me they..."

"You are correct. At that time, Rakia had a mobile inferno under its command. They didn't bother with strategy or planning. They just annihilated everything in their wake with overwhelming firepower."

Victory after victory, undefeated and invincible, a god of war who couldn't lose.

She says that no one knew how to stop Rakia when it was blessed with magic swords.

"Rakia was too aggressive. Their wars changed the very face of our world. Thus, prairies and cities alike were burned to ash, leaving nothing behind...And then their flames reached a forest inhabited by elves."

It's said that humans and demi-humans and elves didn't interact very much before the gods descended to this world. There are some very close-minded people around now who still don't.

The best examples are the elves. I've heard there is a group of them who are so proud that they absolutely hate interacting with other races. They've shut themselves off from the rest of the world in a forest somewhere.

So basically, that means…

"They were chased out of their home, those elves? The forest they lived in was destroyed by a war?"

"They were smoked out, to be more precise. Their homeland went up in flames."

Their forest burned to the ground.

I gulp down a mouthful of air once the meaning of those words hits home.

Lyu finishes her story by saying that the surviving elves sought help from other gods. They joined *Familias* in the surrounding nations, received blessings, and took revenge on Rakia.

Unfortunately for the kingdom, they no longer had magic swords in their arsenal. Lyu said that those elves got their retribution relatively easily.

"Rakia's soldiers spread devastation as if it was a game. For those on the receiving end of magic swords, hating the Crozzo family might be a case of misplaced anger…However, there are still many elves who haven't gotten over the past."

"…"

"So that is why the name Crozzo is impossible for elves to ignore."

"…What about you, Lyu?"

"No, I harbor no ill will."

Her quick denial surprises me.

I've heard that elves consider their entire race to be a family, filled with pride in themselves and one another.

Lyu says that's an exaggeration, and that her own homeland was not directly affected…I'm absolutely stunned.

Of course, Syr—and the others as well—cares for me, but to think Lyu hasn't known me very long at all, yet shares something like this and worries about me so much…She's very important to me.

"Be-ll! Sorry to keep you waiting!"

"…It's time. Mr. Cranell, please be careful in the Dungeon today."

"Ah, yes…"

Lyu gives me a slight bow as Syr comes through the door.

She goes back inside the bar without another word. I watch in silence as the door closes behind her.

"I'm a little late…"

I'm speed-walking my way through West Main. Morning bells ring out from the east as I make my way through an ever-growing crowd of people. Lilly and Mr. Welf are waiting for me at the base of Babel Tower. I have to get there as soon as possible.

My feet are moving, but my thoughts are somewhere else entirely. I'm so wrapped up in what I just heard from Lyu that I don't even notice a person walking right up to me.

"Oh, this really *is* your route."

"Ah," I say as everything comes into focus. It's Mr. Welf, and he's waving at me.

Isn't this strange? I told him we were meeting at the same place as yesterday…Did he want to meet me halfway?

"Hey, Bell. Mornin'."

"Good morning. Umm…Mr. Welf, what are you doing out here?"

"Got a message for you from Li'l E. She can't join us for dungeon crawling today."

"Eh?"

He explains that he was waiting at the base of Babel when a very animated Lilly rushed up to him. She said that on top of being busier than usual recently, the gnome she works for collapsed. She's the only one around who can take care of him. Apparently she bowed enough times to make Mr. Welf dizzy watching her.

Hearing that I always arrive from West Main, he decided to come out and meet me.

"So, what do we do? Hit the Dungeon as a two-man cell?"

"W-well, ummm…"

We won't be able to collect as many magic stones and drop items without Lilly with us. But if we don't go into the Dungeon, I won't have anything to do all day…I'd like to avoid that.

Should I go grab my old backpack and gather stones and drop items, like I did back in my solo days?

"...Bell. If you've got nothing else going on, can I have some of your time today?"

"What?"

I tilt my head to the side at his suggestion.

The corner of his mouth rises in a grin; his hands wave from side to side.

"I made you a promise, didn't I? A full set of new equipment."

"Y-you know, Mr. Welf, I'm fine with just the light armor..."

"No need for modesty. A smith never goes back on his word."

Mr. Welf is heading somewhere at a brisk pace and I'm doing my best to keep up.

I know I already agreed to it, but the thought of receiving brand-new equipment for free makes me feel like I'm taking advantage of him...I feel kind of guilty.

I try a few more times to decline the offer, but he just waves me off, saying, "Leave it to me." I watch his black coat swish back and forth as we make our way up the street.

"Bell, I don't pretend to know everything, but you should go after the best stuff you can get. Adventurers never know if there's a tomorrow. Because you don't know what's coming, you should always have the best weapons and armor on you at all times—right?"

"Yeah..."

He makes a very good point. I can't help but agree.

Everything is pointless if you die. I don't know how many times Eina has said that.

And I promised the goddess that I wouldn't leave her alone. All things in moderation, but...the most important thing is not to make the big mistake, I guess.

I think about it for a while, but in the end I decide to take Mr. Welf's offer.

The moment I say, "I'm looking forward to your work," Mr. Welf grins from ear to ear and says, "Coming right up."

"Mr. Welf. Can I ask you where we're going?"

"My workshop."

Workshop? He must've looked over his shoulder and seen the confusion on my face, because Mr. Welf starts to explain.

A workshop is where a smith creates armor and weapons. He says everything he needs to create my new equipment is already there: a forge, various metals and tools, etc.

Apparently his *Familia* assigned him his own workshop...and that's something special about being a member of *Hephaistos Familia*.

"You mean everyone having their own workshop isn't normal?"

"Doubt it. It'd be much cheaper to have everyone use the same space; be more efficient, too."

"Then, why?"

"So that other smiths don't see your techniques. My way is *only* my way, yeah?"

Must be an artisan thing...Or maybe it's his pride as a smith?

Members of his *Familia* are also his competition. That's got to be one stressful working environment.

"Don't be thinking I'm doing something shady, now. Lady Hephaistos wanted it this way."

Laughing at his own joke, Mr. Welf starts to pick up speed.

We're moving along Northeast Main Street right now.

Large and small shops on both sides of the street have awnings over their entrances. Shops selling tools and other items are all over the place, with not a bar to be seen. The people around here are wearing all kinds of different worker's gear as they get ready to start the day. Only a few of them have *Familia* symbols on their clothes, so I guess most of them are free workers. I can see large, boxy buildings all over the place...I bet they're factories.

If I remember right, all of the magic-stone products that Orario is known for are made along Northeast Main.

The Industrial District, that's what it's called.

"We're turning up there."

I'm distracted for a moment by a dwarf lumbering along the side of the street while carrying a massive tree trunk over his shoulder, but I follow Mr. Welf.

Our path suddenly narrows as we turn off the main street. It's still morning, but the sun's rays have yet to reach this stone-paved side street. It's quite cool back here. The brilliant blue stripe of sky above us is absolutely magnificent.

All the buildings around here are made of stone as well. Just when I think we're going to go all the way to the city wall, Mr. Welf comes to a stop.

"Whoa…"

After winding our way through so many back streets, here it is.

A compact, one-story building stands in front of us.

Burn marks and soot cover the stone walls, but this is the real thing! The aura of an actual forge oozes out of every inch of this place. A smokestack juts out of one corner of the roof. The whole building is rather charming.

"You might already know, but this is the area most workers call home. Can't walk two steps without seeing another workshop or factory. My *Familia*'s home is just around the corner."

Of course, this is all news to me. "Oh, I see," I say, my head on a swivel as I take in all the sights.

Mr. Welf's workshop is quite a ways away from Main Street. This area reminds me a lot of my home, being a bit dark and out-of-the-way.

Echoes of metal on metal ring out from every direction…I can feel the presence of other smiths already hard at work, as well as hear them.

Above all, it sounds like *Hephaistos Familia* prepares a workshop for each of its members in this area.

Each member is in charge of taking care of their own area…but still, it's really generous.

"What're you standin' around for? Come on in."

"Ah, sure."

I say a quiet thank-you as I follow Mr. Welf into his workshop.

The first thing I notice is the strong smell of iron. Mr. Welf opens the shutters, bathing the dark room in the crisp morning light.

A wide array of tools hanging on the wall starts glistening. Hammers, tongs, random utensils...A lot of them. I've never seen anything like any of these before.

A large fireplace is nestled in the corner, behind a medium-height bench. Isn't that thing called an anvil?

There are no dividing walls in here, just one big space devoted to forging armor and weapons.

Now *this* is a smith's workshop.

"Sorry, bit of a pigsty in here. Can you put up with it for a bit?"

"Don't worry about me, I'm fine!"

Actually, I want to see him in action...Starting to get excited, I take another look around the room.

Mr. Welf pulls up a chair for me and motions for me to sit down.

"For starters, I'm going to need your measurements. I can handle everything else on my own after that."

"You need my measurements?"

"Yeah, I'll be customizing the armor for you. Would be a shame if it didn't fit just right, now wouldn't it?"

The armor sold in shops has to accommodate a wide range of body shapes and sizes, so there are always spots that aren't snug or that stick out a little bit. Adventurers can make little adjustments themselves, but the ideal is to have armor and weapons made to fit perfectly.

"I'm thinking 'bout making some greave-style shin guards. Any requests, Bell?"

"Hmm, ummm...?"

"If there's a piece of equipment you'd like me to make, just say the word. Like maybe you feel naked without a shield, things like that...So yeah, if there's an item you want, speak up. I'll make anything for you."

Mr. Welf has his back to me, collecting various tools from the wall.

Clink, clank. I hear him set tools on his workbench while I'm sitting in my chair, racking my brain.

I suppose my preferences would be short blades and light armor? I don't want to be pushy, but I can't think of anything else I'd want, no matter how hard I try.

Well…it wasn't a shield, but having a protector was nice. Maybe I should ask for another one?

Wow, that's a huge blade…

I catch a glint of light out of the corner of my eye. I look over there and see a series of shelves in the opposite corner of the room.

Several weapons are lined up on them. Probably some of Mr. Welf's past work.

In the middle of all of them, I spot a broadsword that reminds me of the cleaver I used in my fight against the Minotaur.

"…Mr. Welf, would it be asking too much to try this out?"

He suddenly appears next to me as if he'd been yanked over by a rope. His eyes follow mine to the massive sword on the shelf.

It's not here as decoration, but its silver blade and proportionate balance as a weapon are absolutely stunning nevertheless.

I could say this about the armor I wear into the Dungeon, but it was very clearly made by Mr. Welf.

"It's not 'too much,' no…The shop sent that one back to me 'cause it wouldn't sell."

"But I-I'd like to use it."

I ask him if I can take a few practice swings. The confusion in his eyes is as plain as day, but he gives me permission to try.

Shung. I grab the hilt and lift it off the shelf. I swing the blade from the floor up to the ceiling, carving a silver arc in the air. I can't help but smile.

I try a few side swings next. It's so much heavier than my knife, and it won't move the way I want it to.

"…"

"…? Is something wrong?"

After swinging the blade a few times, I notice that Mr. Welf is frozen in place.

When he finally responds, Mr. Welf's lips hardly move as he speaks.

"You really…weren't after a magic sword."

Wha? I tilt my head again, wondering if I heard that right. "Huh?"

"How was I supposed to know you'd be more interested in a shop reject than a magic sword after coming all the way here?"

He looks happier and happier with each passing second. "Ummm," is all I can say.

That's right! Crozzo's magic swords...I was so excited about seeing the workshop and all these weapons that I completely forgot. Everything comes flooding back in.

I don't know how to respond to that, but Mr. Welf suddenly has a mean smile on his face.

"So, what did she tell you? Your goddess...What did Lady Hestia tell you about me?"

"?!"

"One of the guys working in Babel told me. A young-looking goddess was asking around about me."

The blood drains from my head as Mr. Welf calmly explains the situation.

He knows that I've been talking about him behind his back?!

"I-I'm so sorry! My goddess didn't mean anything bad by it, she's just...well, worried about me...It's all my fault!"

"I couldn't care less. Someone from another *Familia* has started working with one of her own. She's gotta stay on top of things."

"That's a good thing, isn't it?"

Mr. Welf responds with a lighthearted smile. It looks like he really doesn't care.

I breathe a deep sigh of relief.

"I was worried you'd look at me differently...once you found out. Sorry to test you like that, but I had to know."

He genuinely looks sorry with that grimace on his face.

...So that means he was trying to see if I would ask for a magic sword, if given a chance. If I would use a descendant of the magic swordsmiths to get one for myself.

Having a famous family name like Crozzo must've made him really sensitive to those words.

Huh. So that's what he was getting at earlier.

"Got a bit sidetracked, but I'll ask you again. Other than a big sword, is there anything you want?"

"Ah, yes...umm."

I never did figure that out, so let's see. Maybe I should ask for a shortsword? Wait a minute, maybe something on Mr. Welf's shelf will give me an idea.

I turn my back to him and take another look.

"...Hey, Bell. I've been wondering this for a while, but is that a drop item strapped to your back?"

"Eh? Oh."

I look over my shoulder and see that Mr. Welf is pointing at my lower back, where the Divine Knife, my dagger, and the Minotaur Horn are.

"This is...Yes. It's a Minotaur drop item...but for some reason I just can't let it go."

A scorched horn with bits and pieces of red showing through. I don't really consider it to be a good-luck charm, but I can't shake the feeling that selling it off is wrong somehow.

...I can't turn my back on everything that I went through with that Minotaur.

At the very least, I should leave it as it is.

Although it is kind of useless, carrying it around like this...

"...How about making something out of that?"

"Eh?"

"Using that horn to make a piece of equipment. I could make one hell of a weapon from the Minotaur Horn."

My eyes go wide.

Of course! The direct contract—I bring him drop items from the Dungeon, and he'll make weapons for me!

Mr. Welf's suggestion is like an angel's song to my ears. This way I can always keep it with me, and the drop item won't go to waste. I nod my head as fast as I can.

"Yes, please!"

"That settles it, then."

I hand the Minotaur Horn to Mr. Welf.

He holds it in his hands for a moment, looking over every inch of the item.

"...Were Minotaur Horns always red?"

"What do you mean?"

"Never mind, not important...It's in pretty good shape, and quite a bit denser than usual. Little bit of shaping, some elbow grease, and it should become one fine blade..."

Mr. Welf is getting more and more excited as he looks at the Minotaur Horn.

Talking under his breath and scrunching up his brow, he takes his eyes off the horn for a moment and looks up at me.

"Bell. Can you let me do my own thing? I want to take my time making this."

"S-sure. I'm not a smith, so I wouldn't be able to tell you what to do, anyway..."

"Thanks, that helps. Since we're only using this horn, your options for a new weapon are kind of limited..."

One shortsword or two daggers.

That's the Minotaur Horn "menu" that Mr. Welf presents for me.

He says that trying to stretch it out into a shortsword would make the blade very thin, so he recommends the latter option.

The Divine Knife is one thing, but my dagger was provided by the Guild...It might be time for an upgrade. I don't think that a weapon of the lowest rank would be much use against the monsters I'll face in the middle levels.

This might be a good opportunity for an upgrade. I've used my dagger for about two months already, so I decide to hang it up for good.

I ask Mr. Welf to make the daggers.

"All right, that's what I'm talking about. I'll just make one for now and use the leftovers to make another once I learn Forge. Wait and see what I come up with then!"

"Ah-ha-ha-ha..."

Mr. Welf has a very excited glint in his eyes, and I can't help but chuckle at his enthusiasm.

He doesn't waste any time in getting my measurements after that. Grabbing measuring tapes and different tools from a metal bucket, Mr. Welf works his way around me, measuring as he goes.

He asks me to take off my boots and spends a great deal of time recording the shape of my feet.

"You can head home once I'm finished here."

"Um, Mr. Welf, about that…"

"Yeah?"

"Would it be okay with you if I watched…?" I manage to ask as he looks over the palm of my hand, specifically where the hilt of the blade would sit.

I really want to see what a smith does and how weapons are forged. Coming all the way out here has piqued my curiosity. Mr. Welf works his way up my shoulder as I'm trying to picture what's about to happen in this place.

Mr. Welf doesn't know how to respond to my honesty. "You're a strange one," he says while tilting his head to the side. But he agrees to let me stay.

I promise over and over not to get in his way. I don't know if it's because I'm getting excited, but my cheeks are suddenly very hot.

"It gets pretty damn hot in here; it'd be a good idea to take off your armor."

"Eh, ah, yes."

Not really understanding what he meant, I follow his directions.

Down to my undershirt, I set all of my armor in the corner and turn to face Mr. Welf. He's in the opposite corner, next to the forge… lighting a fire.

"Wh-what are you doing?"

"Heating up the drop item."

"You're going to burn the monster's horn?!"

I yell out in surprise despite promising I wouldn't interfere just a moment ago.

Animal horns are just like bone, aren't they? Well, I'm not sure, but…they'll turn to ash in a fire…?

"There's something like metal inside a monster's horns and claws."

"Metal…?"

"Yeah. Ever heard of adamantite?"

Adamantite…I feel like I've heard of it before, but I can't place it.

All I can think of is that it's an extremely rare metal…

"Adamantite can only be found in the Dungeon. When it comes to making weapons, it's the best stuff out there. Very sturdy."

"People find it in the Dungeon?"

"Yep. Sometimes pieces of it just fall out of the dungeon walls, like the monsters. But that's once in a blue moon. Every so often I hear of someone finding it in the upper levels, but most adventurers bring it up from much deeper in the lower levels."

It can only be collected in the Dungeon…That means that it can only be found in Orario.

Apparently, adamantite weapons are a specialty of Orario's. Since it's a very difficult material to acquire, its value puts magic stones to shame.

"…So then, it's possible that monsters born in the Dungeon have adamantite inside them…?"

"Hit the nail right on the head. Exactly. On the other hand, it's not as pure as the stuff that comes out of the dungeon walls. It's a bit weaker."

In that case, it might not be strange that monsters born in the Dungeon are affected by this material.

Mr. Welf tells me that only a few of them have adamantite in their fangs and claws, but they're perfect for making weapons.

…This horn. This horn broke that thick cleaver during our battle.

"Minotaur Horns also have a metallic element to them. Heat them up just right, and you can shape them at will."

Okay, now I get it. He's going to make the Minotaur Horn hot enough to forge, just like a piece of metal…This is just the first step.

An image of the red-hot horn pops into my mind. It kind of looks like a piece of candy.

From there, Mr. Welf is going to take all kinds of tools to it, just as if he were working with metal.

"Sorry to bug you, Bell. Could you open the door and the shutters up all the way?"

"N-no problem."

Mr. Welf wraps a hand towel around his head at the same time he speaks to me.

I go around the room, opening every window and door.

I turn back around to find Mr. Welf poking and prodding at the fire he just started. There is a rock at the base of the forge, a drop item from a monster known as an Inferno Stone…The flames it can produce are so intense that average people can't buy one.

"Just like adamantite, this horn ain't gonna bend unless I heat it just right."

Mr. Welf keeps his eyes glued to the forge while talking.

In no time at all, a roaring flame erupts from the stone and intense heat swells within the forge. The heat wave reaches me a moment later. I'm a good distance away from it, but I've already broken a sweat. I can't imagine what it would be like if I still had my armor on.

Mr. Welf is completely focused on adjusting the temperature within the forge. I sit back down in my chair and watch from behind.

It's still only midmorning. I don't even think an hour has passed since I got my lunch from Syr. I bet Babel Tower is swamped with adventurers making their way into the Dungeon by now.

Yet here I am in a dim room, surrounded by gloomy back streets with only this forge for light.

Looking at the massive furnace, its red mouth wide open, everything feels mysterious.

I can only see part of Mr. Welf's face, but his intensity matches the flames that dance in front of him.

"You look like you've got something on your mind."

"Huh?!"

"Come on, ask away. We have a direct contract. I don't want to have any secrets."

A few moments pass in silence. His preparations complete, Mr. Welf withdraws his face from the forge and looks at me.

I freeze on the spot, stunned by his sudden request…How did he know?

It's not that I have a specific question to ask him, but there's something that's been on my mind for a while. Every time I hear about

Mr. Welf, my curiosity grows and grows to the point that if I'm not careful, the words will spill right out of my mouth. I guess he must've caught on.

He has a gentle aura about him. A light smile on his lips. I can see a look of trust in his eyes...At least I think so.

I swallow all the spit in my mouth and take that first step to finding the answers from Mr. Welf himself.

"Why don't you...Why don't you make magic swords, Mr. Welf?"

I can still remember how happy he was when I became his client.

If he would just make magic swords, he would have more clients and money than he would know what to do with.

He already has a famous name that would draw in people from all over. That's the power of the Crozzo family.

I have to know the reason why he doesn't even try.

"Well, there are a few reasons, but..."

His mouth curling into a grimace, he casts his gaze back into the flames.

"I *hate* magic swords."

Then he starts to explain the reason why he despises them so much.

"Truth is, I told you my work doesn't sell, but I've had a ton of clients...Nah, still do."

"Eh......?"

"It's so simple that it makes me sick. All these people see my armor and weapons in the shop, but once they see my signature, 'Crozzo'... they come knockin' at my door, beggin' me to make a magic sword for them."

Mr. Welf pumps more air into the forge, using a tool at his feet.

"They completely ignore *my work*, it's all just magic sword, magic sword, magic sword...That's all everyone other than you ever said. I know and realize I don't have much experience, but...You know? It hurts."

The slightest of wrinkles appears below his mouth, the only dark shadow on a face blanketed in an orange and red glow.

A magic sword that is said to be strong enough to burn away

the sea, probably the strongest ever. Everyone was after the magic swords of the Crozzo name, not Mr. Welf's armor or weapons.

None of the customers who came to him looked him in the eye… Could they only see the value of the Crozzo bloodline?

All they saw were the magic swords.

"Um, Mr. Welf…How did, um, you know…"

"Yeah, things went downhill fast. Lots of yelling. 'Get lost, you bastards!' and 'Who would listen to the likes of you?!' I chased them all away."

"Ha-ha-ha-ha…"

I'm lost for words; all I can give him is an empty laugh. However, I get it. I understand.

He's angry at the people who wouldn't give his armor and weapons any attention. Well, part of it could be that he's angry at the Crozzo blood flowing within him.

I hear what he's saying and I get it…But.

"Um…Is that the only reason?"

I feel like there's something more.

He said he hates magic swords, but there has to be a deeper meaning.

"…"

An answer doesn't come right away.

Taking his eyes off the forge, Mr. Welf walks over to his workbench and looks down at the Minotaur Horn. Picking up a chisel and hammer, he sets to work on breaking the horn in two.

After about fifty shrill impacts, the Minotaur Horn finally splits right down the middle. Setting the relatively larger half off to the side, he carries the smaller half back to the forge and sits down.

"Do you know why the Crozzo family can make magic swords in the first place, Bell?"

He pinches a piece of the horn with a special tool and thrusts it deep into the heart of the flames.

"I don't…" I respond as I watch him move onto the next step in the weapon-making process.

"There was once an ordinary man named Crozzo. It was his

descendants who made his name what it is now. We call him The Ancestor. All this happened before the gods came down here."

We call the time before the gods came to this world "the Old Age." That era ended about a thousand years ago.

The Crozzo family history can be traced back that far?! Wow…

"The story goes that The Ancestor was a smith down on his luck. Nothing would sell. And of course, he couldn't make magic swords. However, it's beyond a shadow of a doubt that he's the one who started it all."

A breath.

"The Ancestor risked his life to save a member of a certain species from a monster."

"A certain species…?"

"A fairy."

—"Whaa?!" My voice hits the floor in shock.

Mr. Welf smirks at the surprise on my face and continues his story with even more enthusiasm.

"The fairy did everything it could to save the life of the man who was bleeding out on the ground. It cut part of its body and gave him some of its own blood."

"S-so that means the Crozzo family has…?"

"Yeah. We've got fairy blood in us."

—Fairies.

Nymphs, spirits, elementals, jinn…Their mysterious race has many names here on Earth. Their population is extremely small compared to the other races.

"The most loved of all the children." "Children of the gods."

Humans and demi-humans have many stories about them, but the one common thread is that fairies are the ones closest to the gods themselves.

"The Ancestor made a full recovery, like nothing ever happened. A full-blown miracle. However, after that day it was said that he could use magic despite being human…and he could make magic swords."

Fairies are capable of so much that other races pale in comparison. They're magic users, like the elves. They can call forth flames, summon wind, create their own ponds deep in the forests, and even produce precious metals out of thin air.

It might be accurate to say that their power rivals the gods'.

Basically, they can perform miracles.

"So did, did the Crozzo family become heroes…?"

"Nah, nothing like that. Good or bad, The Ancestor was just regular townsfolk."

Fairies appear in many stories, especially stories about heroes— and many of those stories are based on truth. Gramps told me that.

The fairies in those stories use their power to guide the young hero, sometimes lending him strength, and using their power of miracles to help him fulfill his destiny when the time comes.

Usually, they impart magic on the hero or give him a powerful blade, not unlike what Mr. Welf just said. I even heard about a fairy who turned its own body into a weapon.

Fairies play a big part in heroic deeds of the main characters in each story, and are sometimes directly involved.

In the time before the gods, having a fairy on your side would have been the equivalent of a Falna today.

"The Ancestor died at a ripe old age, but his blood was passed on. It's probably due to more fairy magic, but it's still around today more than a thousand years later. The gods and goddesses who witnessed everything from above can tell that I'm a member of that line."

It's said that once the gods came down to this world, more fairies began to interact with other races. Be that as it may, most of them avoid us. I don't know if they're whimsical or too proud.

Gnomes are a race of fairy that lives alongside us very well. They may look like little old men and women, but their knowledge about jewels and valuable materials has made them a valuable part of our society.

Blessings from the gods and goddesses have made fairies less appreciated compared to the Old Age. However, their mysterious nature still captivates human and demi-human alike.

"Even though they had the fairy blood of The Ancestor within them, the first few generations couldn't do much with it…That is, until a Crozzo received a god's blessing. That changed everything."

"…Skill?"

"Yep. One that let them make magic swords. Every member of the family acquired it the moment they received their blessing. Nothing to it."

A hidden potential awakened within them as soon as a Crozzo family member received a Status.

Even after all this time, that fairy's power is still at work.

"Li'l E already told you what happened next. Magic swords were much more powerful than anything else available, and the Crozzo family sold their work to their king."

Mr. Welf explains that by this time they had become subjects of a kingdom.

To sum everything up, The Ancestor used fairy blood that was given to him in order to make magic swords before any family members received Falna. Then they became known as a family of magic swordsmiths because…that blood they all shared unlocked the ability to create powerful magic swords.

The source of the Crozzos' fame comes down to the quality of their bloodline.

"They really lived it up after that, doing whatever the hell they wanted. Their swords granted the king's armies unbelievable power; the compliments from the king himself and rewards for their work kept flowing in. They stuffed their faces with the finest delicacies, nearly drowned themselves in expensive ale…Smiths behaving like royalty—what were they thinking?"

Mr. Welf's words trail off in hesitation, his eyes not leaving the flame.

Silence falls.

For the longest time, the only sounds in the workshop are those of the crackling flames in the forge.

"…The Crozzos got full of themselves. They forgot that they owed everything to the fairy blood in their veins. Started thinking that their Skill was their power, that magic swords were their right… Blinded by greed, they kept making more and more."

—"So they were cursed."

Mr. Welf speaks more clearly than he had all morning.

"The kingdom used Crozzo's Magic Swords in war after war… earning the hatred of the elves in the process by burning down their homes…"

"I-I know."

"It wasn't just elven hatred they wrought, but that of the fairy who saved The Ancestor as well."

"?!"

"Fairies love to be at one with nature. They surround themselves with it. The magic swords scarred their mountains, scorched their ponds, annihilated their forests…Just like the elves, the fairies were chased out of their own homes."

This was the source of the elves' grudge, just like Lyu said.

Did Crozzo's Magic Swords become the fairies' sworn enemy, like how the elves swore revenge on the Kingdom of Rakia?

"The elves took out their anger on the country. But the fairies, their grudge was with the Crozzos."

"…"

"And then, just before another battle like any other, all of the magic swords crumbled without warning. Never-been-used magic swords, fresh out of the forge. It goes without saying that the kingdom lost that battle without its greatest weapons."

"Did the fairies do that?"

"I'm sure of it. At the same time, the Crozzos lost the ability to make magic swords. They were cursed by the fairies."

So that's what it means to be cursed…?

When did my shoulders get so tense?

"The kingdom lost over and over after that. The Crozzo family took the blame and was stripped of nobility. That's the fall from grace. By the time I was born, there was nothing left from the old days."

From heaven to hell. You reap what you sow, I guess…

That explains the Crozzo family's fall into ruin.

But, wait. Hold on a second…

"You said that the Crozzos couldn't make magic swords, right? But I've heard you can, Mr. Welf…?"

"Yeah. I can. No clue why."

Maybe the effect of the curse wore off, or maybe the fairies were satisfied with their revenge. There might also be something special about Mr. Welf.

Even though the reason is unclear, the one thing that he's sure of is that he's the only Crozzo who can make magic swords right now.

But Mr. Welf ran away from home and broke free from the Crozzo family...He says that he was nothing but a wanderer when Lady Hephaistos found him.

"I know they were trying to restore the family name, but I'm grateful to my old man for cramming all these forging techniques into my head. Thanks to him, I learned the joy of creating something useful."

My body feels a few degrees warmer. I've completely lost track of time, but Mr. Welf seems to know what's going on. Sensing the right moment, he pulls the drop item out of the forge and places it on the anvil.

Although the piece of Minotaur Horn is still in its original shape, it looks like it could melt at any moment, glowing red like that.

"Probably because I didn't hate it. I didn't hate being a shop hand, working alongside my old man and his tools in a workshop covered in soot.

"That feeling the first time I struck metal..." he says in a voice so quiet I have to strain to hear him.

A wet sound reaches my ears at the same time.

"However...once they realized I was good at it, my old man forced me to make a magic sword. He said it was to return the Crozzo family to glory."

Mr. Welf takes a deep breath as he grabs a hammer with his right hand.

His lips go flat into a straight line as his eyes open wide.

This is the first time I've seen him like this—Mr. Welf's smith face.

I hold my breath.

"...Make *a tool* the king would appreciate, is what he was saying. But he left that part out."

A moment later, Mr. Welf brings the hammer down on the Minotaur Horn with incredible force.

"It's not the same. Weapons aren't like that, not even close."

The impact of metal on metal sends a shock wave of sound through the room. The forging has begun.

Mr. Welf hits the drop item with his hammer as if he's trying to drive his thoughts into the material.

"Even political tools are no reason to get excited. But weapons, they become part of their wielder."

A series of shorter, more precise strikes sends out a new chorus of high-pitched echoes throughout the workshop.

All of the strength he's built up in the Dungeon makes each blow much stronger than that of a normal man.

"No matter what desperate straits someone is in, they must always be able to count on their own weapon. From the moment they grip the hilt, it becomes an extension of their arm."

He starts mixing strong hammer blows with short strikes, the rhythm of the echoes changing every moment.

The material lengthens with the heavy impacts; the quick hits adjust the shape.

He doesn't wait for me to respond to him. He just keeps talking as the hot object beneath him takes a new form.

"It's our job as smiths to make weapons that last."

His passion for reliable armor and weapons is pouring out of him. It's almost as if Mr. Welf himself is on fire.

It's pure devotion to his craft.

"We face down metal at its hottest—at our hottest. A weapon can only be made when we bring everything we have to bear. What'll happen if we half-ass it? Fail to pour our sweat and blood into it? What if we forget our own ambition?"

Mr. Welf is slamming his whole world into each strike.

As if his blood is boiling, as if he's possessed by something unseen.

I wonder what he's seeing in the middle of that lump of molten metal...

"I hate magic swords. They will always break before their wielder."

© Suzuhito Yasuda

Showers of sparks fly, red beams of light flash.

Flakes of burned metal are launched from the horn with every blow. And yet they all just flow harmlessly off of Mr. Welf's black coat and to the floor. I wonder if it has some of the same qualities as adventurer's armor...

Wait, that's it.

His black coat is in such rough shape because it's his work clothes.

Its black color and worn condition are all proof of how hard he's worked, how many pieces he's made.

"I absolutely despise magic swords. That kind of power rots people's souls. The user, the smith's pride—anyone and everyone. At the very least, Crozzo's Magic Swords do."

The all-powerful magic swords that corrupted their creators.

"Cursed magic swordsmiths."

I think I finally understand what those words mean.

"I won't make a magic sword. And even if I did, I'd never put it up for sale."

Sweat dripping down to his chin, Mr. Welf raises the hammer again.

Another round of echoes rings out. The workshop is drowned out in a fierce melody of impacts.

I've been so wrapped up in the spectacle that I forgot to wipe the sweat from my face.

The metallic smell that hit me when I first walked in.

It was so strong that I wanted to cover my nose. But now it seems so far away.

I continue to watch Mr. Welf strike the horn over and over again.

🔥

I take a look outside the shutters and see an evening sky. It's almost nighttime.

At last, Mr. Welf is almost finished.

"...That should do it."

"Whoa...!"

Mr. Welf emerges from the corner of the workshop carrying a shallow box in his hands. He places it on his workbench.

I lean over the bench to get a good look and see a dark red blade inside.

The cutting edge of the blade is so thin I can almost see through it. It's just a little bit shorter than the Divine Knife. The blade color matches the Minotaur Horn almost perfectly.

The hilt is a reddish maroon color and is probably shaped to fit my hand.

"T-this…this is…really, really good…!"

"I had good material. Out of all my work so far, this has gotta be my best."

Mr. Welf smiles from ear to ear with the satisfaction of a job well done.

He's being modest, but I can tell by the look in his eye he's very proud of this one. He wouldn't use the word "best" if he wasn't.

I bow my head over and over to show my gratitude.

"Ah—sorry. Didn't have time to make a sheath. I'll have a custom one ready by tomorrow, so can you put up with a generic one for tonight?"

"S-sure, of course! Actually, it doesn't have to be tomorrow…It's already late."

"Nah, it's better to finish everything when it's still warm.

"That's how metal is," he says while rotating his right shoulder.

That's just what a smith would say. Hang on, he actually is *a smith.* I grimace at my own train of thought.

I wonder if all smiths are people like Mr. Welf. Images of their daily life pass through my head as I space out for a moment.

"Now, this guy needs a name."

He leans over in front of me and takes a long, hard look at the dark red blade.

His eyes narrow as he scratches his chin with his right hand.

I've never seen someone focus so hard on something before…He slowly opens his mouth to speak.

"The Young Bull, Ushiwakamaru……No, the Bull Dagger, Minotan."

"Wait, wait, wait, wait, wait, WAIT! Isn't the first one so much better?!"

"Huh? You like Ushiwakamaru better, Bell?"

"I don't even have to think about it!"

I speak so vigorously that spit flies out of my mouth and toward Mr. Welf.

I do my best to convince him to go with the first name. "Okay then…" he says with a very sad look in his eyes, but he accepts it.

"All right, take it."

"Thank you so much, Mr. Welf!"

I grab a sheath from his weapon shelf as he holds the dagger out to me.

I say one more thank-you and reach out to take it from him…

Woosh! Suddenly the blade is pointed right at my chest!

"Ehhh?" My jaw slacks in surprise.

"That's it."

"Wh-what's it?"

"That's the last time you call me that uptight name."

His words just add to my dumbfounded shock as my eyes peel back.

"We haven't known each other for long, and I can't say we completely trust each other, either, but call me something like I call Li'l E.

"Something like friends," adds Mr. Welf—no, Welf—with a grin.

A smile floats to my lips as I respond.

"Gotcha, Welf."

He flips the hilt of the blade forward and I grab hold.

EPILOGUE   NEXT STAGE

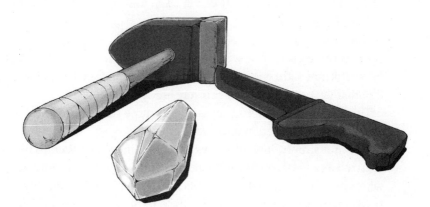

The Guild was as busy as ever that day, many adventurers coming and going.

However, none of their footsteps or voices reached the inside of the consultation box in the corner of the lobby.

Bell and Eina sat across from each other, on either side of a desk inside the soundproofed room.

"Crozzo? I apologize if I'm wrong, but is he part of that black-smith family...?"

"He is...So they really are that well known?"

"I believe so, yes. Whenever adventurers or people in this vicinity hear the name Crozzo, that's the first thing that comes to mind."

A week had passed since Bell received his new weapon and he was just now passing on the information to his adviser. Eina forced a smile as she listened to Bell talk about his new ally and contracted smith. The young man's name alone was enough to start a new conversation.

"But, it's surprising."

"Eh?"

"That there's someone with the name Crozzo in Orario. He should be well known throughout the city by now. A famous blacksmith like that isn't someone who can stay hidden for long."

The reason for Welf's anonymity was quite simple: He rejected all clients who requested magic swords.

To put it simply, it would be extremely difficult for Welf to be rec-ognized as a Crozzo without making magic swords. The only people who knew the truth were members of *Hephaistos Familia*. By con-trast, the prospective clients who didn't know the details tended to treat Welf as a "fake" Crozzo.

"A Crozzo who won't make magic swords is useless to me." With the people who sought Welf out saying things like that every time, rumors of his existence had never emerged from the shadows.

While he wasn't disappointed in Eina…Bell was sad to hear that the average person's reaction to the name Crozzo was only to think about their magic swords.

"Excuse me, but back to what we were talking about before."

"Ah, yes…Well, can I see it, please?"

Switching gears, Bell reminded Eina why he'd come in today.

A suddenly nervous Eina stood up, her face stiff as a board.

Bell followed suit. Turning his back to her, he took off his armor and inner shirt.

Bell Cranell

Level 2

Strength: G 267   Defense: H 144   Utility: G 288   Agility: F 375

Magic: H 189

Luck: I

"…"

Eina's jaw dropped when she saw Bell's Status. Her lips quivered for a moment before she forced her mouth shut.

Only ten days had passed since he leveled up to Level 2. Despite that, his highest Basic Ability rank was already *F*, three levels up from the lowest rank of *I*.

Just how many barriers was he going to shatter before he was satisfied?

Bell pulled his inner shirt back on as he sat down. He thought now was as good a time as ever to ask his burning question.

"My battle party is a three-man cell. Is it okay for us to go to the middle levels?"

Bell's ruby-red eyes radiated determination as he looked Eina square in the eyes. His demeanor catching her off guard for a moment, Eina took a deep breath to steady herself and closed her eyes.

The first two floors of the Middle Fortress, the thirteenth and fourteenth floors, were recommended for Level 2 adventurers with Basic Ability levels ranging from *I* to *H*. Which meant that Bell's status was more than adequate now.

That left a relatively capable Level 1 smith and a supporter with a very low Status. It might have been a three-man cell, but it was very unbalanced. Be that as it may, monsters encountered on the thirteenth floor were not much different from the twelfth in terms of strength. Monsters like the Hard Armoreds were also encountered in the middle levels.

As long as they didn't stray too far from Bell, there was very little danger of them being wiped out on that floor.

Their battle party just barely qualified for permission to enter the middle levels.

"…Wait a moment."

Eina opened her eyes and left the consultation box.

Bell twiddled his thumbs for a moment, but Eina returned quickly. She was now carrying three pieces of paper that looked like tickets.

"Bell, take these."

"Are these…"

"They're coupons for salamander wool. Take them to Babel Tower and you'll get a discount."

Seeing the confused look on Bell's face, Eina explained in further detail.

"I grant you permission to go to the middle levels. However, on one condition: Everyone in your party must be equipped with salamander wool."

"S-salamander wool?"

"It's a cloth infused with spiritual protection. Without it, you must never, *ever* go into the middle levels. Is that clear?"

"V-very clear!"

Eina was leaning forward, her finger in Bell's face. Bell forced his answer through his mouth, with sweat rolling down his cheeks.

Her thin, half-elf eyebrows standing on end, Eina finally relaxed and sat back down in her chair.

"Bell, I forbid you to try to do too much. You are to retreat at the first hint of danger. Can you promise me that?"

"…Yes, ma'am."

Bell nodded in response to Eina's stern emerald gaze.

Eina wanted to make him understand the anxiety that came from not knowing what was waiting in the middle levels.

She paused for a moment so that her words could sink in.

"Give it your best."

Her eyebrows relaxed, Eina gave him a sincere smile.

Bell left the Guild and headed off toward the Dungeon, where his friends were waiting for him, that smile fresh in his mind.

"RugyaAH?!"

An arc of red light, and a silverback fell motionless to the floor.

The red light came from a dark red dagger in Bell's left hand. It cut through the Dungeon's fog like a torch's flame through darkness.

Sensing a new monster charging through the thick fog, Bell wasted no time in bringing the Hestia Knife into position.

"Hyaaa!"

"GEEH?!"

Stealing the first blow with speed beyond Level 1, Bell cut into his target with a high-speed counterattack.

An imp screamed out in pain before the pieces of its body hit the grassy floor.

"The fog is going away!"

Bell heard Lilly's voice at his side, through a fog so thick it made the tenth floor look like a walk in the park.

They had reached their destination on the lower twelfth floor: the room that connected to the thirteenth.

The fog only filled about half of the square room. As soon as they made it through, there would be nothing to cloud their vision.

Prums were known for their great eyesight, and Lilly was spot-on. They were closing in on their destination.

Shuff-shuff-shuff. The three of them stayed close enough to hear one another's footsteps in the grass. Welf stayed close by, careful not to get separated as they advanced farther into the room.

"!"

The white fog wavered like smoke for a moment as they walked into the clear.

A swarm of monsters greeted Bell's eyes as he quickly scanned the room. The back wall looked like jagged boulders stacked on top of one another behind the beasts.

The other walls up to this point had been an odd yellowish color, but now ash-colored rocks were starting to take over. A massive hole sat in the middle of the back wall.

—That was it!

The entrance to the middle levels.

Thump, thump. Bell's heart was in his throat.

"Haa!"

He left Welf and Lilly behind and charged forward.

Ignoring the intimidating roars of the monsters, Bell used his Agility to weave through them with ease.

"——?!"

One swing of his red dagger, and a Hard Armored disintegrated into ash.

Despite aiming slightly lower than its chest, the shock waves generated on impact hit the monster's magic stone and destroyed it.

'The Young Bull, Ushiwakamaru.'

It was a dagger about 15 celch in length. Made by Welf from the Minotaur Horn, it was much different from the Hestia Knife's precise slashes in that it utterly destroyed everything in its wake with sheer power.

Two arcs of light carved their way forward, one of purple and one of crimson.

Bell mixed his Agility with a double-bladed attack as he left a trail of dead monsters in his dust.

"Now that's how it's done...Hell yeah!"

"Hegyaaaa?!"

Welf charged forward with his longsword over his shoulder. Watching Bell tear through enemy ranks with the weapon that he forged brought a smile to his face. Just ahead of him, Bell sent two more imps to the ground with spinning kicks.

"OOWWWOOOOOOOOOOOOOOOOO!"

"You've come to play, too…!"

The floor shook as a massive body emerged from the fog.

Welf changed course to engage the orc that had a natural weapon clutched in its grasp.

"—KIIIIIIII!"

"?!"

However, a shrill shriek pierced his eardrums before he could close the distance.

It came from a bad bat, flying just overhead.

Welf was disoriented by the intense screams of the monstrous winged rodent and took a knee to steady himself.

The orc wasted no time in seizing this opportunity and swung its club down at Welf with all of its might.

"Mr. Welf?!"

"!"

Lilly's yell alerted Bell to what was going on behind him. He knew immediately how dangerous the situation was and moved to assist.

Since the monster had Welf pinned down, Bell didn't have a clear shot. Firebolt was not an option.

He made a split-second decision.

Slamming his foot in the ground and launching himself toward the orc, Bell set a course to engage the monster in close-quarters combat.

"Lilly, the broadsword!"

Bell's voice cut through the chaos.

Lilly instantly realized what Bell had in mind.

She jumped forward and wrapped her hand around the hilt of a broadsword that had been strapped to the outside of her backpack.

Pulling to release the restraints, she brought the sword handle up to her side. The weapon itself still hung in a side strap. The blade as long as she was tall, their combined shadow made a perfect plus sign in the grass.

Putting her body directly in Bell's path, she spun her back to him.

Bell reached out and grabbed the hilt, withdrawing the silver blade as if Lilly herself was the sheath.

"—!!"

Full speed.

The orc's club was a mere heartbeat away from crushing Welf's head when Bell crashed into their battle with everything he had.

"OOOOOOOOOWWWWW!!"

"HAAAAAAAAAAAAAAAAA!!"

The orc's downward stroke was intercepted by Bell's upward diagonal slash.

The broadsword took the brunt of the orc's attack and sliced the natural weapon in half.

"BUBEEH?!"

A cry of surprise.

The orc's pupils shrank in shock as it watched its powerful attack fail.

Bell's speed and momentum had combined into an attack strong enough to overpower the orc's attack head-on.

Welf saw an opening for his own strike and jumped up and over Bell. Spinning in midair, he separated the orc's head from its shoulders in one gallant stroke.

"...Sorry 'bout that."

"It's okay...We're friends, aren't we?"

Welf scratched the back of his head as Bell grinned and nodded.

His eyes going wide, Welf's expression suddenly became serious.

All of a sudden: *Twang! Splat!*

Lilly's aim was dead-on as her arrow brought the bad bat crashing to the floor.

"Let's go over this one more time."

The last of the monsters in the room defeated, the three of them knelt in a circle.

The grass between them had been cut so short that the stone floor was showing through. Lilly used her knife to carve simple pictures to explain her plan to the others.

"The path through the Middle Fortress is all gravel, so we'll form ranks. First, Mr. Welf will take lead."

"You sure I'm cut out for that?"

"On the contrary, that's the only place for Mr. Welf. Lilly's not exactly paying you a compliment, however...Moving on."

Lilly moved her knife to point at the middle of three circles carved into the stone.

"Mr. Bell, take the middle. Support Mr. Welf in combat. Be warned, Mr. Bell will have to be mindful of attack and defense. This is the most difficult position in the formation...Is that okay?"

"Not a problem."

Seeing Bell nod, Lilly continued by saying, "By process of elimination, that leaves Lilly at the back." She pointed at the final circle of her diagram.

"Lilly thinks you understand this already, but this party is very unbalanced. Since Lilly doesn't have much attack strength, she can't cover you when the tables turn against us. Regrouping would be meaningless."

"So we're toast if we make one wrong move. Harsh."

"Shall we turn back now? It's not too late, you know."

"Don't be stupid. I'm gonna be a High Smith, mark my words. Like hell I'll turn my tail and run after coming this far."

Bell quietly listened to their banter as the three of them started to get into position.

He wasn't really paying attention, but he snapped to attention when he noticed the two of them were glaring at him.

"The heck are you grinning at?"

"Huh...? I-I'm smiling?"

"Yes, very much so...Does Mr. Bell realize how dangerous a place the Middle Levels are?"

Bell put his hands to his cheeks, and he was indeed smiling from ear to ear.

He quickly apologized to both of them.

"Don't have to apologize, but why you grinning like that? Bit worried."

"Um…Well, this is exciting, isn't it?…It feels like the three of us have become an actual battle party, and that makes me…I don't know, happy."

Bell blushed and looked at the floor as Lilly and Welf exchanged glances.

"And also, isn't this kind of exhilarating? All of us working together, going on an adventure."

Bell's excitement was beginning to boil over, his cheeks a bright shade of pink as he flashed another grin.

This was what being an adventurer was all about.

Taking that first step into somewhere you've never been, working together with your allies to make new discoveries.

Getting excited about the unknown, fighting side by side and sharing the spoils with people you can call friends…It was all very exciting.

His eyes full of youthful enthusiasm, Bell decided to ignore the teaching that adventurers must not go on adventures.

"…Keh-ha-ha-ha-ha-ha! You're right, this is one hell of a thrill! Couldn't call myself a man if I didn't get excited about this!"

"Lilly can't exactly agree…but Lilly understands Mr. Bell's feelings."

The three of them looked at one another in turn. A smile bloomed on Welf's face big enough to rival Bell's, as Lilly's expression softened as if she could giggle at any moment.

His own emotions urging him forward, Bell couldn't help but smile happily right back at his allies.

"Well, then, shall we move forward?"

"Yeah, I'm ready. Let's do this!"

"Yes."

The three of them stood in their single-file line and took their first step toward the rocky entrance as one.

The entrance to the Middle Levels was encased in the blackest of black rocks. The only light from within came flickering up from the floor far below.

The moist, dank rocks smelled like soil. Completely uneven and spread out all over the place, they added to the tension that descended on the group. New, powerful monsters they had never seen before lay waiting for them at the end of this path.

His skin covered in goose bumps, lightly clenching his fists, Bell took a confident step forward and looked straight into the heart of the Dungeon.

…Nothing to worry about.

He was not alone. They might not be family or part of his *Familia*, but they were friends who shared a strong bond.

Together, they could do it, somehow.

All these thoughts ran through Bell's mind.

…Here we go!

A golden light of aspiration held tightly at the core of his thoughts. Bell took his first step into the middle levels.

【WELF·CROZZO】

BELONGS TO: *HEPHAISTOS FAMILIA*
RACE: HUMAN
JOB: SMITH
DUNGEON RANGE: TWELFTH LEVEL
WEAPON: LONGSWORD
CURRENT WORTH: 94,000 VALS

《BLACK JACKET》

- NORMALLY USED AS WORK CLOTHES. VERY STRONG AGAINST FIRE AND HEAT, BUT NOT GOOD FOR DEFENSE.
- ARMOR IS USUALLY WORN ON TOP OF IT.

Lv. **1**

STRENGTH: C 617   DEFENSE: D 521   UTILITY: C 645
AGILITY: D 509   MAGIC: I 70

《MAGIC》

【WILL-O'-THE-WISP】
- ANTI-MAGIC FIRE
- TRIGGER SPELL: "BLASPHEMOUS BURN!"

《SKILL》

【BLOOD OF CROZZO】
- ABILITY TO FORGE MAGIC SWORDS
- STRENGTH OF MAGIC INCREASED AT TIME OF PRODUCTION

《LONGSWORD》

- A WIDE-BLADED LONGSWORD WIELDED WITH ONE HAND. A LARGE BLADE.
- FORGED BY WELF. STRONG ENOUGH TO OVERPOWER ANY MONSTER IN THE UPPER LEVELS.
- IT HAS NO NAME, SINCE WELF MADE IT FOR HIMSELF. HE ONLY NAMES PIECES THAT HE PLANS TO SELL TO OTHERS.

✳ "Quest X Quest" and "A Campanella to the Goddess" are updated versions of short stories that were first published in *GA Bunko Magazine*, May 2013 and *GA Bunko Magazine*, February 2013, respectively.

QUEST

QUEST

It's a clear blue sky.

The weather's been very calm these past few days. It's been a while since I've seen a cloud in the sky over Orario.

Many people of all shapes and sizes go about their business, carrying many different things with them underneath the gentle sunlight.

A woman is balancing a basket full of fruit on top of her head, a man is carrying a bag full of what looks like dirty clothes, and a well-dressed merchant walks between the two of them. Horse-drawn carriages work their way down the middle of the street and into the throng of people.

The streets are alive with people of many races, human and demi-human living side by side in harmony.

"T-today was rough..."

I take in the view while willing my wobbly knees forward, as I work my way down West Main.

Aiz has been teaching me how to fight for the past three days.

We start training in the darkness before sunrise, which means my body is beaten to a pulp before going into the Dungeon. I think I take more damage from her than all the monsters I encounter down there combined.

People are laughing, running around on Main Street. Meanwhile, it takes all I've got to keep putting one foot in front of the other on the stone road.

This is all so I can get stronger.

So that I can catch up to her, my instructor.

I keep telling myself that over and over and ignore my aching joints as I make my way to the spot where Lilly is waiting for me.

"Bell...Be-ll..."

A monotone, almost lazy voice reaches my ears.

I come to a stop when I realize it's calling my name. I scan the crowd for a moment and find the owner of the voice right away.

She's a chienthrope, a dog person named Nahza belonging to *Miach Familia.*

She's slowly waving at me from between two buildings that mark the entrance to one of the backstreets. As usual, her clothing is quite strange. Her shirtsleeves are two different lengths, the left sleeve ending just above her elbow, but her right sleeve goes all the way down to her wrist. Her right hand is covered by a glove. Looking farther down, I can see her thick, bushy tail sticking out from underneath a long skirt. I watch it sway from side to side for a moment before looking up at her half-open eyes. She motions for me to come to her.

I quietly nod and look both ways to make sure the coast is clear before making my way through the bustling crowd toward her.

"Um, good morning. What are you doing out here—is something wrong?"

"Yes, a little something…"

This is the first time I've seen her out and about in this area in the morning.

I tilt my head in confusion as she looks back at me with a groggy stare. Her expression unchanging, her lips start to form words.

"I was waiting for you, Bell. I thought if I was here, you would pass by…"

I always travel down West Main whenever I go to the Dungeon after leaving home. Nahza must have known that and waited here looking for me.

As for the reason why…She pulls a rolled-up piece of paper from her pocket and hands it to me.

"A quest. Was wondering if you'd be willing to take it up…"

"Qu-est…?"

"Yep, there's even a reward…Could you bring me what's written on the memo?"

She and I lock eyes for a moment before she lowers her head in a bow and I look at the "memo" in my hand.

"Think of it as helping out Lord Miach and me…Please."

"S-sure…"

"There is no time limit, but the earlier the better…Thanks a bunch."

Swish-swish! Showing more energy than she had up until now, Nahza waves a few times before turning around and going down the backstreet. I blink a few times as I watch her go back toward *Miach Familia*'s home.

So, I'm doing a job for them, I guess…?

I unroll the piece of paper and have a look. It seems like there's a monster name on top with a whole bunch of Koine, the common language, scribbled out underneath. I stare at it for a moment, scratching my head. In any case, I should go meet up with Lilly.

"A quest?"

I nod back at Lilly as she looks up at me in a daze.

We are in a corner of Central Park, very close to Babel Tower. We use this spot as our meeting point because of the wide leaf tree growing here and the brick planter it's in is at the perfect height to sit on.

The sun's bright rays make their way through the gaps in the leaves and onto my face while I tell Lilly about my conversation with Nahza.

"This is unusual. No matter how friendly their *Familias* are, Lilly's never heard of anyone giving a low-level adventurer a quest directly."

"Are quests like that?"

"Yes. It depends on the item they're looking for, but most quests issued by *Familias* are accepted by high-level adventurers."

Lilly's been a supporter for a long time, so she knows far more about the Dungeon and its ins and outs than I do. It makes sense that she would know more about adventurers as well. "Can I see that, please?" she says, pointing at the memo. Something in her voice sounds like it doesn't add up. I hand her the paper.

"Well, if it's something like this, Lilly doesn't see a problem with a Level One adventurer accepting this quest…"

The request written on the paper is to collect the drop item Blue Papillon Wings.

Lilly's round eyes look up at me, a very ho-hum look on her face.

"Mr. Bell. Is it possible that Mr. Bell is being used? Has Mr. Bell confirmed that the reward is prepared and ready? Lilly feels like you have been sent on an errand…and for really cheap."

"I-I don't really think…"

…*that's true.* I can't finish my sentence out loud.

Thinking back on all the times that Nahza has practically forced me to buy potions from her…It might be a little rude for me to think this, but for a moment there, Lilly's accusations make sense.

I quickly change the subject to hide the sweat starting to pop up on my brow.

"Um, well, what exactly are quests, anyway? I feel like I've heard about them somewhere before, but…"

If I remember right, way back when I first became an adventurer, Eina warned me that I shouldn't "accept any strange quests." However, I've been so focused on getting stronger since the day I met Aiz that I haven't really had time for anything else.

Lilly scratches her chin with one of her tiny fingers as she thinks about my question.

"Mr. Bell has a point, all adventurers will need to know about them eventually…Okay, shall we spend the day working on this quest?"

She looks right at me as she says that last part and smiles.

"Eh, but…"

"This looks like a good opportunity. Mr. Bell seems to be very *tired* recently…"

She adds that as if she can see the part of me that wants to scream out, *I have no time to waste relaxing if I'm ever going to catch up with her.*

The look that she shoots from the corner of her eye makes me flinch. I've kept her in the dark about my training with Aiz, but Lilly seems to know something's going on…

"Resting is important, too, Mr. Bell. Let's have an easy day and accept this quest."

"...Okay, let's do that, then."

Part of me feels like she's leading me around by the reins.

On the other hand, she seems worried about me. So I decide to take her suggestion without any complaints.

And what she's saying makes a lot of sense, too.

"First things first, let's go to the Guild. Lilly thinks it would be good for Mr. Bell to learn about quests for the future."

She seems kind of happy as she grabs my hand and pulls me out of Central Park.

"In short, quests are requests made to adventurers."

The two of us are walking up Northwest Main Street.

Known as "Adventurers Way," it's a bit wider than the other main streets in order to accommodate all the adventurers traveling through it.

"People who make these requests are called clients. They're looking for an adventurer to solve various problems. It is the client's responsibility to prepare a reward that fits the items requested. It's the adventurer's responsibility to collect their reward after the quest is complete."

"Umm, that sounds an awful lot like the Blessings that the gods give us in exchange for our support..."

"Very much so. The gods even have a saying for it: 'give-and-take.'"

The sounds of many boots hitting the stone pavement fill my ears.

It's still pretty early in the morning, so many adventurers are visiting the Guild or buying items at one of the shops on this street to prepare for a day in the Dungeon.

Momentarily distracted by a party of elves dressed in beautiful robes and armor, I accidentally run into Lilly, my hand brushing across her upper thigh. I apologize over and over as her cheeks swell up in anger. I shift my focus completely to her explanation when she starts speaking again.

"To give an example of the average quest in Orario...When a client isn't strong enough to retrieve an item themselves, they submit a request for an adventurer to go into the deepest parts of the Dungeon to find that item in their place."

"That sounds just like the 'Labyrinth City.'"

"Hee-hee-hee, sure does."

We ride the endless wave of adventurers until a large white building made of marble comes into view, a beautiful structure that looks like a large temple: the Guild Headquarters.

We make our way through the front garden and into the busy lobby, adventurers sliding past one another through the narrow doors.

Lilly, who has already "transformed" into an animal-people child, leads me through the crowd and stops in front of a long bulletin board. I follow close behind, watching the wolflike ears on top of her head twitch from side to side.

"Most quests are posted by the Guild here. These are the quests available now."

Pieces of paper are pinned all over the bulletin board. Some of them have information about the Dungeon or tips for adventurers, but most are the quests Lilly's talking about.

I can see item lists and rewards as well as client signatures and *Familia* emblems written on the papers.

"Let's see...'Hellhound Fangs x10'...'Twenty-fourth floor—I would like to trade the items listed below for the fruit of a jewel tree'... 'Recruiting battle-party members to face a floor boss. *Attention— Only adventurers Level Three and above will be considered'..."

I can feel the muscles in my cheeks tightening as I read through the requests.

Looking at them from a difficulty standpoint, most of these are still well out of my league. The only one that I find that looks doable is a request for "Orc Hide x30."

I don't think anyone could take care of that in one day...Sounds very difficult, actually.

"As Mr. Bell can see, most quests take place in the middle levels and below."

Middle levels: the area of the Dungeon that starts on the thirteenth floor. Adventurers need to be at least Level 2 to survive.

Adventurers who level up are known as upper-class adventurers. Only they can enter.

"Why aren't there many quests on the upper levels?"

"Because most *Familias* and adventurers are strong enough to go get those items themselves. Unless they're not cut out for being an adventurer, as long as they have time and form a battle party, almost anyone can go as far as the lower seventh."

Oh, I get it.

Most of the adventurers in Orario have yet to level up. They're still at Level 1.

Which means that most *Familias* can operate in the upper levels, but only a select few can reach the middle levels. Fewer still can go deeper than that. It only makes sense that the number of quests increases as the number of adventurers who can complete them goes down.

That must be what Lilly meant by "most quests are accepted by upper-class adventurers."

"However, the only quests that the Guild posts here are from clients like *Familias* and smiths, and are very appealing to adventurers."

"?"

"In other words, the Guild has guaranteed the rewards…They can be trusted."

Lilly must've read the confusion on my face and added one more thing.

We leave the bulletin board behind and exit the Guild.

"The point is that there are some *really* fishy ones as well. Sometimes the client's name will be hidden, and the request is absolutely absurd."

"…Or maybe the client refuses to give the reward?"

"Very sharp, Mr. Bell. Lilly is happy Mr. Bell realized that."

She's smiling at me like a teacher would when praising a student.

"Lilly's pulled that one off before, by the way," she continues with her grin plastered on her face. I do my best to force a smile and nod again.

Just how deep does your grudge against adventurers go, Lilly…?

"Anyway, shady quests not approved by the Guild, or requests from townspeople, can be found in bars like that one over there. Most of them are very dubious in more ways than one."

Lilly points to one of the bars built along the side of West Main.

It looks like it's run by a *Familia*. A place other than the Guild where adventurers can take up quests—albeit a little under the table—from average people. I blink my eyes a few times to get a better look and, sure enough, that billboard looks like a *Familia* emblem.

In addition, *Familias* that operate taverns like this one also act as a place for people to gather information—a knowledge shop of sorts.

Running a *Familia* as a quest-and-information brokerage…Not a bad idea.

There really are a lot of different types of *Familias* in the world…

"All of this means that if you don't want to wind up in a sticky situation, don't accept any quests that haven't been approved by the Guild…even if asked directly by a friend from another *Familia*."

…So that's what she's been getting at this whole time.

Lilly went through all of this to teach me that from now on I shouldn't accept quests that aren't posted on that billboard. That includes requests from people like Nahza, who isn't that trustworthy to begin with.

But Nahza isn't some person I've never met hiding behind a sheet, and she sought me out personally. So I don't think there's any reason to worry…

"That's exactly why Lilly says Mr. Bell is too kind. Bad people will take advantage of anybody, use that kindness to gain trust. It will come back to haunt Mr. Bell, but Lilly didn't say that."

…Is she reading my thoughts? Or is it written all over my face?

I think she's aware of it, too…I can't respond to that.

"Fear not, Mr. Bell, for as long as there are still lights in Lilly's eyes, she shall protect you from those traps.—Now, that's enough studying for today. Let's move on to the main event."

"Ah, sure."

I take another look at that memo in my hands as we stroll down the main street.

I read back to myself what Nahza requested, making sure I understand every word.

Hmmm. That's right, Blue Papillon Wings...

"Aren't blue papillons one of those...what are they called...'rare monsters'?"

"Yep. They're found in the upper levels, so it won't be all that dangerous for Mr. Bell...Finding one, however, that's easier said than done."

"Of course..."

Nahza said there was no deadline but...this quest that I took up might end up being a real pain.

My head and shoulders droop. Lilly flashes a big smile at me in an effort to ease my fears.

"Don't worry, Mr. Bell. Lilly has a plan. When Lilly is done preparing, let's head to the Dungeon."

...Lilly has really helped me out at every turn.

I really am grateful to have a supporter who I can rely on and who can cover my weaknesses so easily. I'm sorry that she has to work so hard, though......

"Blue papillon."

It's a butterfly monster that is said to appear on the lower seventh floor.

Its light blue wings are so thin that light can pass through them. Tiny scales fall off of them as it flies, leaving a beautiful sparkling trail in its wake. I've heard it's so beautiful that even the most hardened adventurers will stop to admire it.

While the blue papillon is a sight to behold, it's also well known as one of the harder monsters to encounter.

We adventurers call monsters that are extremely difficult to find on any level of the Dungeon "rare monsters." The blue papillon is one of them. This goes without saying, but rare-monster drop items are even rarer and sell for a very high price.

I remember hearing somewhere that the blue papillon is relatively easier to find than other rare monsters…but if we just walk around the Dungeon like usual, it's going to take an extremely long time to find one. The fact I've never seen one before is proof enough of that.

Remembering the monster encyclopedia that Eina had drilled into my head not too long ago, the more I think about it, the more I realize that this quest won't end in a day.

"…We're pretty far out, aren't we?"

"Yes. We'll be in the southern corner very soon."

We're on the seventh floor. Lilly and I made our way down here to find the blue papillon after making a quick stop at an item shop.

Following Lilly's instructions, I make my way through a very thin corridor. I'm pretty sure we've been down here for more than an hour. Rather than staying on the path that leads to the lower levels, we took one heck of a detour and are headed to the deepest corner of the lower seventh.

I've gone deeper into the Dungeon than this, but I haven't explored the outer rim of any of the levels. This unfamiliar terrain gets my blood pumping with excitement as I quickly dispatch all the monsters that appear in front of us with the Divine Knife and the baselard.

Lilly quickly withdraws a magic stone from the killer ant I just took down.

"Lilly, what's waiting for us at the end of this path?"

"The Dungeon's pantry."

"Pantry?" The moment I echo Lilly's words the path in front of me begins to change.

The pale green walls, the lights in the ceiling, the path under my feet—everything is starting to get uneven. The farther I walk, the less my surroundings look like the Dungeon I know. It almost feels like I'm lost in the belly of a cave.

Suddenly, the luminescent spots on the ceiling start to go dim.

My heart pounds in my chest as a shroud of darkness descends around me.

That light…

There's a soft greenish glow coming from around the rocky corner ahead.

I stop for a moment and turn to face Lilly. She doesn't say anything, instead giving me a silent nod. I take a deep breath, face forward, and turn the corner.

My heart is pounding so fast that I can feel it in my lungs.

I've gotten used to crawling the Dungeon, so it's been a long time since I've felt like this. Going someplace new, facing the "unknown," it's exhilarating and terrifying at the same time. My inner adventurer feels so alive!

I follow the glow through a few more turns in the cave, only the sound of our footsteps in the air. The source of the glow is waiting for us at the end of the path.

"____"

Words leave me the moment I emerge from the rocky path.

This is a very, very big area.

I've never seen a space this big, even in the levels farther down in the Dungeon.

My eyes instantly lock onto a towering pillar of quartz in the back of the room.

The massive column of powdery green rock stretches from the floor all the way up to the ceiling. The whole thing is jutting out of the back wall. But the surface isn't smooth, bits and pieces stick out like tree bark. This whole thing might as well be a tree made of quartz.

The entire structure is emanating a green light. So this is where that green glow was coming from…

Those are monsters…

A clear white sap drips out from between the breaks in the rock, enough to make a large pool at the base of the "tree."

I can see killer ants and purple moths dotting the surface of the tree and a needle rabbit dipping its tongue into the pool. They're all drinking the sap.

"Is Mr. Bell surprised?"

"Lilly…"

"This is a pantry…a place that the Dungeon stores food for the monsters to eat."

Clearly enjoying the awed look on my face, Lilly strikes up a conversation and explains what's going on.

Monsters born from the dungeon walls are alive, so it makes sense they would get hungry. While they can feast on stray adventurers or other monsters, it looks like most of them get their subsistence from their "mother," the Dungeon itself.

This wide area is a source of nutrients for the monsters.

I can see why it's called the "Dungeon's pantry."

"…So then, does the blue papillon also…?"

"Yep. Rather than bumbling around in the Dungeon for who knows how long, Lilly thinks our chances of finding one are better if we wait here."

I agree.

Lilly explains that there are two or three pantries on every level of the Dungeon except for the first two. As long as we stake out one of them and keep our eyes open, a hungry blue papillon will show up sooner or later. After that, we can make our move.

Set up a trap and ambush our prey. So this is hunting…

"Don't just stand there, Mr. Bell. We need to hide ourselves. Lilly doesn't want to think about what will happen if the monsters see us."

"Ah…Yes, let's do that."

I can feel her hands on my lower back as Lilly pushes me out of the entrance and off toward one of the sides.

Taking another look around the room, there are many entrances to the pantry. Even now, monsters are streaming in from ten, twelve other places. If even one of them realizes we're here, we'll have to fight every monster in the room to make an escape…I don't want to think about that, either.

We make our way into a corner of the room.

"Well, then, excuse me."

Lilly sets her backpack down and withdraws a large piece of cloth from it. The whole thing is a mossy green color and matches the dungeon walls on this floor almost exactly.

Lilly whips the fabric around through the air like a massive cape and wraps the two of us from head to toe in a green cocoon.

"So that's why you bought this..."

"That's right. None of the monsters on the lower seventh has a good sense of smell, so as long as we're quiet and stay out of sight, Mr. Bell and Lilly will be fine."

She bought this at the item shop right before we entered the Dungeon. I had no clue what she was doing...This is what she had in mind.

Our camouflage seems to be working. None of the monsters has noticed us; even the ones that look in our direction think we're just part of the dungeon wall and go back to their meal.

"W-w-wait a second, Lilly. Aren't you a bit close?"

"Lilly has no choice. Lilly has to hide the backpack, too, and this cloth can only hide so much. Oh, it's still sticking out! Lilly has to get closer!"

She slides her small body up against mine, making me flinch.

Lilly slips under my right shoulder and wraps her arms around my chest, as if she were giving her body to me, and squeezes. A soft pressure brushes against my ribs through my inner shirt. My face feels like it's on fire.

I understand why...but if I didn't know better, I'd say she's enjoying this. It has to be my imagination.

The two of us talk in hushed voices as we twist and turn to find a comfortable position.

"...H-hey, I have a question. You know how there are items that can draw in monsters, right? If there's a place like this where they can eat as much as they want, why do those items work...?"

I strike up a conversation to get my mind off of her body fitting snugly up against mine.

I swear she is in such a good mood that if she were a cat, she'd be purring at the top of her lungs right now. She answers my question right away.

"Isn't it boring to eat the same food all the time, Mr. Bell?"

"Ahh..."

"Fu-fu, that's why. Monsters like a little variety, too."

I keep becoming a little bit smarter every time I ask Lilly about something that doesn't make sense. So I keep the questions coming.

First I ask her why adventurers completely ignored this really good hunting spot. She explains that this place is too far out of the main path. In fact, every single dungeon pantry is so far removed from the usual route that it will take hours to get to one of them. Even if you manage to find one—and are strong enough to survive fighting everything in here at once—it's more efficient to collect the magic stones that are worth more from monsters farther down.

But the most important reason is that if you make even one mistake, the danger of being overwhelmed by sheer numbers is very real.

These are the reasons why most adventurers try to avoid turning these places into their battlefield.

...It could also be that they don't want to ruin such a beautiful place.

At least that's how I feel, looking out across this tranquil scenery from under our camouflaged cloth.

A wide cavern bathed in soft green light.

The clear crystals emerging from the tree are absolutely breathtaking. Light reflects off the pond beneath it like the moon off a still lake at night. The pond's surface glistens in silence.

White flowers with blue stems are blooming in bunches all around the lake. Every so often a needle rabbit pokes its head out from between them. Purple moths fly through the flowers and land on the crystals above, resting their wings. Soft splashes fill the air as a small group of killer ants makes their way through the pond toward the quartz tree on the back wall.

The green light makes everything look calm, almost gentle.

It's hard to believe that monsters that should be violent and horrifying can look this beautiful.

Of course, I fully realize that these beasts are the enemy of humanity.

They're extremely dangerous and will attack if I try to confront them.

Even still, I don't want to do anything to disturb this awe-inspiring scenery.

Looking across the cavern, taking in the light, the monsters, everything, I can't help but feel this way.

"…! Mr. Bell."

"!"

Lilly's shoulder stiffens as she grabs and shakes my arm.

My mind comes back to my body as I sit up and follow Lilly's eyes to the pond at the base of the tree. I spot them immediately.

Butterflies with blue wings fluttering gracefully among the flowers.

A group of four blue papillon, the target of our quest, has appeared in the pantry.

"It was worth coming all the way down here."

"Y-yes."

We get up in unison, preparing to leave at any moment.

The butterflies' elegance and refinement match the cavern perfectly. Each one of their bodies is much more delicate than a purple moth's, their two sets of wings flowing like water. The light blue trails they leave behind are pretty enough to make my heart skip a beat.

While the blue papillon pose no threat in combat, the scales that flake off their wings heal the injured monsters around them. The reason that Nahza wants blue papillon drop items is because they would make an excellent ingredient for healing potions. Of that I'm sure.

"We mustn't make a scene in here. Let's watch them and follow them out of the pantry."

"Okay, got it."

My mind back in questing mode, Lilly and I wait with bated breath for a chance to spring our trap.

A light breeze caresses my face.

Closing one eye to shield it from the gentle wind, Lilly and I emerge from the base of Babel Tower with big smiles on our faces.

"That went very well."

"Yes, to get this many drop items at once is very lucky."

Lilly looks up at me with a happy grin on her lips. Our plan worked without a hitch. Follow the group of blue papillon, take them down, collect the drop items, and return to the surface.

Just as Lilly said, all of the blue papillon left behind drop items. We couldn't be happier that we finished this quest so quickly.

Five wings altogether...I have no doubt that Nahza will be more than happy with this haul.

"If Mr. Bell took these to the Guild, they're worth at least nine thousand vals. The fact they're in good shape might make them worth even more...Too bad we're going to trade them~."

It sounds like Lilly's only excited because these drop items are from a rare monster. I force a smile at my unusually high-spirited partner as we make our way through Central Park and toward West Main.

That was just what I needed to cheer me up...

That amazing scenery put my mind at ease.

I wasn't planning on taking a break, but I'm glad I did. Sure, I still ache all over, but it feels good. I've got a little pep back in my step.

"Good afternoon! Anyone here?"

"...Bell?"

We enter *Miach Familia*'s home, a shop in the backstreets.

Nahza watches us come through the door from her chair behind the counter, her drowsy eyes opening just enough for me to notice.

"Don't tell me, you've already finished the quest...?"

"Yes. We've dropped by to finish up."

I take a box roughly the size of a shield out from under my arm and open it to show her the contents.

A rare, energetic expression runs across her face the moment that Nahza sees the beautiful blue hue of the Blue Papillon Wings. A smile is on her face in the blink of an eye.

The fluffy dog tail beneath her long skirt is happily swishing back and forth.

"Thank you, Bell... You're good; never knew how good."

"I-it's nothing..."

"I always believed you could do it if you tried, Bell..."

I shyly scratch the back of my neck, my cheeks on fire, as Nahza gives me compliment after compliment.

She steps up to me and pats my head, almost like a reflex.

"Sorry to interrupt your moment, but shall we trade the goods for the reward?"

Lilly hadn't said a word since we came into the shop, but she steps in to speed up the process.

Nahza freezes and looks down at her before forming a very innocent smile on her lips.

The two of them have never met before. Nahza must have figured out that Lilly is a member of my battle party because she nods and says, "...Of course," before making her way behind the back counter.

"Mr. Bell, now is not the time to get sloppy."

"I-I don't think I was being sloppy..."

"Remember this well, Mr. Bell. The quest isn't over until you have the reward in your hands."

"...Huh?"

I've never heard her say something so profound. She didn't even look at me when she was talking, just kept smiling in Nahza's direction.

I tilt my head and look at her for a moment before I hear Nahza return with a wooden case in her hands.

"Here's your reward: two dozen potions."

"T-two dozen?!"

I normally buy the cheapest potions that *Miach Familia* has to offer, 500 vals apiece. So twenty-four of those...12,000 vals!

I'm overwhelmed with gratitude for her for adding on extra potions as hazard pay.

Liquid happiness runs through my veins as I look at my first-ever reward from the quest. I'm about to hand the box containing the Blue Papillon Wings over to her, when suddenly—*Shoup!*

A small hand comes out of nowhere and grabs hold of my wrist.

"L-Lilly…?"

"Please wait a moment, Mr. Bell."

Keeping her gaze locked squarely on Nahza, Lilly swiftly reaches out toward the box of potions.

She withdraws one of the vials full of blue liquid in the blink of an eye.

"Hope you don't mind. Lilly will pay you back later."

"Eh, what are you…?"

Without waiting for permission, Lilly flips open the top of the vial and brings it up to her nose.

A few quick whiffs, and she stares at the color of the liquid. A surprisingly flustered Nahza looks on as Lilly pours a drop of the liquid onto her hand and takes a lick.—The next moment.

"—Fu-fu, is this potion worth five hundred vals? What a lovely business you're running, enough to make Lilly jealous."

Lilly sounds absolutely terrifying while wearing the face of an innocent child.

"""_____"""

"This potion, it's been watered down quite a bit, hasn't it? It's less than half as potent as it should be. There're extra ingredients mixed in to give it the right color and sweetness. Yes, this is a common scam."

Shock rips through my body. Is it true?

Nahza and I stand in silence as Lilly drives her point home with that same innocent smile plastered on her face.

"These potions might be worth two hundred vals. It seems you've been drastically overcharged, Mr. Bell.—Of course, this reward is nooooooowhere close to the value of the drop items."

I can practically see the blood draining from Nahza's face.

Even with her eyes half closed, sweat is pouring down her cheeks. The tail that was happily swaying back and forth before is now bent at a very awkward angle.

I don't know what to think anymore.

"So, how do you propose we fix this?"

Lilly narrows her eyes and smiles like a little devil as she takes one step toward Nahza.

"My apologies!!"

Lord Miach forcefully throws his head down in a bow.

The red evening sun shines through the open windows, casting everything in a crimson hue.

Standing next to Lord Miach, with his hand firmly clasped behind her head and forcing her down, is Nahza.

"One of my own has caused you a great deal of trouble, and for that I am deeply sorry, Bell! I will return every val that was taken from you this instant."

"Eh, um, please, Lord Miach, it's not a big deal. Raise your head…"

He straightens up little by little. I can see his downtrodden face but he won't look at me. "My apologies," he says one more time.

Lord Miach's build is very tall and lithe. Wearing his aquamarine hair longer than most men, he carries himself like an aristocrat. The fact that his gray robe is in rough shape doesn't hurt at all; in fact, it adds to his charm.

Nahza's god looks every bit the part of someone from Deusdia, except that right now Lord Miach's expression is very dispirited.

"This has caused you problems, too, Hestia. Taking what little money the both of you have available…"

"What's done is done. Be extra careful that something like this doesn't happen again and teach her right. You've helped me out of a few jams, Miach, so we can let this slide."

"Yes, it will be done…"

After Lilly had finished grilling Nahza, all of us, including my goddess, Hestia, had gathered at *Miach Familia*'s home for an apology session of sorts.

Lord Miach had been unaware of Nahza's shady activities until now, and he has been doing all of the apologizing.

His hand is still firmly placed on the back of Nahza's head, not allowing her to stand up.

"I must say, Miss Supporter, great job catching this in time. I'm relieved to see that you're taking such good care of Bell. Thanks."

"No, no. Lilly is just happy to be of service to Mr. Bell and Lady Hestia."

T-taking care of…?

I break out in a cold sweat as I watch the goddess nod with a happy smile on her face and Lilly respectfully bow a few times. It almost feels like they're bound by some kind of contract that I don't know about…

"…Nahza. Why did you do this?! Answer me!"

Lord Miach's voice thunders.

The moment he releases his hold on Nahza, she turns her back on him.

The half of her hair that isn't tied back floats on air as her head flicks around to look at the wall.

"Our *Familia*'s bank account—it's always moments away from collapse…And the clueless rabbit was a sitting duck."

My eyes go wide at the same time as Lord Miach's. What did she mean by rabbit and duck…?

She doesn't look or sound any different than usual, monotone voice with droopy eyes, but…her bushy tail is shuddering beneath her skirt.

"You fool! What happens when you rob people blind?! This world moves on honesty and trust, especially the business world. You've risked the trust of a valued customer for spare change?!

"How foolish can you be?!" he continues with a glare strong enough to make the bravest of people crumble to their knees.

Nahza casually looks over her shoulder, clicks her tongue, and stares down Lord Miach's gaze with her own.

So she *can* show emotion.

"How can you say that, Lord Miach, when you give out free potions to anyone and everyone? That's why we never have any money. And on top of that, girl after girl is drawn to you like a moth to the flame and you give them the wrong idea…If I had a val for every time I've covered for you…!"

"What…what are you talking about?! I don't draw in anyone, nor do I try to deceive anyone!"

Lord Miach seems to have been caught off guard by Nahza's retort. The goddess's and Lilly's gazes have gone cold.

I'm sure Lord Miach has stolen many hearts with that smile and the way he carries himself like royalty…but I guess he doesn't realize it, otherwise he wouldn't be so confused right now.

"I have wronged Bell…but at this rate, it will be impossible to pay back the loan and it'll only get worse…!"

Eh? That gets my attention.

I take a look around to see if other people heard that, too. The goddess has a very serious look on her face.

Loan…?

Lord Miach is looking more and more uncomfortable by the moment. Between him and the painful look on Nahza's face, I get the feeling something suspicious is going on. Something that Lord Miach doesn't want to talk about…

In that moment—

"FU-HA-HA-HA-HA-HA-HA, I'm coming in!!"

The room shakes with a roar of laughter, and again as the door gets kicked off its hinges.

"?!"

"You got my money for this month, Mii-ahh-chhh?"

A middle-age god with graying hair and a beard appears in the doorway.

I can tell he's quite a bit older than the gods and goddesses I know, but he still has that perfectly chiseled face they all share…But at the same time, his aura is completely different. All that handsomeness is wasted on him.

His cheeks peel back in a sickening grin as he looks around the room like he owns the place. He's wearing an extravagant gold robe with intricate embroidery. Did he choose his wardrobe today just to rub it in Lord Miach's face…?

"Dian…!"

"I dragged myself all the way out here 'cause you never showed up. Be grateful, you ruined beggar, bwa-ha-ha-ha-ha-ha-ha!"

…I think I have a pretty good idea what this god is like.

"I see your shop is just as dusty as always! Gotta make this a quick visit, being here too long's gonna make me sick. Oh, I see misery loves company! Hosting some more beggars so you won't get lonely?"

Nahza's eyes are burning like this god is her father's sworn enemy. Lord Miach turns to face the intruder with a very sour look on his face. "Huh?" Lady Hestia's voice rings out as if trying to get out of the way of an explosion of sparks.

"He's Lord Dian Cecht."

"Lilly…"

"He's the head of a *Familia* that is well respected by adventurers and makes healing items and medicine. Since Lord Miach sells healing potions…they're business rivals."

I nod as Lilly whispers information into my ear. That explains Lord Miach's and Nahza's reactions, as well as Lord Dian Cecht's taunting tone. There's got to be a deep connection between these two, and it's not a friendly one.

"Well, Miach, where's my money?"

"Well, it's…!"

"Fu-fu-fu, do you have it or do you not have it? Gu-HA-HA-HA-HA-HA!"

—*chit chit chit*. I can hear Lord Miach's and Nahza's teeth rattling from over here.

"I've given you extension after extension out of the goodness of my heart, but I've had it with your unpredictability. If you don't have this month's payment by tomorrow, I'll run you out of this place and sell your home to cover your debt! You might as well kiss this place good-bye!"

Lord Dian Cecht laughs so hard that spit flies everywhere.

"FU-HA-HA-HA-HA!! We're leaving, Amid!"

"Yes, sir."

A little girl standing behind Lord Dian Cecht moves out of the way as her god heads for the door. She must've been standing behind him the whole time.

The girl is rather short and looks more like a doll than a person. Amid bows to us as her god walks briskly through the broken door, she turns and rushes to keep up with him.

The storm having blown through, the five of us sit in silence.

"Dian Cecht and I have never seen eye to eye, even in Tenkai......"

Lord Miach begins to tell his life story bit by bit.

After what just happened, I couldn't exactly just go home and pretend everything's okay. So we stuck around to find out about what's been going on inside *Miach Familia*.

"Once we came down to this world, we butted heads at every turn. Our rivalry extended to the children we took under our wing when we got into the same business..."

"I broke that cycle to pieces."

Nahza jumps into Lord Miach's story when his words begin trailing off.

"I used to be an adventurer."

"Eh..."

"I used to crawl the Dungeon like you do, Bell, saving up money... But one day, I screwed everything up. Got thoroughly wrecked by a monster, and it *ate my right arm*."

She tells me before I could even ask.

Nahza looks down at her strangely uneven-sleeved shirt and starts rolling up the wrist-length right sleeve.

All the breath in my body leaves me a moment later.

"A silver arm...?!"

"Lord Miach got it for me after I lost my real one…it's from that *Dian Cecht Familia*. He practically begged them."

I can hear the shock in Lilly's voice.

Just as she said, Nahza's right arm is completely made of a silver metal.

It's as smooth and shiny as a freshly polished sword. While looking almost exactly like a human arm, it's easy to see the gems embedded in the joints of the appendage.

Once she takes off her glove, I can see that her right hand is constructed with exactly the same silver metal.

"*Dian Cecht Familia* makes medicines and other things. Besides selling potions, they also take custom orders from adventurers and make special items to suit. This airgetlám, or 'silver arm,' is one of them."

Click click. Nahza extends and flexes her arm, showing us how it works.

"Lord Miach took out a loan so he could buy this arm for me. The other members of our *Familia* turned their back on Lord Miach when they found out…and left, everyone."

…She says that *Miach Familia* used to be in the middle of the pack in terms of rank. At that time, it was strong enough to compete with *Dian Cecht Familia* on the open market selling potions.

Then after Nahza's accident, everything fell to pieces almost overnight.

"All that stayed with Lord Miach was a useless former adventurer and a colossal loan," she says with fire still burning in her eyes.

"The way I am now, fighting monsters is impossible. I was able to change jobs and become a chemist only because my former compatriots taught me the tricks of the trade…But I can't make enough money to make a dent in the loan. I'm utterly useless."

"Nahza."

"I'm the reason we have to pay anything to that abomination. It's all my fault—me!"

"Nahza, that's enough. Stop there."

Nahza looks like she wants to say something more on the subject, but Lord Miach convinces her to close her mouth with his quiet voice.

A heavy silence descends over all of us.

I can't find any words. Nahza used to be an adventurer, her arm is fake, and everything else is too much to handle at once. Lady Hestia must not have heard that Lord Miach had been demoted as well. She's just sitting there, arms folded across her chest and her eyes closed. Meanwhile, Lilly's calmly looking at Nahza.

Nahza may have scammed me out of some money recently...but if I were in her shoes, I might have done exactly the same thing.

I would've done anything to try to support the one god who didn't abandon me, the one who always extended a helping hand when I needed it most.

That has to be the most difficult thing in the world.

So hard that I'd want to scream out every day.

"...Well, then, what are you going to do? We know what happened, but right now we need to focus on what's in front of you. Dian's threatening to sell your home, isn't he?"

The goddess broke the silence and asks if there's any way they could have the money ready by the end of tomorrow.

Lord Miach scrunches up his face and looks toward Nahza from the corner of his eye.

She meets his gaze for a moment and slowly nods.

"There is one way..."

Nahza's voice is so soft, it's like it could be snuffed out at any moment.

"But with just me...and Lord Miach, it's impossible..."

The last of the evening light comes through the window glass, making the room glow red.

We're a good distance away from Main Street, but I can still hear the din of many voices and footsteps mixing together on the stone road.

Nahza's body droops as she avoids eye contact. I wonder if she feels like she doesn't have the right to look us in the face. The very words "help us" must feel so far away after everything she's put us through.

The silence is making me uneasy. I glance at everyone around the table in turn before looking at the goddess as if she's our last hope.

She looks back at me with a mysterious blue warmth in her eyes. She tilts her head to the side as if to say, *Well?*

In other words, she's asking me to decide what to do about this. At least that's the sense I'm getting from her.

Her eyes, it's like she's looking at her own son…So many emotions are welling up inside me, but I take a deep breath and go for it.

My mind scrambles to find the right words. Now all I have to do is speak loudly enough to break through this dark silence.

"Ah, ahhh…Lilly. Back to what you were talking about before, couldn't we take up another quest? The last one wasn't enough…and I still have a lot to learn."

My acting skills need a lot of work. At the very least, the topic will change one way or another.

Lilly's eyes pop open. Then she must've realized what I was trying to do because she grimaces for a moment and hides a chuckle. She jumps into my "act" a moment later.

"Lilly agrees, Mr. Bell. But where in the world is there a client willing to bestow a quest onto hardworking people such as ourselves?"

Lord Miach and Nahza look on in surprise as Lilly takes my side with an almost giddy smile on her face.

Lady Hestia's lips perk up in a grin. She turns her head to face Lord Miach.

"So how about it, Miach? Do you have any work for these two? Think of it as helping them out. Their energy has to go somewhere. They'll do anything if you ask, including helping you pay back that loan."

"Hestia, are you really…No, my apologies. You have my gratitude."

Nahza looks at me with embarrassment—or is that shame?—from beside Lord Miach as he thanks us over and over.

"Bell, are you sure…? After all I've…"

"…It's thanks to you, Nahza, that Lilly and I are still alive today."

It was the day that I was surrounded by a horde of killer ants.

No matter what the actual price was, the fact that she talked me into purchasing a magic potion was the deciding factor in a desperate battle.

But above all, I can't just abandon someone who helped me in the past.

I relax the muscles in my brow and smile at her. Her eyes open in disbelief for a moment before she hides her face.

"I'm sorry…Thank you."

Her last words barely louder than a whisper, she jerks her head down in what is an unmistakable bow.

Quest accepted

- Client: *Miach Familia*
- Reward: original healing item
- Content: retrieve monster eggs
- Comment: Let's do our best. They're counting on us.

We leave the city early the next morning.

I was told as much last night, so I cut my training with Aiz short and meet up with Lord Miach to help with preparations. Lady Hestia and Lilly join us after we hire a horse-drawn cart for the day from another merchant.

Two divine beings and three humans of different races. I doubt anyone has ever seen a party like ours. We arrive at the city wall as the sun reaches the mountains in the distance.

"Bell, you're such a hard worker. Getting up extra early today to help Miach get ready like this."

"Ha-ha-ha-ha…"

Just like Lilly, I haven't told the goddess about my training with Aiz, either. I really don't want to think about what would happen if she ever found out.

Apologizing over and over in my mind, I quickly engage Nahza in conversation before the situation gets out of hand.

"Hey, um, Nahza. So, as you said yesterday..."

"Yes. There is no time to prepare money for payment by the end of today. So the plan is to turn the tables on them and create an original healing item to sell to *Dian Cecht Familia* to cover the costs..."

She responds in her usual monotone voice. She's wearing rather loose clothing compared to her usual strange combination of garments.

Once we finish some rather monotonous paperwork, we receive clearance to exit Orario's East Gate. A vast prairie spreads up before us, greens and golds swaying in the breeze.

"Lilly asked yesterday, but will this plan actually work? Making a new item from scratch is not easy..."

"Not a problem, I've got an idea..."

Nahza answers Lilly's question with a quiet confidence. As usual, Nahza looks like she could fall asleep at any moment. *Shff, shff.* Her tail is lazily swishing back and forth behind her.

"I didn't hear where we're headed today. Where's this cart taking us?"

"The Deep Forest Seoro. It's not too far away, but we'll be in this cart a while. Since we're all here together, now would be a good time for bonding."

This time it was Lord Miach who answers Lady Hestia's question. He looks at Lilly while saying that last part.

This wooden cart is a lot more cramped than I thought it would be. My shoulders brush up against my neighbors every time the wheels hit a bump in the road. All of us are sitting in a circle with Lord Miach closest to the driver, me next, then Lady Hestia, Lilly, and finally Nahza on the other side of Lord Miach.

The morning sun shines down directly on us because this cart doesn't have a canopy or roof of any kind. Feeling the warmth on our faces, we take Lord Miach's advice and strike up a conversation.

"Miss Nahza. Lilly knows that you successfully switched from adventurer to chemist. Does that mean that Miss Nahza has learned Synthesize as well?"

"Yes, I have…I learned enough by helping make medicine to gain the correct excelia and was very lucky…"

"Um, is Synthesize one of those…?"

"It's an Advanced Ability that allows a person to create higher-quality items and medicine, Mr. Bell."

So that means that an adventurer could learn an ability called Synthesize when they level up, if they have the right excelia. Lilly goes on to explain that it allows a person to create a potion so powerful that it can close wounds on contact, just like a healing spell.

It sounds a lot like the Advanced Ability Forge, in that only professionals tend to learn it and it has a deep connection with creating strong weapons and potent items.

Even if two different people create the same item using the same ingredients, the results will be completely different if one of them has an Advanced Ability.

"Wait, you have an Advanced Ability, so that means…"

"Yeah. I'm Level Two…"

My eyes shoot open as wide as they go.

N-Nazha is just as strong as other upper-class adventurers…

"I made it down into the middle levels, but a monster nearly burned me alive down there…Then it started eating chunks of my arms and legs."

"Oh no—"

"It took a lot of work to get my left arm and legs back to normal, but my right arm was beyond saving. The beast ate everything, even my bones…Ever since that day, I haven't been able to fight a monster. Just standing in front of one of them…My body won't stop shaking."

Chills run up and down my spine as I listen to her gruesome tale.

The stench of charred flesh all over her body.

The feeling of being on her back and utterly defenseless as a monster devours her right arm.

All of the traumatic memories of pain and fear that have literally been burned into her revive every time she faces any monster. She tells me everything.

"…Sorry, I didn't want to scare you."

"Ah, i-it's okay…"

"Anyway, don't let your guard down while crawling the Dungeon…It took me six years to level up…but it only takes a second to lose everything you've worked for."

I clear my throat and take Nahza's warning to heart.

"But that arm of yours, it's very, very well-made. Do you ever have any problem using it?"

"No, I can move it naturally…"

"It cost an incredible amount of money, but I ordered the best item that Dian had available. While it pains me to admit this, I can trust that anything his *Familia* makes will be very high quality."

The deities in the cart change the topic and clear the air. The mood quickly changes from dark and uncomfortable to light and friendly.

We're following one road that leads from Orario's East Gate and through a blanket of green that spreads in all directions. Since Orario is the home of the only dungeon in the world, well-kept roads are required to sell magic-stone goods outside the city. The road that we're on is made of a white stone and is very smooth.

"Lord Miach doesn't recognize my feelings for him at all… although I'm glad he doesn't notice all the other girls looking at him with hearts in their eyes…Sometimes I wonder if he really is a god…"

"Ahh, I know the feeling. My Bell is just as dense. I don't know how many times his cluelessness has made me cry."

"Hee-hee, but in Lady Hestia's case, Mr. Bell's keeping his distance out of respect and doesn't see Lady Hestia as a girl. It would be a good idea to realize that, you know…And Lilly gets treated like a little sister."

"…"

Why did all the girls suddenly get so scary, and why does it feel like the cart is shrinking?

I can hear them whispering to each other, but Lord Miach and I can't understand what they're saying. All I know is I suddenly feel very small.

We pass by many carts heading toward Orario on our way down the road that cuts through the expansive grasslands.

We finally reach our destination with the sun high overhead.

"S-so this is…"

"Okay, I can see why they call it the deep forest."

The goddess and I marvel at the scenery. This is the first time either of us have come here.

Deep Forest Seoro.

It's an incredibly dense forest located at the base of the Alb mountain range, directly east from Orario.

Every single tree in front of me reaches high into the sky, their trunks many times thicker than any other tree I've ever seen. The ground is covered in vibrant wildflowers and moss. This green realm is truly ruled by nature.

All of us quickly hop out of the cart and grab each of the bags we brought with us.

After telling the cart driver we hired to wait for us outside the forest, all of us step into the wilderness together.

"We're going to get some monster eggs, right?"

"Yep. They're not drop items, but actual eggs…"

We came all the way out here to find eggs that were laid by monsters. Nahza must need them as an ingredient for her new healing potion.

The monsters that escaped the Dungeon in the Old Age learned to live on land and reproduce on their own. Their descendants are scattered all around the world even today. Considering that they're still alive, the fact that they lay eggs should make perfect sense…But now I'm so used to the fact that monsters are born from the dungeon walls that the thought of them laying eggs just feels weird.

I keep my head on a swivel, looking for monsters as we make our way through the forest.

"…Bell, stop there."

I was leading the group down a thin path through the trees when Nahza calls out to me and I stop moving.

She can see something up ahead: a wide, round depression in the ground.

Nahza starts giving out orders a moment later. First, she tells Lord Miach and Lady Hestia to wait here. Then she puts Lilly in charge of protecting them.

Last, she waves her hand and motions for me to follow her.

"Bell, here."

Keeping her shoulders low to the ground, Nahza brings me some equipment.

A heavily worn broadsword and a backpack with something inside.

"Wh-what's this for?"

"These guys are tough without a weapon this big...Put the backpack on."

I break out in a cold sweat, pondering what she meant by that. Nahza goes a few paces ahead of me and stops in the shade of a tree just in front of the depression.

Sniff, sniff. I can hear Nahza taking in all of the smells as the dog ears on her head arch back and open wide.

The tension in the air is starting to make me nervous. My heart begins to pick up the pace when suddenly—Nahza moves.

She reaches past my shoulder and swiftly opens the top of the backpack.

"Uck...?!"

My sinuses erupt in pain the instant a new stench wafts up my nostrils.

I know the smell, but I can't quite place it. Nahza salutes me as I rack my brain for an answer.

"I wish you luck, Bell. Sorry."

She takes off before I can even say, "Huh?"

She darts through the trees with the speed and agility befitting a Level 2 adventurer and leaves me behind.

I stare at where she was for a moment, blinking, when...out of nowhere, *splat.*

"...eh?"

A strange goo falls down from overhead.

I can feel the warm, clear liquid running down my shoulder. Slowly but surely, I look up.

"UuuUuu..."

What greets my eyes is the drooling mouth of a large *dinosaur.*

Then it hits me: I remember where I've smelled the stuff that's in the backpack. Blood is racing so fast in my veins that I could pass out at any moment.

It's a trap made of raw meat that draws out hungry monsters.

"UUOOOOOOOOOOOOOOOOOOOOOOOOOOOOOOOOOOOO OOOOO!!"

"DDAAAAHHHHHHHHHHHHHHHHHHHHHHHHHHHH-HHHHHHHHHH?!"

Scream and roar mix.

I turn my back to the massive chin and take off at full speed.

"Uh, isn't that a large-category monster?!"

"Whaa, B-Bell?!"

"B-bloodsaurus...?!"

Hestia was the first to yell out, followed closely by Lilly's shriek of surprise.

A five-meder-tall, carnivorous, red dinosaur had appeared.

It let out one bloodcurdling roar after another as it rampaged through the forest, chasing the "rabbit" that was to become its next meal.

"H-hold on a second here. That's a monster that shows up on the thirtieth floor...!"

"There's no problem. Monsters on the surface are much weaker than the ones found in the Dungeon."

In contrast to Lilly's shaking voice, Nahza's response was quite calm.

"Now's our chance to enter the depression. We need to work quickly while Bell leads the monsters away."

Nahza guided Hestia and the others down the slope.

The depression was revealed to be a monster's nest; the group spotted ten or more eggs situated in a space between two trees.

"Wasn't there a better way we could have done this...?"

"No. If we faced all of the bloodsauruses at once, we wouldn't have been able to protect Lord Miach and Lady Hestia."

"My apologies, Bell..."

"Less talking, more grabbing, dammit! That thing's going to eat Bell!"

Hestia scolded the others for pointless conversation as all of them shoved as many eggs as they could into the bags they had brought with them.

Their work done, each of them slung a bag full of eggs over their shoulders.

"Miss Nahza, was that true, about the monsters?"

"It is. Hundreds of generations of reproducing have taken their toll on the beasts. The magic stone in their chests is so small it might as well not be there."

Nahza answered Lilly's question as she adjusted her bag of eggs.

Monsters that were separated from the Dungeon followed their instincts to ensure the survival of their species.

They began relying on strength of numbers as their own physical prowess began to decline. Since each individual needed less power to survive, magic stones became smaller over time.

As each successive generation's magic stone decreased in size, so did each individual monster's in strength. At this point, monsters on the surface didn't even compare with the "originals" in the Dungeon.

"Bloodsauruses on the surface might be a little bit stronger than an orc in the Dungeon..."

Said Nahza as she cast her gaze in Bell's direction.

The boy was currently being chased by three such monsters. Their numbers had increased. Bell's yelps of fright echoed through the forest.

Nahza straightened up and took hold of the weapon strapped to her back.

It was a longbow that stood just as tall as she did. Holding the weapon steady with her silver arm, she nocked an arrow using her left hand.

There was enough space between her and the monsters to prevent Nahza's traumatic memories from triggering. The sun's rays illuminating pieces of the asymmetric light armor equipped over her traveling garb, Nahza narrowed her eyes for an instant before the arrow hurtled forward.

The projectile tore through the air the instant that Nahza lifted her fingers, and it found its target: the eye of a bloodsaurus.

"_____!!"

A deep roar of pain sounded through the trees.

Its balance and vision gone, the injured bloodsaurus staggered into the one next to it at full speed, sending both of them to the ground.

Bell felt the shock wave of their impact and saw the leaves shake around him. He looked over his shoulder and his eyes went wide as he drew the broadsword into position. The last bloodsaurus charging him with reckless abandon, Bell chose to believe in Nahza's support, drove his heel into the dirt, and charged headlong into the monster's path.

"———This makes me so happy."

"YAAAHHHHHHHHHHHHHHHHHHHHHHHHHHHHHH-HHHH!!"

Nahza, grinning from ear to ear, unleashed another arrow at the same time that Bell let loose a battle cry.

The arrow got there just in time, piercing the beast's eye just before Bell got into position. Reeling in pain, the monster was defenseless against the incoming blade.

Bell's jumping strike took a slice out of the base of the bloodsaurus's lower neck. Fresh blood spraying like a fountain, the beast fell to its knees.

Bell went in for another strike to finish it off but lost his balance in mid-swing. Nahza couldn't help but laugh as she watched from her vantage point.

"Nahza, that's enough."

"Okay..."

She turned to face Miach, the same smile still plastered on her face.

Nahza scanned the group, making sure that both Lilly and Hestia had bags of eggs securely fastened to their backs, before looking back in Bell's direction.

The boy emerged from behind a tree, using the broadsword as a walking stick. "Can we go now?" he said with a very pathetic look in his eyes. Nahza smiled and nodded.

"Time to go home, Bell."

Beneath a night sky studded with stars.

A vial containing a dark blue liquid was given to a man standing in the open doorway of a large mansion.

"This is my *Familia*'s latest product. I guarantee its effectiveness."

"Eh, geh...!"

Dian Cecht gasped as he took the vial from Miach's outstretched hands.

After closely inspecting it himself, the deity handed the vial to his assistant, Amid, and asked for her opinion.

The girl took a sip and went silent. Both of the gods waited with bated breath for a moment before she looked up and gave a very curt nod.

"A double potion that restores physical strength and mental energy...This is the first of its kind. Therefore, you would be able to sell them for quite a high price at your *Familia*'s shops. It is sure to meet the demand of many adventurers, don't you agree?"

"Geh, grrrr...!"

"I have twenty of them right here. The profits from their sale should more than cover this month's payment. Please buy them."

"Wh...Why youuuuuuuuuuuuuuuu...?!"

A deep roar of frustration rang out under the night sky.

Bell and the others, waiting on the outside of the mansion's four high walls, knew the transaction was successful the moment they heard it.

"Sounds like it worked..."

"That geezer isn't dumb enough to turn down the opportunity to make a killing. Although I'm sure he wanted to see us squirm... Too bad."

Nahza half laughed as she responded to Lilly's comment.

The group had been waiting just outside the walls that surrounded *Dian Cecht Familia*'s home for Miach's return.

"Whew, that was a long day! There was no time to sit down."

"Ah-ha-ha..."

A battle against time to produce the double potion was waiting for them as soon as they arrived home in Orario after collecting the eggs from the Deep Forest Seoro. While Miach and Nahza worked their fingers to the bone to meet their deadline, Bell, Lilly, and Hestia helped out in any way they could. All of them worked continuously for hours on end.

Bell grimaced as he looked over at his exhausted goddess.

"But you really did a good job making it. And at the last moment, too."

"The people of Orario are obsessed with the Dungeon and don't even try to learn about the possibilities around them...There are so many discoveries out there just waiting for people to find them."

Monster eggs and Blue Papillon Wings. Nahza told Bell she'd created a new item using resources from both inside and outside the Dungeon.

"Oh, Miach. Finished already?"

"Yes. Everything has been settled."

Miach emerged from the gate and returned to the spot where the group was waiting for him. He smiled and said that they no longer had to worry about being kicked out of their own home as he looked to each person in turn.

"Allow me to thank you once again. This was only possible because of you, and you have my gratitude."

"I'm happy to hear that your loan has become a little lighter."

"It was a quest worth doing."

Hestia and Lilly looked back up at him and smiled. Bell followed suit.

Miach finally turned to face Nahza, his thin eyes smiling.

"Nahza."

"Yes..."

"Yesterday, you called yourself useless."

"...Yes."

"I have never, ever thought that even once."

Nahza's eyes opened wide as she listened to Miach's words.

"I am a god whom you have saved many times. Even if we're not as well off as we once were, your presence makes it all worth it. So please, don't be so hard on yourself."

"...Is that an order?"

"No, a solemn request from the god who watches over you more than any of the other children."

Miach stepped in front of her as he spoke, reached out, and stroked her hair.

Caught in the warm gaze of her deity, Nahza blushed for a moment before looking at the ground. "So dense..." she whispered under her breath as he patted her head.

Hestia watched them with a twinkle in her eye as Miach once again said and did things that could be taken the wrong way. She used the opportunity to tease him, and Lilly enjoyed every second of it. Bell forced a smile as both sides made fun of each other back and forth. Nahza took the opportunity to break out of the small circle and walked up to him.

"Bell, thank you for today. Really...Really, thank you."

"Nahza..."

The dog girl gave a deep bow before raising her head and pulling a vial out of her breast pocket.

"Eh, isn't that..."

"A double potion...There was only one left over, but...this is the reward for completing the quest, and my thanks."

In contrast to Bell's surprise, Nahza's face went back to her usual drowsy expression, but with a smile on her lips.

"If you need help with anything, tell me. After everything I've done, I need to make it up to you…"

Bell's surprise faded away as a smile bloomed on his lips big enough to rival Nahza's.

He took his reward from the girl's outstretched hand.

At long last, Bell's quest had come to an end.

A
CAMPANELLA
TO
THE
GODDESS

"Goddess, I did it! I-I slew a goblin!"

"...Ohh?"

Hestia had been enjoying an afternoon of reading on the sofa.

She looked up from her book when the door opened with a loud bang. That's when she saw a white-haired human with a very proud look on his face as he proclaimed victory.

Hestia Familia's home, a hidden room beneath an old church.

The room itself had two parts, one square and one long, coming together to make a *P* shape. While it was the perfect height for people to be comfortable, the sheer amount of furniture and other items in the room made it feel quite cramped. The building itself was rather old. There were cracks in many places all over the stone walls, and the general atmosphere of the place felt shabby and run-down.

The light from the one magic-stone lamp on the ceiling reflecting off her blank eyes, Hestia stared at the only member of her *Familia*———Bell Cranell.

The boy in front of her seemed extremely happy, his face beaming as if he'd just pulled off an amazing feat.

"Goblin...As in that goblin? The weakest monster in the entire Dungeon, that monster?"

"Yes! One of them nearly killed me when I was a little kid, so I've always been scared of them, but...today, I finally slew one!"

"So, um...Just one?"

"Eh?"

"You killed one goblin and came all the way back here from the Dungeon to tell me?"

Bell's face suddenly went cold, his body still for several moments as he thought about Hestia's question. He had indeed killed only one monster, the weakest one, and come all the way back home.

The boy suddenly realized how insignificant his victory was with great dismay. The face that had been sparkling with joy moments earlier became downtrodden and ashamed. Bell turned around on the spot, hunched forward with his shoulders hanging low.

"I'm going back to the Dungeon. Sorry to have disturbed you..."

"Wh-wha—what?! Sorry, Bell, I wasn't trying to accuse you of anything...H-hold on a second!"

Not hearing Hestia's calls, Bell disappeared from the doorway, his ears bright red from embarrassment.

Hestia Familia had been founded three days earlier.

That's when Hestia had found Bell in the middle of the city and invited him to be a member of her *Familia*.

After accepting her invitation and receiving her Blessing, Bell had joined the ranks of adventurers by registering with the Guild. The responsibility of providing for his *Familia* fell squarely on his shoulders. He welcomed this role, but being away from his hometown in a place so different from what he was used to weighed heavily on his mind as he set to work.

Hestia watched over the boy while doing a part-time job of her own. It seemed like she was discovering something new about him every time they were together. A beautiful, young goddess who always wore her heart on her sleeve, Hestia was doing her best to get to know the shy boy struggling to come out of his shell. Even though they had only been together for a few days, they were already on very good terms.

Among all the *Familias* in the city of Orario, *Hestia Familia* was a bottom-tier group that had to focus on earning enough money to make it through the day. The two of them were a team, building on their loose foundation as they started down this road together.

"I was worried for a while there. If something happened and you didn't come home, I would've had nightmares for a very long time."

"S-sorry to make you worry......"

"Ah-ha-ha, what about? This was my fault, saying all that. I'm the one who should be apologizing. Sorry, Bell."

Hestia and Bell were sitting across from each other at the table in their home.

Bell had made it safely home from his second trip to the Dungeon that day and it was now very late. The pair ate a late dinner in a room where the light of the shining moon in the night sky could not reach them.

Bell's total earnings from his first day of dungeon crawling—300 vals, all of which had been used right away to buy a few stiff loaves of bread and eggs. They spent a lot of time making the eggs look more appetizing than usual and lined them up on the table.

Even though it wasn't much, the yolks of the freshly cooked eggs looked warm and fresh under the light of the magic-stone lamp.

"So how was it, Bell, your Dungeon debut? Does it seem promising?"

"Well, I was too nervous to go all that deep, but…I can hold my own against monsters. It got easier after taking down one goblin and a kobold."

The extra effort put into making tonight's dinner was to celebrate Bell's first dungeon crawl.

They couldn't afford to get anything extra special, but Hestia and Bell smiled with satisfaction as they enjoyed their fried eggs on toast.

"But I'm relieved to hear that. It sounds like you'll be able to make a living as an adventurer, Bell. I was a little concerned that you would spend all of your time chasing after girls in the Dungeon."

"I-I'm not doing that, why would I be doing that?!"

Hestia was only teasing, but Bell's face turned bright red as his voice went up an octave or two.

Hestia raised an eyebrow, looking at the panicking boy, and said, "I wonder.

"You're trying to pick up girls, aren't you? Find some cute adventurer ladies and make them swoon as you dispatch monsters left and right. That's when you make your move, is it not?"

"M-make a move…! I-it's not like that! I don't want to get with a whole bunch of girls…Well, a little but…A-anyway, I'm looking for the girl of my dreams, the one I'm destined to be with! Like the ones in tales of heroes!"

"Didn't you say you wanted a harem of your own?"

"A-a harem is a man's romantic dream! It's something that I must strive for as a man, just like the heroes…"

Bell closed his ruby-red eyes, his cheeks a deeper scarlet than before as he talked.

Hestia lightly shrugged her shoulders as she stared at Bell from across the table. Her thoughts went wild as she took in his boyish features.

The more she knew about Bell Cranell, the stranger he seemed to be.

Despite being extremely shy, he was a womanizer. He wanted to meet the ladies but wouldn't make a move. In other words, his personality didn't make sense. For better or worse, something else seemed to be motivating his words and actions from behind his pure and straightforward personality.

Hestia believed that the cause of this inner conflict had something to do with the boy's grandfather, the one who raised him.

That man's fingerprints were all over many of the stories that Bell told, as well as one or two of the thoughts in his head.

Hestia had to marvel at this man whom she had never met and his methods of brainwashing by means of using heroes for role models. She sighed to herself, thinking about what kind of man Bell could have become if he had just had *a proper upbringing*. His roots, even the way he thought, could all be traced back to that one man.

Bell's obsession with girls and his quest to find "the one" all started and ended with him.

The image of this beautiful girl that he left behind, or implanted, in Bell's head must be very powerful.

A boy whose eyes light up with a good story, his mind always in the clouds.

That's who the boy, Bell Cranell, really was.

Maybe it would've been better if he had been born a girl. A very blunt thought passed through Hestia's mind.

"Gramps told me so. Meeting girls is every man's lifelong ambition. So that's why I…"

"..."

Hestia watched the boy vigorously try to explain himself.

Hestia was learning more and more about him, her first family member.

While Bell was in the Dungeon earning money for his *Familia*, Hestia also was busy working at her part-time job.

She was a lot like Bell, in that she hadn't lived in Orario for very long and she was always trying to figure out what she had to do next. Living on Gekai was much more difficult than the life of luxury she was used to in Tenkai. All the other gods kept saying, "Come and experience the charm of Gekai." It was true, she would never have felt these hardships living in the upper world. But these "charms" were starting to get a little overwhelming.

"Here you are, little Hestia. This is today's pay."

"Thanks, Gram."

A female animal person handed her an envelope that contained her pay.

Hestia was working at a street stand that was situated on North Main Street. They sold a snack called Crispy Potato Puffs: mashed potatoes mixed with seasoning, rolled in batter, and deep-fried to make small potato snacks.

Whatever potion they'd been using as a secret ingredient seemed to be working because they did pretty good business every day.

One, two, three...180 vals.

She worked six hours today at 30 vals per hour. Despite knowing exactly how much was inside the envelope before opening it, seeing how little she earned in the palm of her hand made Hestia sigh.

Not too long ago, she'd made a mistake when setting up the fryer and everything exploded in her face—there were zero injuries, other than Hestia's instant breadcrumb coating. The money to make repairs was taken out of her paycheck every day. At this rate, it would be a long time before Hestia could help Bell provide for their *Familia*.

This world called Gekai was extremely harsh on a young goddess who'd only just arrived.

At least that's what Hestia thought, never once taking her own failures into account.

"Hey, Gram, why don't you join my *Familia*? A young adventurer just joined me and we're on our way up in the world."

"Ah-ha-ha, you mustn't say such things, no-no. Good grief, Hestia, you are so persistent."

"But why—? Please—!"

Hestia prepared to leave as the woman laughed at yet another invitation to join *Hestia Familia*, a daily occurrence at this point.

Part of it was that *Hestia Familia* was an unknown group with no reputation, but the biggest problem was the goddess's lack of dignity.

The woman patted Hestia on the head and gave her a potato puff before seeing her out the door—she was a goddess who was being treated like a child. This realization made her sigh yet again.

"What a long day…"

Hestia made her way through the red evening streets, cheeks puffing out as she stuffed the whole potato puff into her mouth at once.

Usually she was home before the sky turned a deep red, so she had, in fact, worked longer than usual today. *Bell might be home already*, she thought to herself as she trudged forward.

Hestia Familia's home, a room beneath an old church, was located on a city block between Northwest and West Main Streets. So Hestia set out due west from the street stall on North Main Street.

At first, her route took her straight through a nice neighborhood built out of bricks and very well maintained. But the farther she went, the shabbier the buildings around her became. Really old item shops, run-down motels, and dingy pubs lined the street until she suddenly emerged onto Northwest Main.

The street was often called "Adventurers Way" because the Guild Headquarters was built on it. Adventurers of all shapes and sizes strutted their way up and down the road. The shops and buildings that lined the street made the ones that Hestia just passed by look like piles of trash.

"...Isn't that...?"

Hestia was making her way across the street, her long shadow mixing with the crowd as the sun set behind the wall that surrounded the city, when she happened to see someone by chance.

A white-haired human boy was standing outside a shop.

Bell...?

The member of her *Familia* had his back to the throngs of adventurers and had his eyes locked on something in the shop's show window. Seeing the boy so intensely fixated on whatever was inside made Hestia come to a stop in the middle of the road.

A few moments went by before Bell's shoulders drooped and he practically tore himself away from the window. At long last the boy took his eyes off the shop and left.

Hestia watched him disappear into the crowd before rushing up to the window. *Tup-tup-tup-tup*, the soles of her shoes echoed off the stone road as she went.

"...So that's what it was."

After seeing with her own eyes what in the show window Bell had been ogling for so long, she knew why he had been so interested.

The show window was filled with different types of weapons. Freshly polished, strong blades of all sizes sparkled beautifully in the display.

Whether Bell had been drawn here when he was passing by or by the power of envy in a wish that he knew wouldn't come true, Hestia didn't know for sure.

No matter the reason, Bell was obviously extremely interested in the weapons at this shop.

"Hmmm...All right, this is it."

Hestia folded her arms across her chest and decided it was about time she did something "godlike," giving her "child" a present. She nodded to herself. After everything that had happened, Hestia wanted someone to realize that she was indeed a goddess. And being the warmhearted deity she was, she resolved to give Bell a present.

She figured that if she spent every val she had saved up since arriving on this world, she could get him something good. A small grin growing on her face, Hestia moved away from the window and toward the front door.

Doing her best to remember the angle of Bell's gaze, Hestia worked out that the boy had been looking at a shortsword. More than likely, it was the one in the back of the display, sticking out of a jewel-encrusted treasure chest. Even Hestia had to admit the blade was a work of art.

Then, she saw the price tag. "Huh?" The sound drifted out of her mouth, her hand on the door handle and eyes blinking.

"Eighty million vals."

Hestia's fingers released the door, her body frozen in place.

Forgive me, Bell.

That's impossible, she said to herself as she turned on her heel and left the shop as quickly as she could, cold sweat dripping down her neck.

That price was too big of a monster to slay. Hestia's life savings were nothing but a helpless goblin at the feet of a dragon.

"Wait, isn't this…"

Looking back over her shoulder at the redbrick building, Hestia realized it belonged to one of her friends.

Masters of the Forge, *Hephaistos Familia*. She had lived with them from after her arrival on Gekai up until very recently.

Being a brand name known around the world, the fact that she couldn't afford a *Hephaistos* weapon should have been obvious. She took one last look at the billboard before taking off at a light sprint. *Know your place, Bell*, she said to herself, feeling defeated.

Robbed of her chance to show her godly prowess, Hestia sighed yet again as she made her way down the stone-paved path toward home, bathed in the last crimson light from the setting sun.

…My hair ties are in pretty bad shape.

Catching a glimpse of herself in another shop's show window on Northwest Main, Hestia stopped to take a closer look.

The two bands that kept her shiny, jet-black hair up in a set of twin ponytails practically had one foot in the grave. Frayed and falling apart, they could break at any moment.

The only thing these hair ties were doing for her now was to make her look less dignified. Running her fingers over them, she looked at her reflection in the glass. Suddenly, the mannequins behind the glass caught her attention.

Each of the statues was wearing a dress as well as all sorts of protective accessories like amulets. Among the shop's standing advertisements was a statue with very cute hair ties.

"..."

She stared at the blue bands on the mannequin's head, mesmerized for a few moments. She jerked her shoulders before vigorously shaking her head side to side. *A goddess can't waste money*, she practically screamed at herself, despite how much she wanted them.

Swish. She flicked her chin away from the shop window to get her eyes off of it. She took another quick glance from the corner of her eye before forcefully turning her shoulders away.

Making up her mind to live with the ones she had for now, Hestia wrapped her fingers around her hair bands and turned off West Main into a side street.

"..."

A pair of ruby-red eyes whose owner had yet to make his way home happened to catch a glimpse of what had just occurred. Hestia, however, didn't notice.

It had now been a week since the founding of *Hestia Familia*.

Hestia looked at the boy in front of her, a worried look in her eyes.

"S-sorry I'm late..."

Bell walked through the door to their home trailing a cloud of dust, armor and clothes so dirty that Hestia could almost hear the fabric cough.

The clock on the wall showed that it was already past nine at night.

"...Bell, aren't you working a little too hard recently?"

"N-no, I don't think so?"

Bell grimaced as Hestia's expression grew more and more concerned. "I'm fine," he said to reassure her.

Bell had come home in this state every night for the past few days.

He'd get up really early, spend all day crawling the Dungeon, and come home late at night. The dirt and damage on his clothes and armor showed just how hard he was working; his body was faring no better.

Of course, Bell might have been a little too excited when he became an adventurer, but there was something different about him recently.

"Goddess, here. This is the money I earned in the Dungeon today."

"Ah-haaa…"

Ka-ching. The coins inside a linen sack rattled as he handed it to her.

Every night, Bell always gave Hestia some of his profits from crawling the Dungeon to help support the *Familia*. It went without saying that he took most of it for himself, to pay for items and equipment repairs as well as to have a little pocket money.

Hestia undid the strap and took a look inside the bag. A quick glance told her there were at least 500 vals inside. Assuming that Bell took around 1,000 vals for himself to prepare for his next trip into the Dungeon, he had been making a lot more money than he used to. Hestia could tell just how much effort Bell was putting into his early-morning to late-evening excursions into the Dungeon.

In that case, the boy had to have a reason to want to make a lot of money as soon as possible.

"…Hey, Bell."

"Ah, yes?"

"Are you hiding something from me?"

A very exhausted Bell had just grabbed a change of clothes and was headed toward the shower room when Hestia stopped him to ask her question.

Whether it was her divine intuition or just a feeling as a goddess that Bell was trying to keep a secret, she didn't know. But she knew something was up.

Bell froze on the spot, something that Hestia saw as a very suspicious reaction.

"Ah-ha-ha-ha-ha…wh-what are you talking about, Goddess? Of course I'm not."

"…"

Hestia lowered her eyelids at Bell's fake and forced laugh.

Ignoring Bell's words that she wouldn't have believed anyway, Hestia locked eyes with him. *Tell me now*, she mouthed at him, her aura on fire.

"…G-Goddess, I'm going to take a shower now, okay?!"

"Gah!"

Bell practically dove into the shower room, clothes in his hand and a nervous sweat running down his cheek. Hestia was surprised by the boy's speed for a moment, but anger built within her the moment the door closed behind him.

There was a part of Hestia that couldn't stand the fact that Bell was hiding something from her.

Over the past week, Hestia had come to like the boy and was glad that she had brought him into her *Familia,* made him a member of her family.

In return, the boy treated her like the goddess she was—and yet she could feel the warmth of the more personal bond with him.

Hestia couldn't help but want to protect the naïve Bell. But at the same time she felt drawn to him, almost safe in his presence.

In this world of Gekai that was extremely harsh on her, Bell was the one who did everything he could to help Hestia.

She loved his smile. It always seemed to melt all of her worries away whenever she saw him.

"I tell you to spill it, and yet you refuse to crack, Bell…"

That could be the reason why she couldn't allow Bell to have any secrets from her.

This feeling eating her from the inside could be the arrogance of a god who'd found something beyond their control or a feeling of betrayal of trust and loneliness as a family member.

Whichever one it was, it was putting Hestia in an extremely foul mood that was getting worse by the moment.

All right, then, if that's the game you want to play...

A threatening light sparkled in her eyes. She glared at the door to the shower room and muttered, "Just you wait," before turning on her heel and walking toward the kitchen.

She silently set to work preparing dinner.

"Um, Goddess..."

"You're tired today, right, Bell? I'll cook tonight; you go relax on the sofa."

Hestia flashed a smile at Bell, who had changed into clean clothes after taking a shower. Bell looked like he wanted to say something, but the goddess's smile sent a wave of relief through him. She must've forgotten about their earlier conversation.

Shing, shing. Seeing that her prey had let his guard down, Hestia smiled again at the "rabbit" while sharpening a knife out of Bell's line of sight.

"So, Bell. Shall we update your Status tonight?"

"Um, sure."

After finishing dinner, Hestia made a casual suggestion.

The white rabbit didn't protest and did exactly as he was told.

The knife behind the smile was already razor-sharp.

Bell Cranell

Level I

Strength: I 49 -> I 58   **Defense:** I 5   **Utility:** I 66 -> I 72

Agility: I 98 -> H 107   **Magic:** I 0

Magic

( )

Skill

( )

Bell lay on his stomach on the bed as Hestia sat on his lower back and looked at the boy's new Status.

As usual, Defense and Agility were at the opposite ends of the spectrum. While genuinely surprised that his Agility was already *H* after only one week, Hestia finished the process as quickly as she could.

—*Now then.*

A moment's pause after the Status update was complete.

Hestia's true nature suddenly emerged as her eyes sparkled ominously before she sprang the trap on the "rabbit" beneath her.

Flop. She had been sitting on his lower back when she suddenly fell on top of him.

"?!"

"—You're not getting away this time, Bell.

"No......" came a very ominous sound from Hestia's lips as she put her head right above Bell's shoulder.

Her voice was low, her mouth close enough to Bell's ears that he could hear her breathing. The questioning had begun.

Bell's body jolted as if he'd just been struck by lightning, his face turning bright red.

"G-G-Goddess?! What are you doing?!"

"An interrogation. Because you seem to be hiding something from me, eh?"

Bell's body shook again the moment he heard the words "hiding something." He could feel the goddess's soft body pinning him down as his body jerked from side to side.

"Did you know, Bell? *No one can lie to a god!*"

"Wh-what are you talking about...?"

"Ohooo. Trying to claim innocence, are you?"

Hestia's eyes narrowed.

His face a full-blown red, Bell looked at Hestia's expression from the corner of his eye. If he wasn't scared before, he was terrified now.

A moment later.

Hestia wrapped both of her arms around Bell's neck and squeeeeeezed as hard as she could.

"Dahh?! G-Goddess—?!"

"Now scream—scream it out, Bell!! And you still might be forgiven!"

"I DON'T KNOOWWWWWW!! I-I-I-I'M NOT HIDING ANYTHING FROM YOU, GODDESS!"

"Very stubborn…!"

"GHHEEEEEEEEEEEEEEEEEEEEEEEEEEEEEEEEEEEEEEEEEE?!"

Hestia's sizeable chest had made contact with Bell's back. He could feel the soft pressure of *something* and heard an accompanying *squish*.

The shirtless Bell felt every inch of those somethings as they pressed up against him. Completely overwhelmed by the feeling of skin on skin, the boy shrieked repeatedly as his entire body blushed red under pressure.

Hestia pulled the boy up with her arms, making sure that he felt every inch of her as she pressed down.

Screams never stopped coming from the floors of the old church that night.

"I can hardly believe that Bell…!"

The next day.

Bell never cracked. Hestia had been in a particularly foul mood because of that all day. Even after coming home from her part-time job, she made no effort to hide the displeasure on her face.

Sitting on the sofa and reading a book, Hestia turned the pages with a lot more force than necessary.

Seriously, it's almost like he's daydreaming about money now instead of adventures in the Dungeon…There's no way he's being seduced by some strange woman, and she's making him buy gifts for her…

Bell's sudden devotion to crawling the Dungeon spurred on thoughts that normally wouldn't have come into her mind. Hestia knew that her own family wasn't that foolish, but her frustration only added fuel to the fire.

Then just destroy everything! She pictured Bell being lured into the lap of some Amazon woman, the two of them getting touchy-feely with each other before suddenly shaking her head. *I don't wanna see that*, she angrily quipped at herself.

"Eh…?"

Clop-clop, the sound of shoes on the stone steps outside the door echoed through the room.

Now he's too early, she said to herself as she waited for Bell to come through the door. She forced her eyes off her book and stared impatiently at the entrance.

The door should open at any moment. *Knock-knock* to dry thumps came from outside the door.

"I've come to pay you a visit, Hestia."

"Huh......Miach?"

Someone a lot taller than Hestia was expecting made his way through the entrance.

Long hair the color of the ocean and a gray robe worse for wear, the god Miach was greeted by a wide-eyed Hestia.

"Word is you've created a *Familia*. I know I'm a little late, but I thought I should at least stop by and say congratulations."

"What, you came all the way out here just for that?"

Despite only recently meeting him after descending from Tenkai, Miach had a lot in common with Hestia, especially in terms of their *Familias*. Since Miach had helped out Hestia a few times, the two of them had become casual friends. Miach took a step inside the room under the church as Hestia's face changed into a warm smile.

"Ha-ha-ha, there is no such thing as wasted time when there's a chance to get a new regular for my *Familia*. Think nothing of it."

"Hee-hee, nothing gets past you."

Miach Familia produced and sold healing items, like potions. Since his *Familia* was not very well known, Miach went to great lengths to reach new customers. After explaining that today was no different, he shared a laugh with Hestia.

"That being said..." he continued as he took a vial of blue liquid from his robe and handed it to the beaming Hestia.

"Think of this as a sample and as a gift to ensure that our *Familias* stay on good terms. Please accept it."

"Ah, thanks! This helps a lot!"

"Sorry to change the subject, Hestia, but have you registered your *Familia* with the Guild?"

Miach asked her as Hestia reached out to accept the vial.

Huh? Hestia tilted her head, a look of confusion in her eyes. The male god took it as his cue to explain.

"Whether members of a *Familia* go into the Dungeon or not, as long as the group resides in Orario, they must inform the Guild. That's what the registration is for."

In name, the Guild was only in charge of overseeing the Dungeon. However, since the Dungeon was at the center of Orario's economy, the Guild was in a position of considerable power within the city. Efficient and fair management had resulted in a peaceful city and considerable growth using the resources provided by the Dungeon. The Guild had presided over the Dungeon since the Old Age, acting as a caretaker of the city as well.

The Guild controlled everything that happened in the city, and *Familias* were required to be a part of the system.

"Oh, so *Familias* have to register just like adventurers do, huh? Well, they let us live here, so it's only natural."

"That's exactly right. Just another one of the charms of Gekai."

"All these complicated things had no place in Tenkai, eh?"

Yup, yup. The two deities nodded in agreement.

"So then, what to do? Since it looks like you haven't registered yet, shall I go with you?"

"Are you sure? Actually, it would help me out a lot..."

"To tell the truth, I have nothing to do after this. So rather than being lonely during my free time, it would be better to help out a friend in need."

"You're the spitting image of what a god should be."

"Ha-ha-ha, I get that a lot."

The two of them left the hidden room under the church, emitting the passivity unique to the gods.

"I should fill all of these in, right?"

"Indeed. Don't forget to sign your name using hieroglyphs."

They were standing in the wide lobby of Guild Headquarters.

Hestia filled in the Guild registration paperwork as well as she could on her own and asked Miach for help when she had a question, as adventurers from many different *Familias* went about their business around them. A feathered quill in her hand, she had to stand on a stool to help her lean over the counter to write.

Light from the evening sun came in through the ceiling windows, casting the white lobby in an orange hue. Considering it was around the time that many adventurers left the Dungeon, many races of human and demi-human were making their way into and out of the Guild at this hour.

A party of smiling prums made their way out of the Exchange; a few animal men were making passes at the cute Guild receptionists across the way; an elf and a dwarf were engaged in a deep philosophical discussion. There was so much to see in the wide, white marble lobby of the Guild.

The only gods in the room, Hestia and Miach watched all of the adventurers with great interest.

"Miach, what is this thing here, *Familia* Rank?"

"A measure of a *Familia*'s influence as determined by the Guild… It's a grade. While the content of a *Familia*'s activities is taken into account, the most important factor is combat potential and overall strength."

Each *Familia* in Orario was given a ranking from *S* to *I*, the same scale that was used to rank an adventurer's basic abilities in a Status. The higher the rank, the more trust and respect was given to that *Familia* by the Guild and other organizations. Of course, fear as well.

The gods who treated everything on Gekai as a game did everything they could to raise the rank of their *Familias* and enjoyed every minute of it.

"A mercantile *Familia*'s rank increases when they make an impact. A high rank means that customers can trust their products, and more adventurers choose to do business with them."

"By the way, what's your *Familia*'s rank, Miach?"

"Ha-ha-ha, it's *H*."

It went without saying that the newly formed and dirt-poor *Hestia Familia* would be assigned the lowest rank, *I*.

Familias were subject to the taxes of the city; the higher their rank, the more they paid.

"If you don't mind my asking, Hestia, what does the child in your *Familia* look like?"

"Well, that question was out of nowhere."

"What? The two of us are hopefully going to be working together for a long time, so I would like to know the child you have chosen to be your first member."

"…A human boy with red eyes and white hair. His name is Bell Cranell."

"Red eyes and white hair, huh…Oh, could that be him over there?"

"Huh?"

Hestia's feathered pen stopped in mid-sentence and her head snapped up.

Following Miach's line of vision to the corner of the lobby, she saw a white-haired human boy talking with a Guild employee.

"Bell…"

"I thought that was him. And…is he trying to give her something?"

The two deities watched as a very nervous Bell held out a small box in front of him and opened the lid to show the girl behind the counter what was inside. The girl, a half-elf looking very sharp in her Guild uniform, glanced down at the contents for a moment before saying a few things and smiling.

"A gift for his lady friend. Heh, looks like your boy's got some skills."

"…"

Hestia didn't respond to Miach's words and just watched the scene unfold in front of her.

The girl tapped Bell on the nose as the boy blushed and hid his face in embarrassment.

…*Soooo, that's how it is.*

Said Hestia in the back of her mind, her eyes sending icy daggers at the two of them.

The reason that Bell had been getting up so early and working so hard in the Dungeon to make money was all to buy a present for that beautiful half-elf.

Hestia's mood suddenly plummeted like a rock.

Hestia felt more and more displeasure watching her make fun of him, Bell's face beet red and hands waving in front of his chest.

"Humph."

"Oh…? Hestia?"

"Sorry, Miach. I'm going home."

Shoving her paperwork to the employee on the other side of the counter and ignoring Miach's attempts to stop her, Hestia left the Guild Headquarters. Leaving behind the boy who'd never even noticed her, she tore through the front garden with quick footsteps.

Damn it, I didn't wanna see that…

Frustrated thoughts filled Hestia's mind as she made her way down Northwest Main.

As for why she hadn't wanted to see, Hestia already knew the answer.

The goddess wanted full possesion of him. No one else, just Bell.

At long last she had a family—something that she had longed for. So seeing him getting involved with someone who wasn't her hurt. *Don't go to her, I'm the only one you need*, and other selfish, childlike thoughts raced through her mind.

Hestia didn't know if she was reacting like this because Bell was Bell.

A new image suddenly jumped into her head. What if Bell wasn't the first child she blessed…? If he hadn't been her first family member, then her heart wouldn't feel like this. She wouldn't care.

Bell, you're such an idiot…

Hestia arrived at her *Familia*'s home an absolute wreck of intertwining emotions.

She walked straight to the back of the room and in one motion plopped facedown on her bed. Eyebrows locked in an angry frown, the sulking goddess pulled all of the sheets and covers into a mountain around her head.

She did her best to chase thoughts of Bell out of her mind. Hestia slammed her eyes shut; no light was getting to them, anyway.

Clink, clack.

The light sounds of dishes being softly placed on the table outside her cocoon reached Hestia's ears.

Hestia gently opened her eyes in the darkness under her bed covers, the noises slowly waking her up.

Blinking over and over, she sluggishly started to emerge from beneath the blankets.

The sudden light from the magic-stone lamp as she popped her head out of the corner of the bed stung for a moment as her eyes adjusted.

"..."

Her vision was blurry, but the first thing she saw was the back of a boy with white hair.

She watched him walk between the kitchen counter and table many times as quietly as he could.

The smell of freshly made soup wafted into her nose a second later.

"..."

Pushing the blanket and sheets off her body, Hestia slowly sat up.

The boy with the white hair noticed right away and immediately came over to her.

"Good morning, Goddess."

"...Unnn."

Hestia nodded at Bell's warm grin.

The clock on the wall read seven o'clock at night. The groggy goddess looked up at it and nodded again a few times in an effort to wake up.

Her twin jet-black ponytails shook from side to side.

"...Did you make dinner?"

"Yes. You looked really tired when I got home so...Sorry I didn't wait for you."

There was a simple salad and skinless steamed potatoes along with soup lined up on the table.

The soup had been poured into cute wooden cups, steam softly rising from them.

"...You're home a lot earlier than usual today, aren't you?"

Hestia's voice was thick with irony as she watched Bell try to win her back with something as simple as a nice dinner.

"Did something good happen?" she said with the same tone, not bothering to look at him. Bell turned red and jumped for a moment before leaving the kitchen.

He went to a bookcase, his back to the goddess as he reached up to grab something. Whatever it was firmly hidden in his grasp, Bell returned to the goddess's bed.

"Um, well...Goddess, this is for you."

"...Eh?"

Hestia looked down at the box being held out in front of her.

Her eyes went wide as she froze before accepting the box with shaky hands.

She lifted the lid to find that there were two hair ties inside.

The bands were decorated with a blue ribbon that was tied to look like flowers and small silver bells.

"Bell, aren't these..."

"T-the ones that you have look like they're about to fall apart, so I, um, well...

"Got you a present..." Bell sounded like he could disappear at any moment.

Hestia was absolutely stunned. She looked up at the boy with wide eyes as he hid his blushing face behind his white bangs.

The hair ties were inside a box that Hestia had seen before— the same box that Bell had shown that half-elf back at the Guild Headquarters.

He hadn't been trying to give the box to her, maybe he was asking for her opinion—a female opinion about whether or not she thought Hestia would like them.

Thinking back to the way that she'd been teasing him, Hestia realized that she'd made a terrible mistake.

And these hair ties...Did he see me...?

A few days ago, standing in front of that show window on Northwest Main.

The ribbon on Bell's present looked almost exactly like the one on the hair bands a mannequin had been wearing that she really liked.

"I-I wasn't trying to hide it, but I didn't want to ruin the surprise and, um…I'm sorry."

"…"

Hestia softly smiled as she watched Bell fidget uncomfortably.

But a part of her also felt a little sad behind her blushing cheeks.

She'd given up on giving him a present that day, but he had done exactly the opposite.

His feelings for her were stronger than hers for him, and much more admirable.

"So you've been working so hard in the Dungeon just to give this to me?"

"You see, um…Yes."

"Such an idiot…"

These hair ties couldn't have been cheap, Hestia thought to herself as she looked at the quality of the materials.

Coming home absolutely exhausted every day, all to earn enough money to buy these as quickly as possible. He'd probably faced danger many times over.

Hestia closed her eyes as her face broke open into a smile.

"Bell."

"Y-yes?"

"These—put them on me."

"Huh?"

"They're a present from you. I want you to put them in my hair."

Bell didn't know how to react so Hestia smiled, grabbed his hand, and pulled him to the side.

After climbing out of bed, Hestia led Bell to the table and she sat down in her chair. "Quickly," she softly said while looking up at him from her seat.

Sweat rolled down Bell's face, as if something was about to explode, until finally he reached out and picked up the hair ties as if he'd made up his mind.

"Bell, thank you…And, sorry."

"Eh?"

She giggled. "It's nothing." Hestia's still-blushing face shifted into a warm grin as the timid boy started touching her hair.

Watching the look of sheer concentration on his face in the mirror across from her, Hestia felt a soft thump in her chest as the boy struggled to get her hair through the bands.

She practically purred like a cat every time she felt his fingers run through her black hair. Hestia enjoyed every moment of this special time together with Bell.

"…Hey, Bell."

"Yes?"

"Meeting you, bringing you into my *Familia*…made me happy."

Bell stopped moving to listen to the goddess's quiet voice.

A moment later, the boy was beaming with an elated smile.

"I'm glad that I met you, too, Goddess."

Hestia couldn't help but smile and blush again as she watched the boy's face in the mirror.

—There was no doubt she would grow to love this boy.

The little goddess knew that now.

All she wished for was to always be able to watch over him and to follow his story through the Status on his back.

And so it was that silver bells jingled atop clumsily attached hair bands.

They sounded with every movement of her jet-black twin ponytails.

Afterword

Ever since I was a child, I've thought of blacksmiths as "Strong!" "Austere!" "Cool!" just like in *Dragon Quest*! I knew right away that I wanted the hero's partner to be a male blacksmith. Now, at long last, he's in the story. It's particularly moving for the character to be male because of the number and diversity of female characters that have already been introduced.

The blacksmith who appears in this story isn't particularly strong or simple, nor can he make the Seikou Juuji Ken. He's a struggling blacksmith covered in smoke who can't sell anything. However, when I started writing the scene of the forge, I remember saying, "Uhooooo!" out loud as my fingers moved, trying to capture the images flowing into my mind. The character became a dedicated craftsman.

I get particularly excited when I visualize a blacksmith in a dimly lit workshop in front of the red-hot forge, the high-pitched sound of metal shaping metal as he or she pounds their heart and soul, hopes and fears into a weapon of their own design over and over. No matter how many works they complete, blacksmiths remain the physical embodiment of passion in my eyes.

I live for that moment they emerge from the workshop carrying a truly unique weapon in their arms and present it to their client. While I know this scene almost never happens in today's world, I can't help but be fascinated with it.

Since the fourth installment of this series was more of an interlude in terms of the overarching story, I included two short stories that were first published in *GA Bunko Magazine*. The first story,

"Quest X Quest," takes place in the middle of book three, between chapters two and three, while the second story, "A Campanella to the Goddess," takes place before the events of book one. I hope you enjoyed them.

The time has come for me to express my gratitude.

To Mr. Kotaki, this book would not have become a reality without your guidance. To Mr. Suzuhito Yasuda, thank you for always taking time out of your busy schedule to create beautiful artwork to bring this world to life. To Mr. Yuuji Yuuji, for agreeing to share part of his work with a smile. Your support made me very happy.

Also, I would like to thank the combined efforts of Mr. Kunieda and Mr. Kurebito Misaki for their beautiful work on the limited edition releases of this series. In addition, I'm extremely grateful to *Young Gangan* and Square Enix for their support of Mr. Kunieda's work on the comic series based on my novels. I look forward to every new installment.

Lastly, I would like to thank everyone, including the readers who picked up this book, from the bottom of my heart.

I hope you'll all be looking forward to the next volume.

Fujino Omori